the WICKED

Printed in the United States of America.

Published by Thomas & Mercer
P.O. Box 400818
Las Vegas, NV 89140

ISBN13: 9781612182209
ISBN10: 1612182208

the
WICKED

MICHAEL WALLACE

THOMAS & MERCER

ACKNOWLEDGMENTS

I would like to thank some of the people who have given me support as my ideas for this series have changed and evolved. Thanks go to Megan Jacobsen at Thomas & Mercer, who took that leap of faith to acquire *The Righteous* for larger distribution, as well as to my editor, David Downing, who understands exactly what I'm trying to do and helps me realize it. Many thanks also to my agent, Katherine Boyle, and to fellow writer Mel Comley, for encouragement while I was writing *The Wicked*.

And thank you to Gordon Ryan, who is not only a strong writer, but an excellent human being. His feedback reminded me to always take my characters and their beliefs seriously. Our conversations helped bend the story arc of the overall series in a small, but significant way.

Finally, I am grateful for my wife's support and happy that I can finally reward her patience.

CHAPTER ONE

Allison Caliari watched the Dumpster through a pair of binoculars. The lid lifted, a head emerged, and then a young man crawled out and dropped into the alley below her, letting the lid bang shut behind him. He was a boy, really, only nineteen or twenty and heartbreakingly thin, dressed in rags and wearing a scraggly beard. He carried half-eaten slices of pizza and a bag of moldy bread. Somewhere, Allison imagined, the boy's mother made desperate phone calls, hung fliers, begged the police to do something, *anything*, to find her son. Or maybe—and this was almost worse to imagine—his parents thought he was still in school, with no idea the boy was fighting rats for his breakfast.

Two young women emerged from the Dumpster and crouched next to the boy on the broken asphalt. Allison caught her breath. She'd watched from the empty top deck of the parking garage next to the alley for two hours, since just before dawn, had seen the boy crawl inside twenty minutes earlier. But no girls. So where had they come from?

My God, did they sleep in there? All three of them, crammed together down there?

Before she could see the girls' faces, hoodies came up and scraps of food garbage disappeared from the pile on the ground while the three ate. Why garbage? There was a soup kitchen at the Salvation Army, but they never visited it, and she never saw them at the Portland Rescue Mission, or anywhere else you could get a warm bed and a hot meal.

Mom, don't you get it? Madeline had asked. *I'm done, I don't want you anymore. I don't care about work, or school, or those stupid boys I used to hang out with. The sooner you get that through your head, the better.*

"No," Allison whispered. "I won't. I *won't.*"

It seemed laughable now that she'd moved her daughter west in part to get away from Allison's devoutly Catholic parents. From Catholic school, the extended Italian family, a repeat of her own suffocating childhood. What she wouldn't give now to see her daughter attending daily mass and praying the rosary. Anything but this.

Allison lowered the binoculars, took off her mittens and blew into her stiff, cold hands, and tried to figure out what to do next. The kids were growing wary, and she didn't want to spook them like after that crazy thing with the produce truck. She still couldn't understand what they'd been doing. Iceberg lettuce? That wasn't even real food.

Allison thought she had spotted her daughter in the lettuce-stealing group, but she wasn't sure. When she'd approached, they'd scattered into the night, leaving the back of the truck open and heads of lettuce strewn across the street. The kids had abandoned their bivouac underneath the Hawthorne Bridge, and it took two weeks to find them again, this time on the other side of the city. One more scare and they might leave Portland altogether.

She'd drive to Argentina if she thought she could get to her daughter, but she had to be realistic. What chance would she have if Madeline left Oregon? None, that's what, so she'd wait here all day if she had to, until she was sure it was her daughter down there. And then she'd block the alley somehow, do whatever the hell it took. Allison lifted the binoculars back to her eyes.

The three of them had stopped eating and now sat with heads bowed. Each person placed a hand on the shoulder of the person to their right, until it completed the triangle. What were they doing down there? Praying?

And then a hand fell on Allison's shoulder as she leaned over the concrete wall. A light touch, but enough to throw her off balance. She flailed and dropped the binoculars, which had been on a cord around her neck, but now slipped off and tumbled end over end. And then she started to go over the edge herself.

The hand grabbed her now, jerked her back. The binoculars hit the street with a pop and smashed to pieces. The three kids stumbled to their feet, faces upturned. The person spun Allison around. Heart pounding, she found herself face-to-face with a handsome young man with a beard, who fixed her with eyes so intense they reminded her of a tiger stalking its prey.

"Allison Caliari?"

She could barely get out a single word. "Yes."

"You shouldn't have come, you know that. We told you, we warned you. Your daughter told you."

She found her voice, and with it, her anger. "I know. I have Madeline's letter in my pocket, and I read it every day."

"Then why don't you listen?"

"Why don't I listen? She's my daughter—I'm not going to walk away. If you think that, you don't know anything about the way a mother thinks."

"The others have learned. They aren't looking anymore. Most of them give up as soon as they're told they're no longer needed or wanted."

"Do you really believe that?" Allison asked. She fought a rising tide of fury and tried to shrug away the hand, but the man's grip stayed tight on her shoulder, and there was enough fear left, standing so close to the edge of the building, with the memory of her near fall still trembling through her legs, that she didn't dare struggle free. "You really think we've all just given up? We haven't. We've found each other, and we talk. We track you and we e-mail, we have support groups online, and we are watching for you and we're not going to give up until we've got our children back."

His eyes narrowed, and she could see she'd made a mistake. Maybe he knew that people were looking for him and his band of brainwashed children, stolen from their dorms, their student apartments. Maybe he knew they wanted him behind bars, let him bunk with Charles Manson. Or dead, if necessary. He and David Koresh and Jim Jones and all the other evil self-proclaimed prophets could form their own cult in hell.

Or maybe he didn't know. Maybe in his narrow focus, it had never occurred to him that parents would keep looking. But either way, it was stupid to point it out.

"They're not children," he said. "Or not *your* children anymore, at least. They're grown-ups and they can make their own decisions. There's nothing you can do."

Her voice grew shrill. "There is something we can do!"

"You can walk away and forget it."

"I know who you are—I know. And I'm not going to forget. Never!"

"Yes, you will. You'll forget and you'll stop looking. You'll stop because a higher power will stop you." He grabbed her arm, and this time his grip tightened until it hurt. "You can either choose to stop willingly, or be destroyed."

She caught her breath, tried to figure out what he meant, if it was just a threat. "Please, for God's sake. I just want to talk to her. Can't you let me talk to her, just for a few minutes?"

"No, you'll never see her again, I promise you that." He let go, turned, and made his way to the fire escape stairs on the opposite side of the building.

Allison stared for a long moment. Her heart still pounded. Once she caught her breath, she turned back to the alley. The Dumpster sat open and empty. A nest of plastic garbage bags, some torn open, lay at the bottom, crumpled down into the shape of the two girls who had slept there last night. The stench lifted all the way to the roof. But the alley itself was empty.

"Allison Caliari."

She turned and found that the man had stopped at the far side of the roof. "What do you want?"

"Next time I find you looking, I won't pull you back from the edge," he said. "I'll push."

CHAPTER TWO

Eliza Christianson didn't recognize the two men as troublemakers, not at first. They weren't drunk, and they didn't smell like pot. They weren't being loud, and they didn't make rude comments to the woman at the ticket window. They didn't come with girlfriends, planning to pair off in a quiet corner of the gardens, only to have some elderly couple complain at the office about "lewd behavior."

What the two men were, however, were polygamists.

And they'd come to find Eliza.

She was tired, and maybe that's why she didn't notice at first. She was moonlighting as a waitress while working four days a week at Red Butte Gardens in the foothills above the University of Utah. Her bishop in the LDS ward was the director of the gardens and had given her the job after she explained how she was trying to earn enough over the spring and summer to attend class full time in the fall. Her brother Jacob was paying her tuition, but she needed living money.

Eliza was tired because twenty-eight people had come into the restaurant just before closing the previous night and camped out in the garden room. Some multilevel marketing thing. It was half meeting, half orders of pie or cornbread, with the occasional appetizer and lots of free drink refills. Seventy-two minutes past closing, the manager finally asked them, politely, to leave. The group tipped a total of $27.92 in singles and change to be split between three waitresses. Technically, she supposed, it was fifteen percent of the total bill. It covered roughly two percent of the aggravation.

And so she was fighting a yawn when the two men came out of the gift shop, pulled on sunglasses, and asked her for a map of the gardens. She handed them a map, gave a brief overview, and then said, "The tulips are in bloom. The weather has been perfect, and they're especially beautiful this year. Go past the fountains and you'll see them on the right."

The taller man said, "Thank you, Eliza Christianson."

She gave him a sharp look. "What? How—"

Before she could complete the thought, he was pointing to the name tag on her blouse. Utahns loved name tags, and she wore one at the restaurant, at the gardens, even at ward socials. She glanced down at the name tag and had started to feel silly about her paranoia when he continued, "The Lord delights in a beautiful flower. It is beautiful in His sight."

And before she could recover, the two men continued into the garden, while she gawked behind them. A prickling sensation worked itself along her spine, and although the sun was overhead in a clear sky and the breeze was warm and gentle, she felt a chill.

"Is there something wrong?" a voice asked behind her.

It was her bishop from the LDS student ward. He gave her a protective look, then followed her gaze. A frown crossed his face. It was the same expression he'd give to overzealous returned missionaries who tried to hit her up for a date between sacrament meeting and Sunday school. *A time and a season for everything, elders,* he'd tell them, *a time and a season for everything.*

Bishop Larsen waited until they were out of earshot. "Those men weren't bothering you, were they?"

"No, I'm just trying to think if I've seen them before. I don't think so."

"Okay, but you've seemed out of sorts all morning. Is everything all right?"

"Late night at the restaurant, and it was a tough crowd. I'm sorry, I'll get my head in the day, I promise."

"No worries," he said. "It's a slow morning. The students are at finals. No events scheduled. Half the people this morning just want to find a quiet corner to bury their heads in textbooks. The rest are newlywed or nearly dead." He smiled at his own joke, which was one she'd heard before, but his smile was so genuine that she couldn't help but respond in kind.

"Anyway, don't worry about whatever is stressing you," he added. "It's a good day to relax and enjoy the gardens."

"Thank you, I do love it here."

"You know, I've got it covered," he said. "Why don't you take a little walk in the sun and see if that clears your head."

It sounded like a great idea. The two men had disappeared in the direction of the tulip beds. She turned the opposite way, toward the children's garden, where a mother watched a pair of preschoolers racing through the rattlesnake maze. Last week an actual rattlesnake had appeared in the maze, slithered down from the hills. After some screaming and a lot of fuss, Bishop Larsen had shown up with a snake lasso and unceremoniously escorted the animal from the premises.

Eliza was still watching the children playing, first in the maze and then on the giant lizard statues, when she felt someone watching her. She turned, but didn't see anyone but a second mother, this one pushing a stroller up from the herb garden. The access trail to the natural areas exited the back of the children's garden, but no one was there, either. Maybe she'd imagined it.

Who were those men? And what did the one mean about flowers? Could her father have sent them to keep an eye on her? Or worse, court her? The same thing, in a way, as Bishop Larsen's eager young returned missionaries, except, this being Blister Creek, they'd find the most blunt, creepy way to do so.

Only that wasn't Abraham Christianson's style. He'd be more likely to show up himself, proudly proclaim to everyone that he was Eliza's father from Blister Creek, and then introduce one of the creepy young men as her future husband. *The marriage will be at the temple the day after tomorrow, so let's go. We've got a long drive.* No, she didn't think Father had sent them.

She could go back to Bishop Larsen, let him be the heavy. He'd be happy to play the role of chivalrous protector. Collar the young men and escort *them* unceremoniously from the premises. But she didn't need a man to handle these particular rattlesnakes.

Eliza put purpose in her stride as she left the children's garden and took the nature trail that looped through the foothills. She ran over retorts in her mind, trying to think of the proper mix of scripture with which to season her outrage. Something like her brother would say. And delivered with Jacob's confidence, too. It would put them in their place.

She walked the trail without spotting them and began to wonder if they'd already left. Maybe all they wanted was to deliver a message and leave her wondering and worrying. Mission accomplished, they'd exited the same way they'd come. Eliza poked her head in the Secret Garden, then came down the hill by the ponds. Her mind drifted from potential confrontation to whether or not to tell Jacob and Fernie what had happened.

And then she saw them.

The lower pond had a pavilion where people could picnic or hold private parties. The men were emerging from the pavilion onto the main path, speaking quietly.

The taller man smiled when he saw her, and the shorter, younger man narrowed his eyes and glanced at his companion, as if waiting for a cue. Eliza stopped and took a step back.

"What do you want?" she asked.

"To bring you home."

"What do you mean, home? Blister Creek? Did my father send you?"

"Not your childhood home, Sister Eliza, your *new* home. Where you shall cleave unto your husband, where the two of you shall be one flesh." He drew uncomfortably close, while the second man flanked her to the left.

Eliza lifted her hands in warning. "Stand back or I'll cry for help. There's a security guard and only one entrance. You'll be arrested."

He laughed and edged closer. "Arrested? For what, for telling you the will of the Lord?"

"I'm warning you, don't touch me."

"Don't fight it, Eliza. Listen to the spirit." He reached for her wrist.

Her cellular phone rang. She snatched it out of her skirt pocket. "Eliza Christianson."

"Eliza? What's the matter, are you okay?"

"What?"

"Why are you out of breath? It's me, Fernie. What's the matter?"

"Call 911, I'm—"

At "911," the two men turned and strode down the trail toward the entrance. The taller man took a piece of paper from his pocket and let it fall as he rounded the corner.

"911?" A rasp of panic dragged across Fernie's voice. "Eliza, what's going on? Eliza?"

"Never mind, don't call. It's okay," she said. "There were two men—well, never mind. They're gone now."

"Don't give me that," Fernie said in a sharp tone. "What's going on there? Tell me now or I really am calling 911."

Eliza forced herself to sound calm. "Really, I'm okay now. They left as soon as I got on the phone. I was afraid, but they're gone, I swear."

It took a few more minutes before she convinced Fernie that it was nothing, just a couple of random guys giving her a hard time. She didn't mention the polygamist connection.

Fernie let out a sigh on the other end. "I had an impression I should call you just now when I was working on the tomatoes. Thank heavens I listened to the spirit."

"Where are you? Does Zarahemla have telephones now?"

"No, Jacob got me a cell phone so I can call when I go into labor. I hate the thing, can never remember to turn it on, and then there are messages and I don't know how to get them. I don't want to find out."

Eliza knew the feeling. Even carrying a phone felt like an affectation, and in most cases, the person calling wasn't someone she wanted to talk to: the restaurant, asking her to pick up another shift, her visiting teaching companion from church, wanting to set up appointments. Some newspaper reporter had got hold of her cell number and kept leaving messages wanting to interview her about the Blister Creek polygamists. No thanks.

It wasn't that Eliza wanted to turn Amish, get a horse and buggy, and give up electricity. Not even her father was like that; Blister Creek finally had reliable cell coverage. But Eliza couldn't see the point of some of the technological geegaws that people in Salt Lake wore attached to their heads or glued to their hands. Half the kids on TRAX spent their commute hunched over glowing screens, thumbs twitching away, barely aware of the real world.

"I appreciate the call," Eliza said, "but I'm fine, really. I'm still planning to come down to Zarahemla on Monday to see everyone. We can talk face-to-face. And I miss those kids." While she spoke, she walked down the bend in the trail and confirmed that the two men had left. She picked up the piece of paper the taller man had dropped.

"Nieces and nephews will have to wait," Fernie said. "We found David."

Eliza had started to unfold the paper with her free hand, but now stopped. "Really? That's wonderful news."

"You won't think it's wonderful when I tell you where we found him, or what he said over the phone when Jacob called."

Her heart sank. "You'd better tell me everything."

The sick feeling only spread as Fernie told her about David. Jacob's contact hadn't softened David's heart—it had turned him mean and dangerous, both to himself and to others.

Maybe he'd listen to me, she thought. *Or is he so far gone that he wouldn't even care?*

After she hung up, Eliza thought about the two men. She opened the paper the taller man had dropped. If there was any doubt that it was a message for her, it disappeared. Cursive lettering spidered across the page:

Give honor unto the wife, as unto the weaker vessel, and as being heirs together of the grace of life; that your prayers be not hindered.

She frowned. What was that supposed to be, his way of courting her? An invitation to marriage?

Eliza thought about Fernie's invitation. Maybe the timing was right for a road trip.

* * *

Two days later, Eliza walked into a bar for the first time in her life. She was three hours by car southeast of the polygamist enclave of Blister Creek, across the border into Mesquite, Nevada. The atmosphere assaulted her: throbbing music, lights, the nauseating smell of sweat and smoke and perfume and beer, all mixed together.

She showed her ID and pushed past the bouncers at the door. She couldn't shake the feeling of shame, that someone would see her, report back to her father, or to the bishop. Maybe she should have brought Fernie, although that might have been worse. They'd have clung together and clenched their eyes shut like two girls being scared by a campfire ghost story.

It got worse. As she made her way in, she realized it wasn't just a bar, it was a certain kind of bar. Three almost-nude women gyrated on a stage. The closest was an attractive but hard-faced blonde woman with breasts jiggling like overfilled water balloons, rigid and at a right angle from her body. The woman caught Eliza's eye, gave her a leering smile, and wrapped her legs around the metal pole that thrust obscenely from the stage. Eliza looked away. She almost turned around and walked out.

No, you're not giving up now. You're strong and you can do this. Eliza pretended it was Jacob's voice urging her forward, and this gave her just enough courage to go on.

And then she spotted her brother, David, sitting alone near the stage, with a drink in front of him and a stack of five-dollar bills. Eliza slid in next to him, but he didn't look up, and instead kept his eyes fixed on the dancer.

"Can I sit down?" She had to shout to be heard over the pulsing music.

"Sorry, no lap dance," David said, without bothering to look at her. "I'm practically tapped out."

David took one of the five-dollar bills and shoved it in the stripper's G-string, already feathered with bills. For this, she gave him a private show that lasted ten, fifteen seconds, before she moved away in an overpowering cloud of perfume, with a strut and a sneering look at the men around the stage that said, *You can look, but you can never touch.*

Eliza found herself repelled by the woman, but then the stripper turned toward the back of the stage to give way to another dancer and the mask slipped. For an instant, Eliza saw behind the catty expression to a tired woman near the end of a long shift. It was a look Eliza saw every night at the restaurant. A student who'd been racing back and forth to the kitchen all night who now needed to go home and cram for his biology final. A woman anxious to get home to her husband, just back from deployment. This stripper, Eliza realized with a pang of shame at her initial judgment, might have a sick child at home, or a rent check due. When the woman reached the back of the stage, she wrapped her legs around the pole and thrust in time to the music.

"Man, those were some ugly tits," David said.

"Then why did you pay her to shake them at you?"

He shot her a sour, unsteady glance and looked away again without really seeing her. "Boobs are boobs. Even the bad ones aren't half bad." David shrugged, finished his drink with a clink of ice cubes, and then waved for the bartender to get him another. "Yeah, they're probably all fake in this joint."

She found herself studying the blonde woman again. All she had to compare them to were her own, and no, her breasts didn't look anything like that. "But how can you tell they're fake?"

"Come on, boobs don't stand up like that. Those suckers float like helium balloons, except they're harder than the bunions on my granny's feet. I can still feel where she whacked me in the head, probably leave a goose egg. Do you girls all have to get boob jobs? I think the average guy prefers them natural, even if they're on the small side."

"I wouldn't know anything about that, and anyway, I'm not exactly comfortable discussing my breasts with my own brother."

David turned with a sharp expression, which widened into surprise. "Eliza? Goddamn it!"

"That's not really necessary. You seem to be damning yourself well enough on your own."

"Who sent you? Jacob? He can kiss my ass. And pass my well-wishes to the old man. He can kiss my ass, too. Oh, and all his wives too, and all my brothers and sisters and half brothers and half sisters. All the whole inbred clan can kiss my apostate ass."

"Is the vulgarity really necessary?"

David scoffed. "Liz, you're in a strip club. In case you didn't notice, you left Utah about twenty miles back. And you left the nineteenth century as soon as you drove out of Blister Creek." He looked her up and down. "At least you got rid of the prairie dress and ponytails—that's something, I guess. Oh, right, you've taken up with the Salt Lake Mormons. What does Jacob want?"

"Jacob didn't send me."

"The hell he didn't. He's the only one who knows where I am. He called and started hassling me about Word of Wisdom stuff."

"Okay, so he told me how to find you, but it's true. I told him I was coming to find you and he just shrugged. He's got bigger things to worry about than one loser of a brother."

"Yeah, like what?"

"Like tracking down other losers, of course. The family is full of them."

A smile cracked his face, and for the first time she saw the playful young boy she used to watch catching frogs down by the reservoir, who used to bury himself in the hayloft and hide, then jump out, screaming, when Jacob or Enoch came to feed the horses.

She put a hand on David's wrist. "Let me take you to Zarahemla. Jacob will be glad to see you. He loves you, and it hurts him to see you like this."

"No thanks." He waved for another drink. "Getting kicked out of the church was the best thing that ever happened to me. You won't get me back to Utah."

"Mesquite is pretty close. In fact, it's as close as you can get to Utah without crossing the state line. What's that about? Doesn't Las Vegas have enough strip bars without driving all the way out here?"

He gave her a bleary stare. "Thank you, Dr. Freud. I like this place—what's wrong with that? And I don't care what you say or do, I'm not about to get sucked back into the cult."

"Nobody is trying to suck you back in. Come on, let's get out of here. We can talk."

"About what?"

"About getting you out of this lifestyle and back where you belong."

"Are you kidding me? I like this lifestyle. I've got a job driving delivery, and nobody gives me crap. After work I come here and spend my money on beer and strippers, and then I go home and sleep like a baby. I don't think about God, or Jesus, or Joseph Smith, or any of that. And maybe I'm going to hell when I finally croak, but you know what? I'm good with that."

"And what about the drugs?" she asked. When David said nothing, she pressed, "David, I know. It's not just pot is it? That's poison. It will destroy you."

"What's it to you? Why are you so damn preachy? You're worse than Father—at least he doesn't give me the puppy eyes."

"And that thing at the bus station in Vegas? You're still bruised around the eyes."

David's stare hardened. The stripper had come around the stage again, but this time he waved her away without a glance. "What, is he spying on me now? He wants to bring me back into his little cult, so he hires a couple of thugs to mug me and beat the shit out of me, then sends my sister out to give me a sad face once I'm softened up, is that it?"

"David, please. I'm not here to talk about religion or the church or any of that. And Jacob doesn't care about it either."

"Not what I heard. He's Father's *numero uno* now, isn't he? And what about this other thing, the Zarahemla compound?"

"Now who is spying on whom?"

"People talk." He downed his drink and waved for another. A slur had begun to work its way into his speech. If what Fernie said was accurate, he'd go home and fill himself with worse things.

"Exactly," she said. "And that's how we heard about what you're going through. Look, we're not building any sort of cult. I'm not even in the church anymore, remember? All I'm doing is trying to help one of my brothers, so he won't be a Lost Boy anymore. Is that so bad?" She put her hand over his.

"I'm not a Lost Boy."

"Well, someone who left, whatever. I know you're not happy here. How could you be? Jacob could help, and he needs people like you."

"What do you mean, people like me? Where do I fit into his church?"

"If everyone who cares jumps ship, anyone who thinks about it long and hard, rather than swallowing every bit of mumbo jumbo, what does that leave him with? Fanatics. People who think the world is coming to an end, the nuts and crazies. More self-proclaimed prophets."

"You left, didn't you? Tell me, if it's so wonderful, what's up with that?"

She nodded. It was a good point, and how could she explain it? There was too much pressure to marry some old guy with a dozen wives, and until Jacob could change the entire culture—and that would take time—she couldn't stay. So she'd taken up with the Salt Lake Mormons. They were different, but they weren't what she'd been taught or what she'd expected. Bishop Larsen—her whole ward in Salt Lake—accepted her eccentricities, and when people discovered her polygamist background, they embraced her all the more. The belief? Well, she didn't know where she stood, but for now she was comfortable.

"That's different. I have a place to go. What are you still doing in Nevada? And living in Las Vegas? Is there a more godless place on the face of the earth?"

He raised his eyebrows. "You're wrong about Vegas. It's a spiritual vacuum, Liz, and anything and everything is flowing in to fill it. New Age quacks, UFO cults, evangelical offshoots, snake handlers, you name it. Oh, and plenty of former polygs. They seem to find their way into every weird sect imaginable."

"Just tell me you're not hanging out with other Lost Boys."

"No, I'm not that dumb. I heard what happened when they tried to come back. Half those guys are in jail or dead. I'm damn lucky I stayed out of their schemes. Whatever else I am, I'm a Christianson boy, not a Kimball."

She breathed a sigh of relief. "Good." Eliza didn't want to think too hard about Kimballs or the hell they'd put her through. "David, you have two choices. You can follow Jacob's path, or you can follow Enoch's. And Enoch is dead."

The bartender brought another drink, and David took a long sip before fixing Eliza with a hard look. "Liz, we all die sooner or later. Jacob is going to be dead soon, too. And if you don't get away from all these religious crazies, so will you."

CHAPTER THREE

The woman couldn't have stood out more if she'd ridden into the compound on the back of an elephant. She wore a short skirt and a sleeveless shirt. Hair at a fashionable mid-neck length, brown with highlights. And makeup, plus jewelry, the most noticeable of which were gold hoops that glittered in the sun. Maybe mid-forties, beautiful. Slender and athletic, like someone who watched her calories and went to the gym every morning.

Eliza joined the other women in looking up from the raised vegetable beds as the woman clicked across flagstones on high heels. She had a proud, confident air and strode toward them with a look of purpose. "Excuse me, I'm looking for Eliza Christianson."

Eliza grew wary. Just what she needed, another reporter.

Women wiped sweat from foreheads with the backs of gloves, or brushed dirt from their dresses. Nobody answered. It was an unseasonably warm week in central Utah for late April, and they were taking advantage of the sun to mix compost into the new beds.

The woman fixed upon Eliza, dressed differently as she was, in jeans and a long-sleeved blouse, and said, "How about you?" She shielded her hand against her eyes to block the sun. "Do you know how to find Eliza Christianson? That's not you, is it?"

Not again. Why couldn't Jacob have spotted the woman driving up and shooed her away? But Jacob was giving booster shots to children in his clinic at the back side of the compound. Most of the other men were brush-hogging the irrigation ditches up in the hills.

"Nope, never heard of her. You sure you have the right place?"

"It *is* you—I recognize you from TV."

"What do you want?"

The woman moved around where the sun wasn't in her eyes. "I want to talk to you about your *Dateline* show."

"That wasn't me."

"It was you, I'm sure now." She glanced at the other women. "Can we talk privately?"

"What I mean is that I had nothing to do with that. They wanted to interview me; I told them no. I know they found a couple of people who kinda sorta knew me, paid them a bunch of money to act like they really *did* know me, and then made up a bunch of stuff. But whoever you are, I don't want to be in the news. So no, that's not me. Find someone else to interview, please."

"Interview? What do you mean?" She looked down, seemed to notice how she must appear to the women from the compound. "Oh, I understand. No, I'm not with the news at all. I didn't come to interview you. I'm in terrible trouble, and I think you can help."

"Oh, you didn't?" Eliza felt herself softening. "Sorry, I thought—well, what do you mean, help?"

"It's my daughter. She's dying, and I think you can save her."

* * *

"I don't like it," the woman said, eyeing Jacob. "Can't we meet alone?"

She'd introduced herself as Allison Caliari, said she was from Portland, Oregon. Jacob and Eliza had followed her down from the compound to a diner in the small town of Manti, Utah. It wasn't one of those retro places like you found in Salt Lake, with an art deco look and waitresses in pinstriped dresses, but the real kind, with vinyl seats split and worn by ten thousand backsides. A short order cook juggling a dozen breakfasts and a splattered apron. Waitresses in polyester.

Eliza sat next to her brother on the other side of the diner booth. Out the window, a group of elderly LDS in suits and dresses crossed the street carrying little suitcases, on their way to the temple, which loomed like a fortress on the hill overlooking the town. It filled the frame of the diner window.

"Why alone?" Eliza asked.

"I didn't think we'd be meeting with the leader of your cult. I wanted to talk one woman to another."

"No worries, my brother's not going to tell me what to do or say. He knows how to stay quiet and listen."

"That's not much better. I know how these things work. I saw the *Dateline* show, I remember the FLDS coverage, and I've read Krakauer and other stuff about the polygamists. I've been reading up on the patriarchal system out here; I know what's going on."

"Come on, give me a little credit." Eliza turned to her brother, who watched with a half smile. "You could help me out here, you know."

"What? Nah, you're doing just fine on your own." Jacob leaned back with a smile. "And I like hearing people talk about me like I'm not even here."

The waitress appeared with Sprites for Eliza and Jacob and coffee for Allison. Eliza waited until she'd left before speaking again. "Don't believe everything you see on TV. That *Dateline* story was a bunch of baloney. Those guys latched onto a couple of lurid details and made up the rest of it. Or worse, they were listening to the attorney general's office, who were trying to cover their foul-up."

"But he was on the inside during the whole thing," she said.

"So? My brother's a doctor who started working with the FBI because they wanted to get their agent out and needed someone on the inside."

"And somehow became the leader of the whole cult," Allison said. "Convenient."

"Interim cult leader," Jacob corrected. "Nobody else wanted the job. In fact, I'm on the lookout for a replacement, as soon as my wife agrees to get back to civilization. You want it? The job is yours."

"Be serious," Allison said.

"I am serious. Well, not about giving it to you, but I don't want it. I'm not a leader, I'm just a guy in the wrong place at the wrong time. Their leader died, and they have nowhere else to turn, except my father. He'd divide up their belongings and assign the single women to new husbands."

Eliza allowed herself a smile. "Jacob's an enlightened cult leader. A kinder and gentler prophet."

"What does that even mean?" Allison asked. "Never mind, I didn't drive nine hundred miles because I'm curious about your church. And with all due respect to your brother, the so-called enlightened cult leader, it's one of these self-proclaimed prophets who is killing my daughter."

"Killing in what way?" Eliza asked. "You think he's brainwashed her?"

"No, I mean he's literally killing her. Well, that other thing, too. Madeline is like a zombie. Last time I saw her, she wouldn't even look me in the eye. She mumbled something and handed me a letter. It's like a letter from a POW camp, written under torture. How else could you explain all the awful things she said?"

Allison stopped, cleared her throat, took a sip of coffee, and Eliza could see she was fighting to keep from losing control. She waited until the woman seemed to recover, then said gently, "In what way is her life at risk, Allison?"

"They're starving her to death."

"What?"

Allison told them that her daughter had been a student at Oregon State University when she started e-mailing home about a Bible study group she was attending.

"I was happy at first. We didn't go to church much after my husband was killed, and I always felt bad I didn't give her more of a religious education. Madeline had been going through a tough time, struggling with depression and…other things. A supportive church community could be just what she needed. But then the letters started to get weird, and she would quote scriptures and talk about Jesus all the time."

"What's wrong with that?"

"Maybe that's normal with you people, but not with Madeline."

"You people?" Jacob asked.

"Sorry, that came out wrong. What I mean is that Madeline was into Facebook and texting her friends about their favorite bands, or the latest episode of *Glee*. She wasn't into the Bible, and she didn't talk about it all the time."

"Maybe not," Eliza said, "but people get caught up in things they're studying. It could have just as easily been nineteenth-century French poetry."

"Sure, but she was using lots of *thees* and *thous* and tossing random scriptures into everything. We were Presbyterian, not Bible-thumpers. And she started to talk about some group called the Chosen Ones. There were enough red flags that I got online and did a little searching. Took me ten seconds with Google before I was freaking out."

"Back up a second. Who are these people?"

Allison explained. The Chosen Ones, it turned out, was a small cult that recruited on college campuses, in youth rehab centers, and even at rock concerts. California, Oregon, Nevada, Utah, Arizona. They would form study groups, pick out a few susceptible individuals, and then move on, taking the new recruits with them, generally after writing a farewell letter to their parents, indicating their desire to permanently sever ties. Nearest anyone could tell, they lived on the streets and in abandoned buildings, eating garbage and refusing any outside contact except with those they were trying to recruit. She believed they had a headquarters, but nobody had found it.

"So one day I get a letter in the mail. Madeline only lived an hour away, and I don't think she'd ever sent snail mail in her life. I had a sick feeling when I opened it. There was some weird language about making this decision of her own free will and choice and that she was an adult and I shouldn't look for her or try to contact her in any way. I took it to the police, but they wouldn't do anything."

"That's what the weird language was about," Jacob broke in. "So the police wouldn't think she was kidnapped."

"But obviously she *was* kidnapped. I don't mean they tied her up screaming and shoved her in the trunk of a car, but there's not much difference. She's eating garbage and living on the street. Cut off from her family."

"Any idea where to find her?" Eliza asked.

"She was in Portland for a while, recruiting, living on the street. But after I found her, they took her away. It could be that she's in Seattle or LA, but if they're trying to isolate her, they've probably taken her to their headquarters." Her voice caught, and she was quiet for a moment, as if trying to regain control. "I've got to get her out of there. Three kids have already died in the past year. Two froze to death—they found their half-starved bodies wrapped in a thin blanket in an alley in Spokane. The third fell to her death from the bridge across the Hoover Dam. Either jumped or was pushed. Nobody saw it."

"What did the police say?"

"They investigated. Death by exposure in the first two cases. Suicide in the third. That was it. Pretty pathetic." She took a deep breath. "There's more. Their leader is a man the others call the Disciple. Original name Caleb Kimball."

Eliza's mouth felt suddenly dry. "Caleb *Kimball*? He's not...is that...?"

Jacob wore a grim expression. "Gideon and Taylor Junior have a younger brother named Caleb. I haven't heard about him in years. If he's going by the Disciple, that would be why."

"Yes, he's from a polygamist background. I don't know anything more than that. That's why I think you can help."

Eliza didn't know Caleb, but she knew his older brothers, Gideon and Taylor Junior. The two older brothers had been struggling over Eliza, as if she wanted anything to do with either of them. And she knew their father, manipulating both of them while he was making a play to take over the church. Taylor Junior had sexually assaulted her, and Gideon tried to force her into marriage in the temple, then kidnapped her into Witch's Warts.

Eliza explained some of this to Allison Caliari, but not the uglier details of the ordeal, and certainly not the part where she'd crushed Gideon's head with a stone to escape. She turned to her brother. "What's Caleb like?"

Jacob looked thoughtful. "A quiet kid, troubled. No doubt bullied by Gideon and Taylor Junior. All those younger kids were."

Allison Caliari said, "I don't know everything the Disciple believes, but I don't think he's teaching polygamy. His soapbox speeches are more like hard-core Pentecostal tracts, but with a dose of crazy. He thinks the world is coming to an end—I'm fuzzy as to the details. These doomsday cults don't keep blogs and send tweets. And I'm probably the biggest expert on this group, so if I don't know, nobody does."

"And what is it you want us to do, exactly?" Eliza asked.

Allison reached across the table and took her hand. "I need you to help me find my daughter before they find her dead in an alley somewhere. She's not safe, none of them are. Please, for God's sake, help me."

Eliza was opening her mouth to ask what exactly Allison wanted her to do, but Jacob spoke first. "You mentioned a headquarters. Any idea where it might be?"

Allison leaned back and the worried look eased, replaced by determination. "Again, nobody has seen it, but I think in Nevada. After I lost my daughter, I spent three weeks searching through Las Vegas, followed one group for a while, but they spotted me again and disappeared. They might be living in the desert. I overheard one of them talking about eating grasshoppers."

Las Vegas. Eliza thought of David and his comments about the religious sects in the area, and how the Lost Boys were involved in most of them.

She glanced at Jacob, and they passed a knowing look. "I think we should show her," Eliza said.

"Show me what?" Allison asked.

"The Book of the Lost," Jacob said.

* * *

David Christianson came out of the house to discover thieves had broken into his truck. He was groggy and his head felt stuffed with rocks, and he didn't recognize at first what was happening. It was only April, but already in the eighties, and he wasn't sure how long he'd been asleep, only that he'd gone inside with a throbbing head-ache and crashed on the couch and that he had three more deliver-ies to make before five. A girl stood by the rear bumper, and when he stepped onto the porch, she banged the side of the truck with the palm of her hand.

David lived in a deserted subdivision on the outskirts of Vegas. For decades, developers had scooped up thousands of acres of worthless sagebrush, thrown up tens of thousands of crappy stucco split-levels and ranches, and landscaped them with thirsty lawns and a few token shrubs. Crappy construction was the richest game in a city full of games, but sooner or later the house always collects, and dozens of developers fled town after the real estate crash.

David stayed rent-free in one of these houses in return for keeping an eye on the whole subdivision, to keep crackheads from camping out in basements or thieves from stripping the houses of copper pipes to sell for scrap. His nearest neighbors were a bunch of unemployed drywall hangers from Guadalajara two blocks over, waiting for work to come back. One of them had told David he was going back to Mexico if he couldn't find work by summer.

The rest of the neighborhood was row after row of empty homes on packed earth, surrounded by brown lawns and the skeletons of trees and bushes. Two streets over lay the bulldozed wreck of a crack house burned to the ground last summer. Nothing left but the foundation. A management firm had hired David shortly after the fire.

What the company didn't know was that David was one of the addicts he'd been hired to guard against. Not crack—thankfully, not yet. Not heroin, either. Well, only once or twice, and he didn't plan to go back. Those two were the worst. But since New Year's Eve he'd moved from the comforting little devil of marijuana to the hulking demon of crystal meth. He'd already been smoking pot at a party the first time he'd done meth, and even stoned he knew it was an asinine move. He met some chick on a balcony overlooking the Strip, and she gave him a smoke off a piece of tinfoil while rubbing her hand on his crotch. Again a week later, and then two days after that. Same girl, same sort of situation. After that, she'd been his almost-girlfriend for a few weeks before disappearing with some dealer. What was her name again?

Oh yeah, Benita Johnson. "Ya know, like BJ." And she had lived up to her name. She also had an endless supply of what all the people at the party called "Tina." He remembered her rasping laugh, the time she'd flapped her arms on the top of the high-rise apartment building as if she planned to fly off the edge and swoop over the Strip.

By then, he was smoking meth three, four times a week. He felt like crap every time it wore off, but even though he always swore he'd never do it again, he'd taken a four-day weekend just after seeing his sister Eliza. When the drugs hit, he felt like he'd jumped off a cliff and was hang gliding over the desert, soaring on thermals, with thousands of square miles of rock, dunes, and a sea of sagebrush below him. Not a person in sight. Only at the end, the wind had died and the hang glider broke in two while he was still three thousand feet above the desert floor.

What the hell are you doing, Liz? Can't you leave me alone? You pushed me into this. I was fine before.

Except that excuse didn't wash, did it? Eliza hadn't given him meth. He couldn't legitimately blame Benita, for that matter.

Whoever was to blame, four days of meth left him a wreck. And now it was Monday, and he had to go back to work. He'd dragged himself out that morning, picked up his shipment at the farm, made his first delivery, and then came back to the house to crash. As he stepped onto the porch, feeling ready to puke, and knowing the best way to knock that feeling down was to tweak himself out again, he remembered the guy at the party last night. Some blond kid with a surfer accent who went by the name of Pedro, maybe ironically. *What about that house at the end of the cul-de-sac? Nobody will know if I set up a little workshop, right? And all the free Tina you want. Things are getting too hot in this neighborhood, know what I mean?*

Maybe he'd have done it, too, but he couldn't get Eliza's visit out of his head. And now, dragging himself from the house to get his deliveries done in time, he couldn't forget the look in his sister's eyes. There was nothing calculating there, only concern and—he was almost too cynical to think the word—*love*. She'd entered the strip club, a place she would have found repellant, because she thought she could save him.

Oh hell, what am I doing?

He stared at the girl next to the truck, without realizing at first that there was something wrong. Slowly, it came. There shouldn't have been anyone on the deserted cul-de-sac. The back door of the truck was open, and he was sure he'd locked it. And who the hell was banging around inside the truck?

"Hey! What do you think you're doing? Get away from there."

The girl smiled at him and didn't move as he ran over. He grabbed her wrist and pulled her away from the truck, and still she didn't resist.

And then three young men poured out of the back. They wore untrimmed beards, and his first thought was polygamists, someone from Blister Creek or Zarahemla come to cut his throat from ear to ear. But their long-sleeved shirts were open at the collar, and he could see bony shoulder blades. No undergarments.

The men fixed him with hard looks, and he let go and stepped back, lifting his hands. "I don't want trouble, just take what you want and go. There's no money in there or drugs. It's a CSA truck—there's only cabbage and carrots and other boring stuff."

The three men came at him. The first blow caught him on the jaw, and his head exploded with pain. They hit him with fists and elbows, and when they had him lying on the hot pavement, kicked him in the face and ribs. David curled into a ball, tried to protect his head, but still the blows rained down. They said nothing. There was no sound but his own grunts and feet connecting with ribs. Through watering eyes he saw others, standing in a half circle around him, silent, watching. Maybe a dozen in all, mute witnesses to the beating.

Then he recognized a face. One of the girls, staring. She was thinner than when he'd seen her before, but her dark eyes were the same. She stared at him, her irises oversized and a look of profound sorrow reaching out to him.

Benita. David lifted his hand to beg her to help, to stop these people, but a kick landed on the side of his head and he flipped over.

Blackness crowded his vision. And then, by some wordless signal, the beating stopped. The whole incident had lasted seconds. He lay there, groaning, eyes clenched shut, and when he finally opened them, his attackers were gone. He spit blood, rolled over, and threw up. There was a ringing in his ears. His left eye was already closing, the same one that had swollen shut after the last assault.

But that one had been a mugging. He'd met some guy at the bus depot to buy drugs, and as soon as he flashed his money, three more guys materialized, took his money, and beat him up for the twenty and two fives in his wallet. They'd laughed and jeered while they did it, and a dozen passersby stopped and watched without comment. An elderly black woman had finally helped him to a bench while her grandson called the police. While waiting for them to arrive, she'd wagged her finger at him and told him to stop consorting with "bad sorts." The police had said pretty much the same thing when he'd claimed it was a random attack.

But this was different. Ruthless, calculating, brutal. And for no apparent purpose. The pain in his gut was like fire, and he knew he had to make it inside and call an ambulance. He lifted himself to a sitting position.

Where had they gone? He could see the end of the vacant cul-de-sac. Nothing but an empty street and empty houses, tumble-weeds piled against front doors. He turned the best he could, but saw nothing in the desert behind the house, either. But there was a dry wash fifty feet beyond the dead grass behind the house, and it cut a jagged scar, fifteen feet deep, up into the foothills.

David rose shakily to his feet and gripped the edge of the bumper so tightly that it cut his hand. When the wave of nausea passed, he took a glance into the truck. Boxes of produce lay overturned through-out the interior, with broken carrots and crushed avocados. They'd knocked over crates of CSA produce and scattered it about. For what? Looking for drugs? That didn't make any sense. There was nothing to steal.

And then he saw it. They'd taken several crates of iceberg let-tuce. Not romaine, not arugula, just the bland, tasteless stuff with almost zero nutritional value. He didn't know why the CSA grew it. Most customers on the route didn't care for iceberg lettuce, except for the nursing home. Apparently there were some older people who complained that the other types tasted bitter.

A wave of dizziness washed over him. More nausea. He bent and threw up again, and there were bloody specks on the few drops that came out.

He'd lose his job over this. And if he called the cops, he could lose both jobs. What if they searched the truck, would they find anything? And if they searched the weeds and sagebrush behind the house, would they find signs of pot and meth? He was in trouble if they got a warrant for the house. That would be the end of his house-sitting gig.

He leaned against the bumper for a long minute and doubled over again, fighting another wave of nausea. This time, dry heaves. He wiped his hand and saw more blood. He had to get inside and call an ambulance.

David saw the letters as he edged around the truck. They'd scrawled something across the side panel. Bits of charcoal lay on the pavement below. He focused slowly, and any hope that he'd been targeted a second time by random thieves now disappeared.

Rev. 8:10.

It had been years since he'd done his memorization exercises, and he'd always known the Book of Mormon better than the Bible. But the mnemonic came back to him, and his mind raced through Revelation 8, starting from verse one: *seventh seal…seven angels… seven trumpets…first, second, third angel…*

He stopped and thought through the tenth verse, then whispered it aloud.

"And the third angel sounded, and there fell a great star from heaven, burning as it were a lamp, and it fell upon the third part of the rivers, and upon the fountains of waters." He stopped and then thought of the next line, but he didn't speak it.

And the name of the star is called Wormwood.

CHAPTER FOUR

"The thing about most Lost Boys is that they can't leave religion alone," Jacob told Allison Caliari. "It's drilled too deep into their heads, and after they leave the church—"

"After they're kicked out, you mean," Eliza interrupted as she set two photo albums on the picnic table.

Jacob's wife Fernie helped Eliza carry Jacob's so-called Book of the Lost—a misnomer, since it had grown into several photo albums—from the shelves in their quarters into the open air of the courtyard. Eliza was confused about the order, except that there was a difference between the brown jackets and black jackets, so she set these in two separate piles on the table.

It was still sunny, but chillier than it had been that morning. Covered arcades surrounded the small courtyard on this edge of the compound. Bullet holes pockmarked the wall on the far side. Jacob had ordered them left unfilled to remind people of the horrific FBI raid last summer. A reminder to the people of Zarahemla, he'd told Eliza in private, that fanaticism always brought misery.

"After they've been kicked out," Jacob said, with a nod, "they usually take up with some other sect or cult. Or start their own in the case of Caleb Kimball—your so-called Disciple. Others slip into a nihilistic tailspin, so convinced they're going to hell that they do their best to get there as soon as possible."

"Why are they kicked out?" Allison asked.

"The official answer is sin, rebellion, pride, apostasy. The real reason is that there are never enough women to go around, so they get forced out. I'm working to change that. It's a long-term project."

Eliza caught a frown on Fernie's face, and she wondered if Fernie was still worried about Jacob taking a second wife. She didn't think Fernie wanted it—she *knew* Jacob didn't—but the difference between the two was that Fernie tried to do what God wanted, and Jacob tried to bend God's will to his own. And Fernie believed that plural marriage came from the Lord, so what choice did she have?

He flipped through one of the books. "These three pages are just the people who disappeared from the Kimball family. Notice, no girls."

Allison tapped one of the photos. "This is the Disciple," Allison said. "He's about ten years older now, but it's clearly the same guy."

It was a boy with a gap-toothed grin and a bowl cut. He looked more like Taylor Junior than Gideon, Eliza thought, but there was nothing particularly sinister that jumped out of the photo.

"That's Caleb Kimball, all right," Jacob said. "Fernie, do you remember this kid? I'm having a hard time pinning down anything specific."

She frowned and looked at the picture. "I remember one thing. The Kimballs came up to Harmony, and the Christiansons had the younger kids over. The sister wives were busy with dinner, so they had some of us older girls babysitting. Caleb was ten or eleven, and I found him in the barn, pacing back and forth, talking to himself. I thought he was making up a story, like kids do. He turned when I came in and said, 'The devil told me to climb into the rafters and jump off.' I asked him what he was talking about, and he said, 'But one of the angels said I'd die and then I'd never get into the Celestial Kingdom because it's evil to kill yourself. I probably shouldn't, right?' There was something spooky in his expression, and I thought he was absolutely out of his mind. And then it went away and he smiled sweetly up at me. 'I was just kidding, just playing a game.' I might not even remember that, except that the barn burned down that night. I always wondered if that kid had something to do with it."

"I remember the barn burning down," Jacob said. "Father thought one of the Kimball kids had been smoking in the hayloft. What was that, ninety-eight, ninety-nine?"

"Something like that," Fernie said. She sat down, her hand over her pregnant belly. "You remember the barn incident, Eliza?"

"Not really, I think I was in Blister Creek. Ninety-eight was the summer I spent with our Harris cousins."

"I never said anything," Fernie continued, "because I wasn't sure. And this was one of those cases where I didn't quite feel like part of the family. He wasn't my real father, after all."

"What do you mean?" Allison asked.

"My dad suffered a nervous breakdown when I was two years old and ran off with a gentile woman. My mother married Abraham Christianson. So I'm Eliza's half sister through my mother."

"And I'm Jacob's half sister through our father," Eliza said, "but Fernie and Jacob aren't related by blood."

"Actually, I think Fernie and I might be second cousins, once removed," Jacob said.

"Third cousins, dear," Fernie said.

"Oh, right."

Fernie smoothed her dress over her belly. "In another few weeks, Eliza is going to have a new niece through two different lines of the family."

"How confusing," Allison said.

"Yes, I know," Jacob said. "The key detail is that Fernie and I are not siblings."

"But wait a second," Eliza said to Fernie. "You'd been with the family for years at that point. You didn't feel you could speak up?"

"I wasn't a Christianson—I didn't always fit in. My mother was busy with the younger kids. I wasn't about to make an accusation I couldn't back up."

Jacob set the book aside and pulled over another stack of albums. "These three are the Las Vegas books." He opened the first one in front of Allison Caliari. "Lost Boys, mostly, but also some girls who ran away and small families we've lost track of. Tell me if you recognize anyone."

The woman thumbed through quietly, her expression growing troubled. The pictures varied, from screenshots of grainy security camera footage, to photos of twelve-year-old boys side by side with computer-rendered pictures showing how the boys might look as adults, to family snapshots, mug shots, and newspaper clippings.

"I don't understand—why do you collect all this?"

"They're people we're trying to bring back," Jacob said.

"So what, you're stalking them? To force them back into your church?"

"They're lost," Fernie said, gently. "We're trying to save them."

Allison looked between the two women, then at Jacob. "I think maybe I made a mistake." She stepped back from the books.

Eliza took her wrist. "Please, wait, let me explain. I think you're misunderstanding. Anyone who wants to leave is free to go, isn't that right, Jacob?"

"More than right. I'm *encouraging* people to leave. I'd leave myself if I could. But it's not that easy. Imagine taking a bunch of Amish and sticking them in Manhattan and telling them to earn a living. Or ripping the burkhas off conservative tribal women in North Africa. You can't just throw sheltered people into the world."

"And some people don't want to be thrown," Fernie said. "I know it's hard for you to look at me, dressed like this, and believe it, but I don't want to be out there in the so-called real world. I want to be with my people."

"And some of the people in these books do, too," Eliza said. "The others could use support while they find their own way."

She pointed to one of the pictures, a troubled-looking kid with an overbite and too-big ears. It was a picture taken by his foster family in Cedar City. He'd stolen the family car and driven it to St. George, where he and two friends had burst into a pawn shop waving plastic guns. The Gulf War vet behind the counter had a sawed-off shotgun to deal with this kind of trouble, but fortunately, he recognized three dumb kids and didn't blow their heads off.

"That's my cousin," Eliza said. "Six more months in the Washington County Jail and then he'll be back on the street. His friends will be waiting. We need to get to him first."

"Most of them are good people," Jacob said. "The ones who aren't are a danger, and not just to us. Guys like Caleb Kimball. We're trying to find them before they kill people."

"Okay. That's awful, but I suppose it makes sense." Allison stepped back to the table.

Jacob opened another book. "A bunch of them end up in some other religious group. They've been fed a diet of religion their whole life and can't leave it alone." He pinched about a third of the new book between his thumb and forefinger. "These people are in a polygamist offshoot called the Church of the Lamb. They're under the sway of some guy who claims he's Joseph Smith reborn." He thumbed through the second half of the book. "And this guy, this guy, and these two brothers are in a group outside Bakersfield who claim they are evangelical Jews, whatever that means. This book and this are Lost Boys who are in trouble with the law, drug addicts, guys trying to fight their way back into my father's church, and other nihilistic types."

"Wait," Allison said. "Open that book again—let me see something. No, that one."

Eliza handed her the book, and she flipped through quietly for a moment. "This one, here. Yes, him. I've seen this guy."

Eliza looked down at the picture with a frown. "Are you sure?"

"I'm sure. I saw him walking along the Strip with a girl I later spotted with the Chosen Ones, someone named Benita Johnson."

"Jacob, look." Eliza pushed the book across the table. "It's David."

"Who?" Allison asked.

"It's our brother," Eliza said.

"Oh my God." Allison gripped her wrist. "You see? He knows her, he knows how to find her."

Eliza nodded. "And I know how to find David."

* * *

It didn't surprise Eliza that Jacob didn't want her to go. But she hadn't counted on Fernie's opposition.

"Absolutely not," Fernie said after she and Jacob had put the kids down and the three of them retreated to the cold, dry air of the courtyard.

"You know I have to," Eliza said. "And you helped me find David, you supported me when I decided to go to Nevada to find him."

"Totally different," Jacob said. "That was your brother. And one guy."

"This is Caleb *Kimball*," Fernie said. "You remember the Kimballs, right?"

"Come on, Fernie, be serious."

"I am being serious. You seem to have forgotten Gideon and Taylor Junior. Caleb is cut from the same cloth. And he's surrounded by fanatics."

Fernie set the oil lamp down on the picnic table. Stars glittered overhead, and a breeze brought the smell of juniper from the desert. A baby cried from somewhere in the compound, then quieted.

Allison Caliari had stayed through dinner, seemingly stunned by the dozens of children, the feeling of an enormous family reunion in the main courtyard. The adults had been polite and welcoming to their visitor, but some of the children had stood a pace off, staring as she ate, as if she were an animal at the zoo. Parents kept shooing the children away, but one by one they would return. Allison

had retreated to a hotel in Manti to wait for Eliza and Jacob to come
to an agreement.

"Fernie's right," Jacob said. "I won't let you go. If anyone is
going to do it, it's going to be me."

"You've got a job at the hospital, you're just holding things
together here, and Fernie and the kids need you, too. This could
take weeks."

"What about me?" Fernie asked. "I could go."

"He's my brother."

"And you're my sister," she said. "I'm not going to let you—I
can't take that chance."

"You're about to have a baby!" Eliza said. "And would you
really leave your kids? Besides, you're both too old. You're almost
thirty, and you heard Allison, they're recruiting college students.
Maybe you could pass for that age, maybe not, but we only have
one shot."

"Then we'll find someone else," Jacob said.

"Come on," Eliza said. "You know it has to be me. Who else
is young enough, knows David, and is smart enough to pull it off?
Sorry, but it's true. The choices are to help me or not, but I'm
going."

Jacob was quiet for a long moment. Fernie closed her eyes.
Eliza guessed she was saying a silent prayer, but whether she was
asking the Lord for guidance or to change Eliza's mind, it was hard
to say.

"It should be a man," Jacob said.

"A man? Oh, please," Eliza said. "Cut the patriarchal crap."

"Liz!" Fernie said.

"Sorry for the language, but you know it's true. And since when do you pull that garbage, anyway?"

"Give me some credit, Liz," he said in a quiet voice. "I don't mean you can't do it because you're a woman, I mean it's more dangerous because you're a woman. What's the first thing these jerks do? Tell all the women to have sex with the prophet. You'll be out heaven-knows-where, starving to death, no doubt, and then some creepy guy will come into your room at night and rape you."

"That sort of thing happens to Lost Boys, too."

"But not as often. Listen, what do you think Father would say?"

"Father? Are you kidding? He tried to marry me off to Taylor Junior. You can be damn sure I'm not taking *his* advice."

"Liz!" Fernie said a second time.

"Sorry."

To Eliza's surprise, Fernie turned to Jacob. "She's right, though. We should let her go. She knows how to take care of herself."

Jacob turned and stared. "But Fernie, we agreed. You said—"

"I know what I said. I was wrong. Someone has to go. It's not just David, or the other lost children raised in the Principle who will join this cult, it's Madeline Caliari and all the others who are dying. That's what your Book of the Lost is about, isn't it? You told me yourself, it's about finding the lost sheep."

"I'm having a hard enough time keeping track of our own people. I can't start looking for other people's lost kids, too."

"Nobody's asking you to," Eliza said. "That's what I'm going to do."

"He's going to recognize you," Jacob said. "I don't mean he'll know you're Eliza Christianson and that your father is Brother

Abraham. But he'll hear your accent, or you'll say something wrong, and he'll know that you're from a polygamist family."

"I'm counting on it. In fact, I'm going to announce it first thing. That's why it's going to work."

"Whatever for?" Fernie asked, her voice alarmed. "You can't tell them, you just can't. It's too dangerous."

But Jacob looked thoughtful. "No, I think I understand."

"If I just show up, they'll never let me in," Eliza explained. "I'll bet people are trying to infiltrate all the time. Cops, private investigators, people looking for a son or a missing sister. Once you ask politely long enough, I imagine you'll try anything. But this guy isn't going to expect someone from Blister Creek to come looking for Madeline. She's a gentile." She turned to Jacob. "Well? Will you help me or not?"

Jacob was quiet for a long time, but she knew what he was going to say before it came. Her brother was the most analytical person she knew, but he also knew when to take a risk, when to seize an opportunity. This was a big risk, no question, but also a big opportunity. There were lives at stake, and not just Madeline Caliari's. Eliza waited for him to finally say it.

At last, he let out a sigh. "Okay, I'll let you go."

She put a hand on his arm, then said gently, "Thank you, but I was going to go whether you let me or not."

"I know, Liz. If you were just asking, I'd still say no. What I mean is, I'll help you as much as I can."

Fernie pulled her shawl tighter around her shoulders. "Great. Now that we're running toward the edge of the cliff, I want to hear how we're going to get down without falling."

"I need more information," Jacob said, "and there's one man who can give it to me."

"You mean—?" Eliza started.

"I do. It's time to pay my respects to the prophet of the Church of the Anointing."

It was still a shock to think of her father as a prophet. Eliza thought of the last time she'd seen Abraham Christianson, after that horrible time in Blister Creek. He'd tried to force her into marriage to the repugnant son of one of the church elders, a man who had sexually assaulted her. Even knowing that, Father had not relented. Now that she was hundreds of miles away, living in Salt Lake, she'd come to a calm, steady place, and she thought she could forgive him, maybe, if he didn't keep trying to drag her back into the church.

"Be careful," she said. "I don't trust him. He's still trying to manipulate you, and if you're not careful, you'll be sucked back into the whole mess."

"We'll be careful, don't worry."

"We?"

"Eliza," he said, "I want you to come with me to Blister Creek."

CHAPTER FIVE

The weakest of the bunch was a boy named Diego. He was nine, maybe ten, but small, starved. Nobody knew who he was or how he'd joined the group. Christopher said he was a homeless boy they'd found half-frozen in Reno a couple of years ago. Benita said no, the boy had a mother. She'd abandoned the child when Lucifer regained her soul and she returned to the crack house where the Disciple had found her.

Madeline Caliari knew that the Disciple's rules of purification were for their own good, but Diego was so young, so weak, that she always felt guilty seeing him devour the meager rations, seeing the pinched, pleading look on his face. He never begged—she'd only ever heard a few whispered words—but sometimes, when the food had been divided and there was nothing left for Diego but a half-eaten apple or crust of bread, a whimper would catch in his throat.

Once, after a sanctification with the Disciple, she'd asked him about the boy while she was putting her clothes back on. "He doesn't belong with us," she said. "We should leave him at a shelter in the city, let someone look for his parents. Or a foster home, if he doesn't have any."

The Disciple slipped into his robe and tied it off at the waist with a braided rope. With his beard and hair, he looked like Jesus. "The Lord delivered him into my hands for a reason. Until I find out what that is, he's not going anywhere."

"He's too young. He doesn't understand, and besides, he's still growing. The purification is stunting his growth."

"Stunting his growth? What does that mean?" The Disciple came and put his hand on her neck. "Madeline, child, there is no growth to stunt. Diego will never grow into a man, you know that. The Great and Terrible Day is upon us, and his only hope of avoiding the fire is to stay with us."

Madeline felt a rush of the Holy Spirit as she stared into his deep, liquid eyes and felt his warm hand against her skin. She knew he was right. But later, lying on the thin, smelly mattress, fighting the gnawing in her own stomach, she didn't think about that warm feeling, or the sanctification. She only remembered the whimper as Diego clutched his half-eaten apple, and the way his hands trembled. The boy was asleep on the next mattress over, his whistling breath joining the snores and night coughs of the others in the trailer. Madeline reached out a hand and stroked his back. Even through his shirt, she could feel skin stretched taut over ribs and a jutting spine.

The next day, when Madeline ventured on a scavenging expedition in the city, she tucked an uneaten cheeseburger into her blouse and kept it hidden until she got back to the double-wide and the two smaller, teardrop-shaped trailers. After the food was divided and devoured—Diego's portion being two limp carrots and a rind of cheese—she took him outside, behind the pile of rotting tires, where they sat on the hood of a wrecked car. She pulled out the cheeseburger.

"Here, take this, but don't say anything, right?"

Diego stared at her outstretched hand, then met her eyes with a quizzical expression.

"Go ahead. Hurry, before someone sees."

He turned back to the cheeseburger and stared. His expression reminded her of a stray cat her mother had once befriended at their house in Portland. Starting with food left on the porch, it had taken Mom weeks to earn the cat's trust, convince it that she wasn't going to kick it or mistreat it in any way. Madeline couldn't afford that kind of patience.

She grabbed Diego, and before he could claw and hiss free, she'd slapped the cheeseburger into his hands. He scrambled back several steps, until his back was against the tires. He eyed it with a ravenous look.

"Go ahead, hurry. Eat."

"Hey! What's that?" It was Christopher. He came around the pile of tires. His voice flared with anger. "Put that down."

And now, finally, Diego moved. He shoved half the burger into his mouth just as the man grabbed him. Christopher snatched up the rest of the burger and chucked it into the desert, then wrapped his hand around the boy's windpipe with one hand and pried at his mouth with the other. "Spit it out. Now!"

"Leave him alone!" Madeline cried. "Can't you see, he's starving? Just let him—let go of him!"

She struggled with Christopher, but he threw her to the side. Diego was trying to get the chunk of burger down, and might have made it if he hadn't bitten off such a huge piece. Christopher opened his mouth, scraped out the hunk of burger, and ground it into the dirt with his bare foot. He shoved the boy out of the way.

He turned on Madeline. "You. Harlot, temptress." He grabbed her by the hair and dragged her to her feet, lifting a hand to strike her across the face.

"Stop!" It was the Disciple. He stood a few paces off. A frown crossed his face. "Do not strike her."

Christopher let her go. "It was her fault. You won't believe what she did."

Madeline took two steps back. She was shaking with equal measures of anger and fear.

"I saw," he said in a quiet voice. He turned to her and there was a deep hurt in his voice. "Oh, Madeline. The Lord told me you might backslide like this. I suppose I didn't take His warning seriously enough. If I had, maybe I could have stopped you. And the boy, too. You have tempted him, and now he will suffer."

"Please, don't punish Diego. It wasn't his fault. He tried to tell me no, but I forced him. I shoved it into his hand and made him take a bite—it's my fault."

"I won't punish the boy," the Disciple said. "God will punish him for his weakness, not me."

"How will He do that?"

Meanwhile, several others had come from the trailers and watched in silence, some with haughty, judging expressions, others with sorrow, and others with worried looks. One of these was Benita, who chewed on her lip.

The Disciple ignored Madeline's question. "And I'm not going to punish you, either."

"You won't?"

She felt a wave of gratitude, mixed with guilt. She shouldn't have done it, she knew that now. It was a weak moment, and it wouldn't happen again. The smug look on Christopher's face faltered. Madeline glanced at the others to see relief on some faces, disappointment on others. There were plenty who'd be delighted to see her walk the desert, or thrust her hand into scalding water. So long as it wasn't their punishment.

"No, I won't punish you. It was weakness, more than a sin. Although I did tell you not to feed the boy, didn't I?"

"Yes, you did."

"And you accept that I am the Lord's disciple, correct?"

"Yes, I do."

The Disciple came and put a hand on her cheek. "Then why?" He sounded sad, as if her disobedience had nearly broken his heart.

"I don't know, Master. Please."

He drew back, and a smile warmed his face. "But if the Lord Jesus can be merciful, it's the least I can do."

"Thank you, I promise I won't do it again."

"I don't think you will, but I need to be sure." His voice rose, and he turned to address all of the Chosen Ones. "The End is coming, and only the most pure will survive. Madeline Caliari, can you be pure?"

Her mouth felt dry. *Pure.* There was only one thing that meant. There was a sudden silence from the others. Only the creak of black tires expanding in the desert sun, a jet overhead. It left a streak of chalk across the blue.

There was a moment, a split second, where she wondered what would happen if she said no, she couldn't be pure. Would they let her go? Would the Disciple even tell Christopher to pour a little gas in the truck and drive her into the city? And if not, surely they'd at least give her a two-liter bottle of water and let her walk. She thought she could make Highway 157, fifteen miles away. And she could walk along the highway until a car came. She'd borrow someone's cell phone and call home.

Mom, I'm sorry, I made a mistake. Could you forgive me, please?

Of course her mother would. She'd wire money to Las Vegas and catch the first flight from Portland. And then she'd take her daughter home and help put her life back together. Madeline could find her old friends, get a job, even enroll in school again.

But the moment passed in an instant. She'd given up too much to get here—she couldn't turn her back on all that sacrifice, and she couldn't face the End, the Tribulation, alone. She needed the Disciple to protect her from the horrors that awaited the earth.

Madeline looked down at her feet. "I shall be purified, if that's what you want."

"It is not what I want that matters. I want to send you inside and tell you not to do it again. It is what God wants that matters. And God wants me to prepare you for purification."

The atmosphere was now electric. The last few Chosen Ones had come from the trailers and stood in a tight knot with the others. They stood rigid, on the balls of their feet. What would be the sentence? The Disciple eyed them one by one. "Benita, go to the root cellar. Bring out twenty heads of lettuce."

A collective gasp passed through the others. Madeline felt her knees go weak. "Twenty?"

"It was a serious transgression."

"But twenty? Nobody has ever done more than ten."

"Nobody has so blatantly defied the will of the Lord."

"No, please. I can't do twenty heads, I just can't."

"You must. The lettuce, Benita," he added in a sharp voice.

Benita stared at Madeline for a long moment, and there was something unexpected in her expression. Was that, could it be, envy? And then the girl turned to hurry for the trailers.

The Disciple looked at Christopher. "Prepare Madeline for the purification."

Christopher stepped forward with a gleam in his eyes. He grabbed her blouse above the collar and tore. Buttons popped off and her shirt came free. She felt their eyes on her thin, bony body, her small breasts, and resisted the urge to cover herself. Christopher made for her pants, but she was already shrugging out of them herself. Then her underwear. A horrid shame flooded through her.

Naked, skin bleached white, she wouldn't last long in the sun without suffering a horrible burn. But this wasn't that kind of ordeal. It wouldn't be long before she'd welcome a sunburn. Twenty heads of lettuce. She would die.

Christopher grabbed her arm and looked to their leader for guidance.

The Disciple looked her over, then nodded. "Bring her to the pit."

CHAPTER SIX

The bullet-dimpled sign read "Blister Creek: Population 2,397." Eliza closed her eyes as Jacob drove past. Beyond that lay two full miles of sagebrush and red rock, but she could see the landmarks without opening her eyes: the spires of Witch's Warts, the Ghost Cliffs looming over the north side of town, the temple, which would grow from a dot until it dominated the heart of town. Together, they breached her defenses with a flood of memories.

Her early visits left a pleasant veneer over the darker impressions. She'd come several times as a child and could remember swimming with cousins in the reservoir. An aunt had taught her how to bake pies; an uncle found her father's old bicycle in a shed, changed the tires, and cleaned up the banana seat, and Eliza had spent hours riding around town with the other girls. She even remembered her brother Enoch catching a fence lizard and letting her hold it. It had closed its eyes and held still while she stroked its sapphire-blue belly. And when she stopped, it squirmed free, scrambled up her dress, and took a leap for freedom.

All of that happened before she was fourteen. Her memories from her later teen years were twisted. Sexually assaulted, traded like a prize heifer, and the horrific moment when she'd dropped a stone on Gideon Kimball's head, crushing the life out of him and sending his evil soul speeding to hell.

"Are you okay?" Jacob asked.

"No."

"Do you want to go back?"

"I can do this."

"Are you sure? Because I can take you to Panguitch, get you a motel room, and you can wait until I'm done."

"Yes, I'm sure. That's not how I want to live my life. I'm going to walk down the streets of Blister Creek, holding my head high. And when I see Father, I'm going to look him in the eye. I have nothing to be ashamed of."

"Good for you," Jacob said.

She opened her eyes when they got to the wide, gridded streets of Blister Creek itself. A pair of women in prairie dresses with several children in tow stopped and stared at the strange car as it passed. They stopped to let a sleeping dog rise, stretch, and stroll to the side of the road. Two boys on dirt bikes slowed to watch them pass, and a pickup truck coming from the other direction made a wide U-turn to fall in behind them as they turned off Main Street.

"Drive a little faster, could you?" she asked her brother.

She stared at the temple as they passed and thought about her brother Enoch, murdered by Lost Boys in the Celestial Room. "I won't let that happen to David," she said.

"I was thinking the same thing," Jacob said.

He drove down Third West, to the old Kimball compound, now possessed by Abraham Christianson, prophet of the Church of the Anointing. Father was determined to hold together the people after the horrors that had nearly destroyed the church, and several years after the murders, he had largely consolidated control. At the very least, members had stopped slipping away to join other sects or find their way to the Zarahemla compound, a hundred and fifty miles to the north.

Abraham Christianson waited on the porch with his arms folded. Even in his sixties, Brother Abraham was still a tall, powerfully built man with the same charismatic aura that Jacob commanded. Eliza found herself wavering when she saw him. Mixed with the anger were memories of a childhood spent worshiping the man. He read to her, everything from the scriptures to Shakespeare, and taught her to swim, ride a horse, and shoot a rifle. But with so many children, a farm to run, and his church duties, she hadn't seen nearly as much of him as she'd have liked.

"Jacob. Let me look at you. What a man you've become— you look like I did thirty years ago. Or should I call you Dr. Christianson?"

"Only if you want me to check your colon for polyps."

Father laughed. "Let's stick with Jacob. Eliza Christianson," he said, turning her direction. "The prodigal child returns." Before she knew it, he'd grabbed Eliza in a bear hug. When he was done, he gave her a critical once-over. "Good heavens, look at you. All grown up and beautiful. You look like your mother."

"Thank you."

"But still unmarried. That's a bit of a disappointment. Well, there's time, you're not a barren womb yet."

"I'm not any kind of womb," she snapped.

He chuckled. "The family spirit, I like it. Well, let's get you two inside. I've got a lot to discuss with Jacob before we get to the subject of marriage."

It was the old Kimball house, but overlaid with the furniture and fixtures of the house in Harmony. There was the daguerreotype of Brigham Young, the framed photograph of the Manti temple under construction, a set of dinner bells carried by Father's great-great-grandmother across the plains, the piano where all the girls had learned to play. A china cabinet that had supposedly been in the family since the faith's earliest days in Kirtland. Even the smell of the rugs brought her back to her childhood.

Father had Jacob sit down, but waved a hand at Eliza as soon as she moved to sit next to her brother. "The women are in the kitchen, getting supper ready. I'm sure they could use a hand."

It didn't matter much to Eliza, so she shrugged her shoulders and turned toward the kitchen. Some of her mother's sister wives would be there, and she hadn't seen them for ages. It would be good to catch up.

"Sit down, Liz," Jacob said.

"It's not worth fighting over. Anyway, it doesn't matter, I don't mind."

"But I do, so unless you'd rather peel potatoes, I'd just as soon you stay with me." The two men stared at each other.

"We have priesthood matters to discuss, son," Father said. "I need Eliza to leave."

"I have no secrets from Liz."

"Oh, is that how you run things in Zarahemla? You let the women into your meetings, so they can peck like hens at everything you say? Whine and complain until they get their own way?"

"Yes, I do. And I've found that the hens only complain when the rooster bullies them."

"No wonder," Father said.

"No wonder what?" Jacob demanded.

"No wonder Zarahemla is such a mess."

"Excuse me? A mess?"

"Don't get me wrong, I think it's clever how you took control after this other man, this so-called One Mighty and Strong, met his untimely demise. But that's the time to tighten your grip." He banged his fist in his hand. "Come down hard, show them the straight and narrow. You can call on the Lord to guide you." He turned to Eliza. "Go help the women—do it now."

She didn't move, but looked to Jacob. "I'll stay if you want me to."

Jacob continued to stare at Father. "Yes, please stay, Liz."

Eliza took the chair next to Jacob's side. "Since you asked so nicely, I'm happy to stay." She smiled at Father. "See how easy that was?"

A tic worked alongside his jaw. "Both of you? How dare you defy me. I should, I should…"

"You should what?" Jacob asked.

"You know what I can do. Don't make me say it."

"Feel free to kick me out," Jacob said. "If that's what you're getting at, go ahead and do it. Do the same thing to me that you did to Enoch, to David, Jeffrey, Caleb, Alonzo, Hyrum, Samuel, and Peter. What you'll no doubt do to Phineas, Brigham, and Benjamin, when the time comes. They're not exactly leadership material, either. Why should I be any different?"

"You want to be a Lost Boy?" He sounded incredulous.

"I know who I am. I won't be a Lost Boy."

"Oh, so you think you don't need me, because you've got these people in Zarahemla eating out of your hand. I'm telling you, the sooner we bring the two churches together, the better. That's why the Lord told me to put you as my first counselor, that way you can convince them it's for the good. You don't want to jeopardize that, do you?"

"Threats only work if you have something to threaten," Jacob said. "I never wanted the job, so if you snatch it away, I'll say good riddance. I'll be my own man."

"You'll be what I tell you to be."

"No, Father, I won't. Nobody tells me who I am."

He sputtered. "I don't believe it. I just cannot believe what I'm hearing. I'm warning you, boy, I've had other rebellious sons. You know what happened to them, what they've become, how far they've fallen. That will be you, too."

"Father, I've got a medical degree and am a respected doctor at a hospital. I am married and have three children, with a fourth on the way. Liz supports me, and Fernie, and several hundred other people who can see that you don't need whips and bullying to lead them."

"You've only accomplished that because of me and because it was the will of the Lord. Now, are you going to obey His servant or not?"

"Come on, Liz, let's go. I can see we're wasting our time." He began to rise.

"No, wait! We need to talk."

Jacob sat back down. "I'll be happy to talk, Father, but no more bullying. You deal with us—not just me, with Liz, too—and you're going to deal with us as equals. If you don't deal with us as equals, we're going to shake the dust from our feet and never visit this place again."

Eliza sat up straight. She had watched the exchange with growing astonishment. In spite of his bluster, Father had been on the defensive from the beginning. In years past, nobody had stood up to him like Jacob, but Father had always won, through sheer force of will and a righteous certitude in his own actions. But not today— today it was clear that Jacob was more than his equal. He was stronger than Father, even on the older man's home territory. And now, the threat to shake the dust from his feet, to condemn Father forever.

Father turned gray. "What do you want?" he asked at last.

"Liz, tell him what we want."

"Look at me, Father," Liz said. She forced strength into her voice, to match Jacob's. "In the eye."

"Do you have to do this?" he asked Jacob. "It is humiliating. I've already agreed to listen. Do you have to rub my nose in it?"

"Do it," Jacob said. "Look her in the eye and wipe the condescension off your face. She's not a child, she's an adult. If you don't do her the courtesy of treating her as an equal, you'll be the one who will look like a fool, not her."

Father stayed rigid for a long moment, then his jaw loosened. He turned his face to Eliza. At last he met her gaze, and she was surprised to see a touch of pride in his expression hiding behind his arrogance. Pride in her, it would seem. "Well, you've certainly learned some lessons from your brother."

"I hope so."

"You know, Liz, you remind me of my great-grandmother, still spitting nails until she died."

"Grannie Cowley?" Eliza asked, surprised at the comparison. Even dead for decades, the woman was something of a legend in the church, and as a child Eliza had visited the abandoned farmstead near the cliffs where the woman had lived alone for twenty years until she died at ninety-eight.

"Strong woman, didn't always have much use for men."

"Thank you, Father. I knew you had it in you."

"Okay, let's not get carried away. She still managed nine children. Why did you come? What do you want?"

"I want you to call back the Lost Boys," she said.

"What? You can't be serious."

"I'm serious. I want you to send word that they're forgiven and they can come back. This is their home and we are their family, and if we can't support them, we have no business calling ourselves saints."

"Impossible. I can't even believe you'd ask. You don't know me at all if you think that I would even consider it. And it's against the will of the Lord, in any case." He turned to Jacob. "Tell her, explain. It's impossible. Especially after Gideon attacked the church, there is no way. And wives for all of these men? Where would they come from? Tell her."

Jacob shook his head. "Talk to Liz, Father, not me."

"Eliza, it's out of the question," he said. "You'll never get that. Never."

She was prepared for his refusal. Eliza and Jacob had discussed it at great length during the drive from Zarahemla to Blister Creek and agreed that he'd balk. But, Jacob suggested, it would open an important door, as well as serve as a wedge for getting what they really wanted.

"Okay then. Call back *one* of the Lost Boys."

"Anyone in particular, or should I just draw names from a hat?"

"David. Call him back."

A moment of silence. "David wandered into the mists of darkness years ago. There's nothing I can do for him."

"You can remove your edict. Send word to Las Vegas that he's no longer banned from Blister Creek or Harmony. That you want the prodigal son to return, and you will kill the fatted calf when he does."

"That won't put him back on the straight and narrow. He's got bigger problems than my anger."

"Nothing that can't be resolved."

"You don't know the half of it, Eliza."

"We know about the drugs," she said. "But if you welcome him, it will make David think. When he sees you've softened your heart, he'll soften his own. And then I can talk to him and maybe he'll listen this time. And Jacob can help, too. Fernie, Sister Miriam, the whole community at Zarahemla. He won't even need to set foot in Blister Creek, not at first."

Father looked at Jacob. "And you agree with this?"

"Yes, of course," Jacob said. "It's a reasonable request, and you would show that you can be merciful as well as just. You'll gain more with this one act than any number of punitive reactions could hope to accomplish."

He said nothing in response, but pulled on the end of his beard. From the kitchen, the gentle murmur of voices and the sound of a pot being placed on the stove, a rolling pin on the board. "All right," he said at last. "David Christianson is forgiven. Nobody else."

Eliza got up and leaned over to kiss him on the cheek. "Thank you, Father. You'll be blessed for this kindness."

"Maybe, maybe not. But I have to warn you, it won't do any good. You have no hope of pulling David out of his spiral into hell."

"Why not?" Eliza asked.

"Because David Christianson is already doomed. An evil spirit has marked him for destruction. I've seen it in my dreams. Only a miracle would save him."

CHAPTER SEVEN

Eliza and Jacob met Fernie and Sister Miriam at a hotdog and cree-mie stand in Cedar City, an hour north of St. George. It was a clear, warm day, and none of them wanted to get up from the outdoor picnic tables and get on with the unpleasant task of sending Eliza into the belly of the beast, Las Vegas. At last Jacob finished his root beer and went off to find a prepaid cell phone for her to use. Eliza got up to use the restroom and came back to find Fernie and Miriam engaged in an intense discussion.

"Of course I don't want to share him," Fernie said. "Why would I?"

"Then why not keep your mouth shut?" Miriam asked. "He'll never get there on his own."

They fell silent as Eliza approached. "No need to stop," she said. "Count me with Sister Miriam. Jacob doesn't want anything to do with plural marriage. I'm not sure why you do, Fernie."

"Who says I do? Who says *any* woman does?"

"I know plenty of women who claim they love it. They love their sister wives, the idea of sharing the parenting and the household chores. And they say they're never jealous."

"Silk slippers on a cow," Fernie said. "You can dress it up fancy, but it still smells like manure."

"What?" Eliza asked, blinking. She turned to Miriam. "Have you seen my sister? I left her here five minutes ago, but she seems to have wandered off."

"Look, Liz, here's how I see it," Fernie continued. "We're not getting rid of polygamy. It's part of our culture. And I know in my heart that it comes from the Lord. Why, I don't know. Maybe it's just His way to make our lives more difficult, who knows? But I also know that when you keep it secret, when you barter women like livestock, it turns out ugly. If you want to get rid of the manipulation, the underage brides, the trouble with the law, you need to bring it into the open." She hesitated. "I might need to set an example."

"What about you, what do you think?" Eliza asked Miriam.

"I don't have any emotional attachment to polygamy, if that's what you mean."

"Well then?"

She shrugged. "My family was moderately religious, but I never had any sort of spiritual experience until I came to Zarahemla."

"It's not like that turned out well," Eliza said.

"I know, I'm still wrestling with that. But in spite of everything, I can't deny what happened to me there. I know God led me to the truth, and I know I was promised I would be the wife of a great leader when the Last Days arrive."

"Meaning Jacob?"

"I believe so, yes. In the Lord's time."

Eliza glanced at Fernie, who said nothing.

"But I don't know for sure," Miriam added. "Right now all I know is that Jacob isn't acting to his full potential."

"How do you know that?" Fernie asked, her voice strained.

Miriam looked surprised. "Don't you think he's falling short of his calling?"

"What I think or don't think is irrelevant. I don't know how you could make a judgment, that's all. Whether or not you'll be married to him someday, you aren't right now, and you don't have any more insight than anyone else in the church."

"I think I do."

"Right, because you were an FBI agent, you think you have a special insight," Fernie said. "Some super exclusive ability to discover hidden motives."

"I didn't lose my skills when I quit the bureau. It's why the Lord brought me here, so I could help Jacob reach his potential. I'm convinced of that. And I'll do what it takes to make it happen."

Eliza didn't understand either woman. Fernie wasn't jealous about sharing her husband's body with Miriam, but sharing insight into his soul was another matter. And Miriam claimed she only wanted to obey the will of the Lord, but Eliza had heard enough claims to know that the will of the Lord matches one's own desires with startling frequency.

Fernie opened her mouth to say something, but Eliza never found out what, because Jacob pulled up in the car, having secured the prepaid phone.

* * *

Eliza entered Las Vegas feeling confident. She knew the limitations of its power. She'd entered the first time as a naïve teenage girl, tagging along with her brother Jacob while he investigated a murder. The city was just as aggressive six years later, still dripping with sin and corruption, but it no longer had the power to frighten her.

It helped to picture the city naked.

There was no reason for Las Vegas to even exist. It didn't have a port, wasn't on a river. It wasn't surrounded by rich croplands and hadn't grown organically from some trade advantage. It wasn't even the capital of the state. Instead, Vegas was surrounded by dry, baking wilderness and survived only by upping the shock value from one year to the next. People came to gamble or be entertained, but these days you could do those things anywhere. What other places didn't have was the continual growth of the lurid and obscene, the promise that every time you came back, there would be some sparkling new thing to catch the eye. A volcano! Pirate battles! The Eiffel Tower! Someday, that sparkle would fade and then the city would die. People would return to live in real towns and cities and leave Las Vegas to crumble in the desert until it became the biggest ghost town of all.

In the meanwhile, the city's outward appearance was a hulking, intimidating monster, but Eliza knew the beast was toothless. What was it Jacob had told her once? *The real monsters live inside us.*

And so she fought down the neon, concrete shock, ignored the lurid, the obscene, and the aggressive, and thought about her brother David. She stepped off at the Greyhound bus terminal, near the Strip, then stood on the curb with her suitcase in hand, while the buses huffed diesel fumes. Her eyes scanned the street for a taxi.

Miriam and Fernie had returned to Zarahemla in the second car while Jacob drove Eliza to the bus stop in St. George, in the extreme southwest corner of Utah, just over the border from Arizona and Nevada. They had stood apart from the others as passengers shuffled onto the bus. Mostly older people, probably heading for Las Vegas for a weekend of gambling. But there were also a few shifty types, with drawn hoods and baggy pants or shaved heads and tattooed arms. One guy wore plugs in his ears and bristled with piercings.

Jacob produced the prepaid cell phone. "Here, take this one, give me yours. This one only cost twenty bucks, so you can ditch it without a second thought. And there's nothing on the phone to identify you. Fernie and I have the number, plus Sister Miriam and Allison Caliari. Nobody else."

She tucked it into her pocket. "Thanks."

"Call me when you get there and every day after that."

"I'll call you when I get there, if I can. But these guys sleep in Dumpsters and eat trash. They don't carry cell phones, and if I'm going to blend in, I can't either."

"You need to check in, Liz. You know I can't let you go if you don't."

"I'll find a place to stash it. Let's say twice a week until I'm out."

He frowned.

Eliza put a hand on his arm. "You've got to trust me. I'll find a way to let you know I'm okay, but it's not going to be every twenty-four hours."

At last, he nodded. "I'm just worried," he said as another dodgy-looking kid made his way past them and onto the bus. "I wish I could tell you not to be afraid, that there's nothing to worry about, no real danger. But that would be a lie."

"I'll sit up front by the driver."

No smile. She was surprised at how nervous he looked. "You know what I'm talking about. Those guys on the bus are about show, about looking like they mean business. The people you're trying to find don't need to show anything, but they're ten times as dangerous. People have died in there, Liz."

"Thanks, that's comforting."

"My point is, only idiots aren't afraid of danger, and you're not an idiot. So you'll be afraid. You can deal with that."

"I'm waiting for the part where you say something encouraging," she said. "As in, 'You can do it, Liz!' or something like that."

"Of course you can do it. But you already know that. Listen to me. Being brave is about *acting* brave, that's all. Like you did with Father. You looked him in the eye and you acted like you weren't intimidated. But I knew your heart was pounding and you didn't want to lift your hands because you were afraid they'd tremble."

Just then, the bus driver leaned out and said, "You ready? We're rolling in two."

"Coming," Eliza said. She turned back to Jacob after the man disappeared back inside. "You're right, I was nervous. But anyway, that's different. Father is…difficult. These people are nuts. And Caleb Kimball…he scares me. I'll bet he's nuts, too."

"You don't know that. You don't know anything about them."

"Of course they're nuts. Look at what they're doing."

"We're nuts too, to anyone who isn't from a polygamist family," Jacob said. "You don't know if they're crazy or sane, sincere or cynical, so be prepared for anything. But what you do know is that you're stronger than anyone you're going to meet in there. Even Caleb Kimball."

"Am I?"

"Of course you are. If I didn't think that, there's no way I could send you to Vegas, let you track down David on your own, find this group and infiltrate it, knowing they might try to kill you. I can only do that because I know you're stronger and smarter and more resourceful."

"There we go," she said. "That's what I was looking for. Maybe you should have started with that part."

"And let you get cocky? I don't think so." He gave her a hug. "Get David, get the girl. Then get out."

"I won't stay one minute longer than I have to."

She had watched him staring at the bus as it pulled out of the station, then pulled out the cell phone Jacob had given her and called Allison Caliari. "I just wanted you to know that I'm on my way to Las Vegas to find your daughter."

"Oh, thank God. Thank you. When you see her, tell her I love her. If she can just come home, we can figure this out."

"I'll tell her."

"Eliza, be careful."

The words were exactly what she'd expected, but there was something odd in her voice that Eliza couldn't put her finger on. It was as if she'd been watching a play—no, make that as if she'd been onstage *with* Allison in one. The curtain had fallen on their scene, and that's when Allison's voice had taken on that odd tone. As if the rest had been an act, but now this, *this* was real. Eliza didn't know what to make of it, but she had other worries.

Now, standing alone in the Las Vegas bus station, Eliza gathered her courage, put a confident expression on her face, and hailed a taxi. Now came the hard part.

* * *

David was in such pain and needing something to kill that pain that he didn't notice that someone had broken into his house. A cast immobilized his right arm past the elbow, he had stitches on his forehead, and his ribs ached with every movement. Angry bruises covered his shoulder and chest, and his face was puffy and yellow-black. His left eye still wouldn't open fully.

Steve at Yost Deliveries had taken one look at him when he'd shown up at work two days after the attack and said, "I knew it, you rolled the truck, didn't you? Jeez, dude, you couldn't bother to call? Customers have been all over my ass."

"No, that's not what happened." He'd carefully worked out what to say next. "I was on the sidewalk downtown, standing too close to the curb. Some drunk clipped me with his bumper and dragged me half a block."

"What? Really? Then the truck is fine?"

"Thanks for caring, man."

Steve had backpedaled, asked about his health and all that. And then still fired him. Never mind that David had been in the hospital, unable to call, fighting for his life against internal bleeding. No, what mattered were the irate customers, thousands of dollars' worth of produce baking in the back of the truck, and that David would be busted up and unable to drive for two weeks.

And so David took a taxi home from the yard, slumped in the backseat, his head pounding, body aching in a dozen places, and shakes working through his hands. As the taxi pulled away, he dragged himself from the curb, squinted against the sun, and then staggered into the house. He had to get to the bathroom, see if he could find something.

They'd given him Oxycontin at the hospital, but he'd gone through a week of pills in the first twenty-four hours. He needed something stronger, something to hammer down the pain. He thought about his meth guy, and the other stuff he carried. The brown stuff, the kind you delivered with syringes. That was just the thing to knock down the pain. But he'd told himself he wasn't going to do it again.

Hands shaking, he emptied the bottle of aspirin in the sink, trying to find a little green pill hidden at the bottom. Nothing. Also nothing at the back of the lower drawers, not even an old joint. He put a hand to his temple and leaned over the sink, thinking he was going to be sick. He'd call Meth Guy, see about the heavy stuff. What choice did he have?

The bathroom door opened behind him. He turned in a panic. The sudden movement hit him with a blackening wave of vertigo and he fell, grabbing at the edge of the sink at the last moment to keep from cracking his skull on the side of the tub. His arm with the cast whacked painfully against the floor. The intruder was already on top of him. He lifted his good arm to shield his face.

"No, David, no. It's only me."

Gentle hands on his. He looked up to see his sister Eliza standing over him, and he was so overwhelmed with relief that he let out a sob.

"Oh no," she said as her face fell. "What happened to you?"

"I was mugged for some lettuce."

"Lettuce? What? Is that slang for some kind of drug? No, never mind. Come on, let's get you out of here. Can you stand up?"

She helped him into his bedroom. He fell back on the bed while she pulled off his shoes. "I'm sorry for scaring you like that. I got tired of standing around in the heat, waiting for you to get back, so I broke in. One of the windows in the basement wasn't latched down, and I forced it open."

"But how did you find me?"

"It wasn't hard. Once Father gave us your fake name, Jacob found the address in about twenty minutes digging around on the Internet."

"Father? Why would he help?" He couldn't muster any anger.

"He's removed his edict. You're not banned from Blister Creek anymore."

"Really? Is he here? Jacob, too?"

"No, just me. Get under the covers. I'll be right back."

She returned with a glass of water and some pills. "I cleaned up the aspirin in the bathroom, and I found some Tylenol. That will work better. Here, take these."

He stared at the white tablets in her outstretched hand. The Tylenol looked about as helpful as Tic-Tacs.

"It's okay, don't worry. I know the bottle says take two, but I figure a third won't hurt this once. You look like you could use something extra."

How about three bullets to the head instead? That ought to do the trick.

But he took the Tylenol and washed them down with water. His empty stomach clenched when they went down, and he bent over, feeling ill. Eliza ran to the kitchen and brought back a big bowl, but the moment passed. As he sank into the pillows, she returned with a hot washcloth, which she dabbed against his forehead. She found the bag he'd brought from the hospital and changed the bloody gauze above his eye. David wanted to cry.

A deep, aching loneliness had seeped into his bones since seeing Eliza at the Girlz Club in Mesquite. What was he doing? Did he want to live like this? And now he had this demon with its claws into him, this demon whispering that maybe heroin was the answer.

It's okay, it whispered. *You're busted up. Just for now, just to help with the pain. You'll just dip and dab a little, give it up once you feel better.*

Except he wouldn't give it up. As broken down as he was, once would be enough. And then the demon wouldn't just have its claws in him, it would climb into his veins and he'd never get it out. And in spite of knowing that, David also knew that if Eliza were to leave now and Meth Guy were to show up with the hard stuff, he would happily take that first hit.

She dabbed at his forehead again. "Do you know someone named Madeline Caliari?"

He opened his good eye and squinted up at her. "Who?"

"Madeline Caliari. She's twenty years old, from Oregon."

"Never heard of her."

"Okay then, how about Benita Johnson? How do you know her?"

David opened both eyes this time and forgot his pounding head. "What? Who are these people, and why do you want to know?"

"That one you do know. I can see it on your face."

"Dammit, Liz."

"Language, please."

"Okay, language. Right. Gosh darn it all to heck. Jumping Judas on a pogo stick. What the flying fetch are you asking all these questions for? There, is that better?"

"Please, David. I need to know how you know Benita Johnson."

"And here I thought this was a mercy mission." He sighed. "Yeah, I know BJ. Met her at a party. She gave me meth. No big deal. We hung out for a while, then she disappeared. I thought she'd run off with some dealer, or maybe jumped in front of a bus. She's got a nasty self-destructive streak. Yeah, worse than mine."

"Are you really doing crystal meth? I thought it was just marijuana. Oh, David, how could you?"

"Easy, when you've got nothing to live for, you don't care anymore. But yeah, it was the meth that got me beat to hell last time. Drug deal gone bad—a bit cliché, don't you think?"

"And this time? Same thing?"

"No, that was BJ's new friends. She's found a new crowd to run with. No idea who, but they're some mean SOBs. They robbed my truck, apparently just for the hell of it, then practically beat me to death. I have no idea why."

"I do. It's an eschatological religious sect."

"Oh yeah? End-of-the-world nutters. Well, that figures."

He told her about the biblical verse on the side of the panel truck.

"Revelation 8:10," Eliza said. "That's the third angel, Wormwood burning from the sky, right?"

"More or less. Damn, I can't figure out how BJ got caught up in that. I think she came from a hardcore Baptist family, but she didn't seem religious to me. More like trying to destroy herself in bits and pieces."

"Kind of like you, then."

"Funny, I never thought of that before," he said with a touch of sarcasm.

And yet, wasn't it true? Wasn't half his self-destructive behavior caused by this worm of doubt that he couldn't cough up? A feeling of despair and failure, worry that he really had caused all the problems in his life, that if he'd only stayed faithful to the gospel he would have stayed in the church. Instead, he'd strayed, been thrust into the Lone and Dreary World as punishment. And it was his own fault. He was damned already, so what did it matter?

Eliza must have been reading his thoughts. She leaned over and put a hand on his cheek. It felt cool against his burning skin. "You can come back. You know that, right?"

"There's no way, not with everything I've done."

"There's nothing you can't repent of," Eliza said, "and forgive yourself, too."

"Really? Nothing? Let me tell you a few things—you'll see. My first day in Nevada, I met a coked-out hooker. Neither of us had any condoms. I was only sixteen. She—"

"Please, it doesn't matter. You made a mistake, you were young. I made mistakes when I was young, too."

"Sure you did, Liz. What, you said a naughty word? Drank a Pepsi? Let me tell you what I've put in my body, then you'll see."

"I don't care about any of that," she said. "Neither does Jacob. He loves you, I love you, we're your family. Whatever you've done, you can turn it around."

"And Father? Does he love me, too?"

"Father doesn't matter. Jacob confronted him and broke him down."

"What?" David blinked. "How is that even possible? Is Father that weak now? He isn't even that old."

"It wasn't Father, it was Jacob. You haven't seen him lately or you'd know. Come back, David."

"Liz, you have no idea where I am right now. Even if I wanted to, it's too late, I'm too far gone."

"It's never too late."

He didn't have the energy to continue this argument. "Who is Madeline...whatever her name is?" he asked.

"Madeline Caliari. She's been sucked into this religious group, and I promised I'd get her out."

Eliza explained about the girl's mother and the other parents who had been searching for their kidnapped—or, rather, brainwashed—children. About the three kids who'd died already. And Eliza's own plan to find the group. She had printed up a bunch of fundy Christian tracts from the Internet and was going to stand on a corner near the UNLV campus, handing them out, until she drew someone's attention.

"And Jacob is on board with this scheme?" he asked.

"More or less."

"More less than more, I'm guessing, if he cares about you at all. It's insane."

"It's a good plan," she protested.

"A good plan for getting yourself killed. Besides, if you go to campus, you might stand there for weeks before anyone notices."

"Do you have a better idea?"

"Apart from going home and forgetting the whole thing?"

"If Jacob couldn't convince me to give it up, what chance do you have?" she asked.

"Fine, then yes, I have a better idea. I think I know how to find them. You could walk up to their door, knock, and ask to enlist. But look at you, you're just a girl. I don't care how smart you are, they'll eat you alive."

She smiled. "Then it's perfect. If you think that, and you should know better, they'll be sure to underestimate me. Where are they?"

"You're serious, aren't you?" He stared at her for a long moment, giving her a chance to back down. She just stared back. Finally, he sank into the pillows and closed his eyes. "Fine. Here's what you'll do."

After he explained about the ravine and his guess as to their location in the desert, Eliza stepped into the other room to call Jacob. David couldn't shake the feeling that he was sending his sister into serious danger. He expected that Jacob would talk some sense into her, but after she relayed what David had just told her about the ravine, all he heard were her replies to what sounded like mild warnings: "Don't worry...of course I'll be careful...yes, I will... Jacob, stop worrying!"

Maybe Jacob would be a little more alarmed if Eliza told him about how the cult members had beaten David nearly to death, but David noticed that she kept these details to herself.

Eliza ended the call and returned to David's bedroom. She may have been hiding information from Jacob, but he could tell from the grim set to her mouth that she suffered no such delusions herself.

"I can see what you're thinking," she said. "Don't try to talk me out of it."

"I already tried that. I'd try again, but I'm guessing it would be pointless."

"You're right." A curt nod. "Okay, I'm ready."

CHAPTER EIGHT

Eliza felt like a migrant, illegally crossing the Sonora Desert, evading Border Patrol agents to enter the United States. She carried a backpack with a gallon jug filled with water and three protein bars in the side pocket. It was the closest to food David could find in his house, and she hadn't wanted to call a taxi to take her to the nearest mini-mart. Better to get started before she could lose her nerve.

David had insisted she wait until morning, at least. "It could be three hours on foot, for all you know. You don't want to be out there at night."

Reluctantly, she'd agreed. It turned out to be a wise decision.

She made it fifteen minutes up the wash before she was already drinking from the water bottle. A racer lizard crossed the sand with a jerky walk and a bobbing head, then ran for cover as soon as she started to move again. She startled a jackrabbit, which exploded from the shade in giant, leaping bounds before tearing off. It grew hotter as she continued, and soon even the lizards and jackrabbits grew scarce. She heard nothing but the hum of insects from the sage that surrounded the ravine.

The sun climbed into the sky and then seemed to stand still. It was only the first week in May, but it had to be over ninety degrees. What would it be like in the summer? At least Blister Creek, with its altitude on the Colorado Plateau, didn't get this hot until June. The Spring Mountains shimmered to her left, snow still covering the highest peaks.

Another stop for a drink. The gallon was half gone. How long now, two hours? Three? The ground at the bottom of the wash was relatively flat, but the sand made walking an exhausting endeavor. And every step took her deeper into the desert.

She wondered if migrants felt the same worry as they set off into the wilderness behind some human smuggler, their money already stuffed in his pockets. Everyone knew that coyotes sometimes abandoned migrants to their deaths when things took a wrong turn.

But at least the migrants weren't dumb enough to enter the desert alone. Eliza's only guide was the footprints that continued in both directions up and down the dry wash. David wasn't wrong. Someone had come down this wash on foot within the last couple of days. She drank more water. Already two-thirds gone. She continued deeper into the desert.

* * *

An hour after his sister set off to search for the lettuce thieves, David left on foot for Meth Guy's place, two miles away. He stopped for an iced coffee at a 7-Eleven, which woke him up but didn't do anything for the headache or shakes.

Meth Guy lived in a basement apartment southeast of the ghost subdivisions. The neighborhood was several years older than David's, and while real estate signs sprouted in half the yards, it hadn't been abandoned after the crash. Some of the houses even had landscaping, including a few short trees. Plenty of cars and pickup trucks in driveways.

David went down to the basement door and knocked. He heard someone behind the door, and a minute later it cracked behind a chain. Meth Guy peered out. "Jeez, man, what happened to you?"

"I was hit by a car."

"You look like shit."

"Yeah, thanks. Can I come in?"

"Depends. You got money?"

"Of course I've got money," David snapped. He felt jittery, angry, and wanted to kick in the door. "What do you think I am?" He pulled a couple of twenties to show.

Meth Guy opened the door. "I have no idea." A flash of teeth. "I don't mean to insult my customers, but you show up on foot, beat to hell, it looks suspicious, know what I mean?"

David came in. The place was like a cave, with blankets over the windows, an old, moldy carpet, its smell somewhat masked by the strange chemical odor that hung in the air. Meth Guy was a pale, wiry man with eyes that darted back and forth from David's face to the street and then back again. Cargo pants and a tank top that hugged him tight enough to show his bony ribcage. He shut the door, and David's eyes took a long moment to adjust to the single light bulb in the room.

"So what happened to Nita?" Meth Guy asked.

"Who? Oh, you mean BJ?" he asked. "I don't know. She hooked up with Pedro."

"The surfer dude selling the crappy stuff? That shit'll put you in the gutter. I thought Pedro left town with some Mexicans trying to kill him. Nita, that little slut. She owes me either five hundred bucks or twenty blow jobs."

"Those are cheap blow jobs," David said.

He shrugged. "Nita's a cheap whore."

David had nothing with Benita, just a couple of crappy, drug-dazed weeks and some equally crappy sex. But he found the fist of his good hand clenching in anger. Meth Guy must have seen the fist, because his hand groped at a side pocket on his cargo pants as if reaching for something.

David lifted his hand. "No worries, man. She's not my girlfriend."

"Of course not, she owes me money, that's all. You gonna pay it?" The hand left the pocket.

"What? Why would I pay it? I barely know the girl. But if I see her, I'll tell her you're looking for her." He shrugged. "For all I know, she's dead."

Except he did have an idea where Benita had gone, and it wasn't dead and it wasn't running from gangbangers with Pedro. The lettuce thieves had her. Could she really have fallen in with a cult? He thought about that terrifying incident on the roof.

About a week after they'd met, David and Benita had been at another party when she said she wanted to go to the roof for some air. She was giggling wildly as they rode the elevator to the twenty-fourth floor, and by the time they climbed the stairs to get up the last flight, he was laughing too, though he had no idea why, except that they were both flying high. Benita wore a black skirt and black combat boots. Black shirt, black hair, black lipstick. As she climbed the stairs above him, he saw that her panties were black, too.

This was late February, and the air outside was crisp. He tried to go back, but she grabbed his arm, still laughing, and pulled him out. "Look at that."

Las Vegas glittered with a million lights. Down below, the Strip was a pulsing, neon thing, like something alive. From this height, it was a blanket of lights, beautiful, with only a few larger signs legible. Benita leaned over the railing at the edge of the building.

"Be careful, you're freaking me out."

She turned and beckoned with a finger and a smirk at her lips. "Come on over."

"I'm scared of heights."

"No you're not, you big baby. Come on." The wind caught her hair and gusted it around her face. "You don't come over, I'm going to climb over the railing." She hooked one leg over the bar, caught him looking at her black panties, and raised an eyebrow. "You like that, huh?"

"I'm serious, BJ."

"So am I. Come over here, and I'll make it worth your while."

And so he went. For a moment, they stood at the edge together, looking down at the city. Then she climbed over the railing.

"BJ!"

"Quit worrying, I'm not going to jump. Hold onto my belt."

It wasn't much of a belt, just a chain of interlocking rings. Two silver skulls dangled off the end. But it was metal, and it was secured tightly around her waist. He grabbed it at the back with both hands as she leaned out with her hands behind her, gripping the railing.

"You got me?" she asked.

"Come back over, I'm serious."

"I'm letting go. Hold my belt."

And before he could protest, she'd released the bar and leaned over the edge, like a rappeller testing his weight on the rope, but there was no rope, just her belt, and she was facing forward, away from him and toward the street below. David might have been high a few minutes earlier, but he felt stone sober at the moment. His hands were cold, growing numb.

"It would be so easy to fall, wouldn't it?" Benita said. He didn't answer, just concentrated on holding on. She leaned out a little farther. "What would it be like? A couple of seconds, like flying."

Benita stretched out her arms, arched slightly behind her, like hawk wings in a dive. And in the light, he saw hatch marks across her arms. Dozens of tiny cuts, like she'd scored her skin with a knife. How had he missed that before?

The wind caught her hair again, billowed her skirt and flapped it against David's arms. Her bare, thin legs trembled.

"I should fly off this building. Maybe I'd soar away like an angel. I won't even land, I'll just fly to heaven."

"You'll fall to your death," he said.

"And what if I do? It will only last a second. I'll be crushed, there will be nothing left. It's what I deserve."

"Don't be crazy. Come back over now."

"I wouldn't be mad, you know."

"Huh?"

"I wouldn't blame you at all."

"What are you talking about?" David asked.

"If you let go of my belt. I'd start to fall, and I wouldn't blame you. It wouldn't be your fault, I know that. And then I'd try to fly, and maybe I would. Or maybe I'd just fall, and that wouldn't make me mad, either."

His arms were aching, muscles quivering from exhaustion. Her words frightened him. His hands wanted to obey, to just let go. He could imagine her tumbling end over end. Would she scream? Would there be a noise?

He gave a terrific effort and pulled her back to the railing, let go with his right hand, and wrapped it around her chest. At last she relented and let him help her back over to the safe side of the railing. For a long moment, he held Benita in his arms. He could feel her trembling and her small breasts pressed against him.

David had almost nothing in common with the girl except for drugs and sex, and a couple of weeks later, when she disappeared with Pedro—or so he'd thought at the time—he was more relieved to be rid of her than anything. But at that moment, with her head against his neck, shivering in his arms and choking down a sob, he felt an overwhelming sense of love and sorrow. He should have said something. Maybe things would have turned out differently.

But then she had yanked away. "Come on, this buzz is crashing fast. Let's go get something at the party."

There had been something in that talk about angels and heaven that now rang a distant bell in David's thoughts. And hadn't she said another time that her parents were strict Baptists? Still, that was a quick shift from dangling over the edge of a tall building, stoned, to member of an end-of-the-world cult living in the desert. And why did she have to run off and leave her dealer looking for his money?

Meth Guy was staring at him. "So what're you here for, anyway? You brought money, what do you want?"

"You know what I want. I'm looking for Tina."

He shook his head. "Sorry man, Tina has checked out of the hotel. Sold out this morning. I've got some weed."

"I don't want weed. You don't have anything?"

"I didn't say I don't have anything, I said I don't have any Tina."

"Well what do you have? Not weed. I hurt like hell, and I need something stronger."

"Tina's checked out, but Mister Brownstone is in the building. Black tar from Mexico, good stuff."

David froze. He felt the claws of the demon break the skin. His body shivered. It seemed to hurt everywhere. "I don't know, that's pretty hard-core. Not my thing."

"Then come back Tuesday, I'll get your shit. You still owe me fifty, by the way. I'll take that now."

"Tuesday? That's three days from now."

"Yeah, no kidding. I'm busy, come back Tuesday."

The demon dug in deeper. He could almost hear it whispering in his ear. Was this what Benita had been feeling when she'd stood on the outside of the railing, leaning over, hoping that David would let go because she was too much of a coward to jump? And the feeling, almost the desire, to suffer at the end, to wake up in hell. Because that's what you deserve.

David pulled out his money. "I'll take the heroin."

CHAPTER NINE

Two heads of lettuce gone, eighteen to go. The other heads sat in a box in the corner of the filthy pit in the desert. Madeline crouched in the darkness, in a hole cut into rocky Nevada hardpan. Overhead, the old dump. Eighteen heads left, but she thought she'd only make a dozen more before things grew scary.

The Disciple had found an abandoned double-wide several miles into the desert beyond the outermost outskirts of Las Vegas. There had been an old road that led to a ghost mining town in the foothills at the base of the Spring Mountains. Sagebrush and sand had overrun the road, but it was still flat and passable to a truck or car with decent clearance. Along the road lay one of the semi-legal dumps where generations of Nevadans had tossed old mattresses, dead appliances, rusting cars, and thousands and thousands of tires. It looked like it had been at least ten years since anyone had used the dump.

The abandoned trailer itself had been home to kangaroo rats and rattlesnakes, but once cleared out gave reasonable protection from the elements. The Disciple had towed a pair of aluminum teardrop campers to the site and propped them on cinder blocks on either side of the trailer. Together, the campers and the trailer served as a refuge for the Chosen Ones while they hid from family or came to learn from the Disciple. He'd ordered one big stack of tires moved to conceal the trailers from the road—should anyone come, which hadn't yet happened—and threw a few on top of the trailers to disguise them from the airplanes that occasionally flew a few thousand feet overhead.

The purification pit lay hidden beneath an overturned refrigerator. Christopher had dragged her to the hole while three others pushed the fridge out of the way. She'd climbed into the pit herself, and then she took the box of lettuce lowered down to her while they lifted up the ladder and slid the fridge back into place. The pit widened at the bottom, to the width of two filthy mattresses. Laid side by side, the mattresses covered the earth.

Madeline huddled in one corner. It was cool in the pit and stank of human waste. She'd awakened a few minutes earlier, unsure if it was day or night and now counted to pass the time.

How long since the last head of lettuce? At least twelve hours, she thought. Maybe as long as twenty. The previous day she'd been convinced they'd forgotten about her entirely. She'd yelled for help, but if anyone could hear, they hadn't answered.

She counted to a hundred and back twenty times and then stopped. She took a swig of water from a milk jug, then got up to pee in another milk jug. Took a sniff from each jug first, to make sure she had the right one. An overwhelming wave of despair crashed down on her. Satan was here, she could feel him. She groped in the dark until she found the exposed edge of one of the mattress springs and started to slash it across her arm before she stopped herself with a heroic effort.

"The Lord is my Shepherd, I shall not want. He maketh me to lie down in green pastures, he leadeth me beside the still waters. He restoreth my soul, he leadeth me in the path of righteousness for His name's sake. Yea, though I walk through the Valley of the Shadow of Death, I will fear no evil, for thou art with me, thy rod and thy staff, they comfort me. Thou preparest a table before me in the presence of mine enemies."

Here she stopped for a long moment, her breath short and shallow. The evil presence had grown until it pressed like a weight on her chest and a blackness swirled in her head, deeper than the black at the bottom of the pit. A moan escaped her lips. The enemy was here, he wanted to take possession of her. Her fingernails dug into the flesh on her arm.

She managed to open her mouth. "Thou annointest my head with oil, my cup runneth over. Surely goodness and...and *mercy*... shall follow me all the days of my life. And I will dwell in the house of the Lord forever." This last part came in a gasp.

Madeline repeated the twenty-third Psalm three times before Satan left her, and with him, the urge to cut herself. The need to eat the lettuce remained.

But if she took too much and they checked, as they sometimes did, the Disciple would double her ordeal. Her only hope was to exercise self-control. How long had it been now? Twenty hours? Could she make it another four?

But just as she thought this, someone banged three times on the fridge at the top of the pit. Madeline let out a sob of relief. She groped in the corner for the crate, but couldn't find it. She felt along the wall, but couldn't find it anywhere, and so she started to work her way around the tiny room. At last it came to her, on the opposite side from where she'd started searching. Either she'd moved it, or she'd become completely turned around.

Her fingers found one of the heads of lettuce, pulled it out, cradled it in her hands.

"Dear Lord Jesus, bless this food and with it purify me before thy mercy."

And with that, she tore off a hunk and ate it. In moments, it was gone. She had a bloated feeling, but that was mostly water. Very shortly, that bloated feeling would dissipate, to be replaced by the consuming hunger.

Twenty-four hours. One head of lettuce. Three down, seventeen to go. She'd been weak and bony when she entered the purification pit. She didn't know if she'd be dead when they carried her out.

* * *

It was almost evening when Eliza found the old road. The dry wash cut a gash through the decades-old pavement. Another hour and it would have been too dark to see the clues, and she would have ignored the road and continued to follow the wash.

But it was still light when she reached the spot where the wash bisected the road, and Eliza was alert. Her water was gone, and she faced the prospect of spending the night in the desert. The air would shed its heat, and she'd shiver all night, only to wake up in the morning still in the middle of the wilderness. Why hadn't she found them yet? Eliza was a strong girl, surely as physically strong as the Chosen Ones. She couldn't believe they'd taken a multiday journey through the desert on foot.

And so she was in the perfect frame of mind when she reached the road. She noticed immediately the tire tracks cutting through the wash from one side to the other. And the footprints stopped.

A new problem, then. They'd walked for hours, yes, but then someone had picked them up in a truck and followed an old road. None of that made sense. Why walk at all? Why not just drive in and out of Las Vegas?

Eliza had to be close. If not, if she had made a bad assumption somewhere, she'd be in serious trouble. Unless she took the road back toward Las Vegas. She could follow it in the darkness and reach the city by morning. Water gone, dehydrated, but alive. For a moment, she hesitated and looked to the glowing city behind her.

At last, she turned away from Las Vegas and followed the road deeper into the desert. Walking on the road was a relief to her aching calves after all day spent trudging through the sand. For a good hour there was nothing but the sound of her footsteps, the wind, and the drone of cicadas in the scrub that lined the wash. The drone faded as the wash snaked away to her left. And then, a snatch of voices, carried on the wind. Her pulse quickened.

She came upon an overturned motorboat, a hole punched through the fiberglass. A little farther, a rusting car, then two washing machines, open to the air as if waiting to be loaded. And then the garbage began in earnest: rusting cans, shoes, metal office furniture, a pile of televisions—the old kind with knobs—and later, a heap of printers, monitors, and other office equipment. A huge tire from a piece of construction equipment, almost as large as the front half of the VW bug that lay next to it. Ahead, she could see several mountains of tires.

The voices picked up as she drew closer to the tires. A woman said something about Jesus, before the wind shifted and the voice died. Eliza slowed down, worked over her story. It was twilight, finally cooling.

Eliza wanted to have a look around, wanted to explore the dump before she announced her presence. Maybe she could even come up to their campfire, or whatever it was, and watch them from the shadows to see if she could recognize Madeline. For a moment she entertained the fantasy of bumping into Madeline, explaining her purpose, and then escaping into the desert before anyone realized the girl was gone.

But she had to accept that Madeline might not want to be rescued. Eliza had seen it a dozen times. A child bride, desperate not to get married, but refusing to testify against her family. Or what about Sister Miriam, an FBI agent who'd infiltrated the Church of the Last Days, but then she became indoctrinated enough in the cult that she'd never bothered to check back in. Even after the FBI tried to rescue her, Miriam had denounced her career and stayed in the Zarahemla compound.

And what if someone heard Eliza snooping around? She'd blow her chances before she could introduce herself. Eliza dialed Jacob's cell phone. He picked up on the first ring. "It's me," she said in a low voice.

This far into the desert, she barely had a signal and couldn't hear his answer. Rather than fumble through greetings and possibly lose the call, she said the agreed-upon words to indicate everything was okay. "Blessed are they whose feet stand upon the land of Zion. Did you hear that? I'm fine."

"Great, but..." His voice broke up again, and then she lost the call entirely.

She found a sofa on its side, cushions missing, the stuffing torn out by animals, turned her phone off, and tucked it inside a torn flap of fabric, among the springs. She didn't want to be caught with it on her person. She tossed the empty backpack. The voices continued somewhere in front of her.

"Hello!" she cried. "Is anyone here?"

The voices stopped at once, like crickets going silent when they hear footsteps. Eliza came around the corner of the nearest stack of tires to discover a double-wide trailer and two of the old-style, silver-colored campers. There were so many tires stacked on and around them that she might have passed right by if she hadn't heard the voices, at least this close to dusk.

"Hello?" She came to a stop fifteen feet from the front door of the trailer. A thin, flickering light—like a Coleman lantern—seeped through one of the trailer windows and then went dark. In that brief glance she'd seen bars over the windows. Someone had been paranoid enough to fortify the trailer as if it were a house at the edge of the slums, instead of an abandoned trailer in the desert.

Still no answer, so Eliza sat down on an overturned refrigerator and waited. After a few minutes, she tried again. "Hello? Can someone come out and talk to me?"

"Who are you, and what do you want?" a man's voice asked. Movement behind one of the open windows.

"My name is Eliza. I just want to talk."

"About what? Are you looking for someone?"

"Not someone, but something, yes."

"Well?"

"Are you the ones who were talking to people at UNLV last week?" she asked. "I talked to a man about the Book of Revelation, but then I never saw him again."

A long, quiet moment, and she could sense the wheels of suspicion turning in his mind.

"I'm looking for Caleb Kimball," she said.

The door opened. A young man stepped down the makeshift cinder block steps to the ground. He was about six feet tall, thin but wiry, with a dirty, unwashed look. He was dressed in a robe, tied off with a cord, and wore a beard and sandals. Apart from looking like John the Baptist, there was a glint in his eyes that Eliza had seen a hundred times before. A true believer. Whoever this man was, he wasn't cynical about his claims. But was it Caleb Kimball? In this light, behind the beard, it was hard to tell if he looked like Gideon and Taylor Junior.

He frowned. "What are you sitting on that for? Get off there."

She stood up and looked around in confusion. "Off what, the fridge?"

He shook his head. "No, never mind. You look too comfortable, considering."

"Considering what?"

"Considering how much danger you're in."

Her mouth felt dry. They'd almost killed David, and that was just to rob his produce truck. She couldn't afford to make a mistake; she needed the same kind of confidence her brother Jacob could wield.

"Of course I'm in danger, the world is coming to an end. I need to make sure I'm on the right side of the Lord. Are you the Disciple?"

"Who told you about us?" he demanded.

"I talked to you, don't you remember? I was reading my Bible on campus and you started a conversation."

His eyes narrowed. "I don't remember you."

"I remember *you*. I couldn't stop thinking about what you told me about the world coming to an end. And when I prayed that night to the Lord, I knew I should find you and talk to you some more. I've been asking everywhere."

"And how did you do that? Nobody else has ever found us."

"But people talk," Eliza said. "You didn't just get here, and you need to go into town to get food and water. Once I figured out where you were, I had a taxi drive me as far as he'd go on this road, and then I walked the rest of the way."

"I don't believe it. Did someone send you? Where did you hear that other name?"

She ignored the last question. "Look at me, I'm just a girl. There's nobody else here, and I didn't bring anything. I don't have a cell phone or food or anything. I tossed my empty water jug an hour ago."

He stepped closer, put his hands on the side of her head, and pulled her face close to his. Intensity burned in his gaze. Eliza forced herself to remain calm, and she didn't look away. "You can't walk in and join. You must be chosen. I'm the one who chooses."

"All I want is what you have. Is that so wrong?"

"Where did you hear that other name?" he asked a second time.

"I'll answer that as soon as you tell me whether or not you're the Disciple."

He let go, then lifted her arms one by one, and pulled back her sleeves to study her forearms. He ran a finger along the inside of her arm, an intimate gesture that made her skin crawl. "They're clean. Have you ever done drugs? Cut yourself? Tried to commit the ultimate crime against God?"

"What do you mean, the ultimate crime? Fornication?"

"No, not fornication, although I'm sure a pretty girl like you must face regular temptation. What I wonder is if you've ever attempted suicide?"

"No, never," she said.

"Then what are you doing here?"

Eliza leaned closer and whispered, "I came here from Blister Creek."

"What?" He drew back.

"I grew up in the same church as you. We lived in Harmony, but my family is in Blister Creek now. And when I heard you speak, I recognized your accent, your way of speaking. You were from southern Utah. Your family practices plural marriage. Am I right?" He said nothing, so she pressed. "You said that you choose who joins and who doesn't. I want to know, who chose *you*?"

"God chose me."

"And God chose me in the same way. I called home and asked around, and they told me that Caleb Kimball had been collecting followers in the desert. I knew it was you and that I needed to find you, because the end of the world is coming."

"There is nobody here with that name. Just me, and I'm the Disciple. When they speak to me, they call me Master."

"I understand, Master. There's nothing else to me but what you see. Can I join you or will you send me away?"

"If there's something else, anything, I'll find it. You know that." The Disciple turned toward the trailer and gave a gesture for Eliza to follow.

She felt a surge of relief, but also fear. If he'd sent her away, she could have struggled back to the road, maybe begging him for water before she left, then returned to Allison Caliari and told her that she'd tried, but it was impossible. As soon as she stepped inside that trailer, it would be too late, she would be fully committed.

As he reached the trailer door, he looked over his shoulder. "Did you bring any money to help with the work?"

"I have about forty bucks, that's all."

"Never mind that. There are other ways you can assist the efforts."

She thought about what Jacob had warned her about during the car ride to Las Vegas. It was his favorite pet theory, but she liked watching how animated he got when he expounded on it, so she had played along, as if she'd never heard it before.

"What are the first two rules laid down by any self-proclaimed prophet?" her brother had asked. "First, consecrate all your money to the Lord. And since the prophet is the Lord's emissary, just go ahead and hand it over now."

"Convenient," Eliza said.

"Second, normal rules of marriage and courtship do not apply to the prophet. The Lord has commanded him to take difficult steps, even though other people might not understand. Even though the prophet himself may be reluctant."

"In other words, obey the Lord when He chooses you to have sex with the prophet."

"Exactly," Jacob said. "And oddly enough, the Lord never chooses middle-aged widows, he always chooses nubile young girls."

"Convenient," she had repeated.

The conversation had seemed hypothetical at the time. It didn't now.

The Disciple grabbed Eliza's wrist, pushed open the door of the trailer, and dragged her inside to meet the others.

CHAPTER TEN

Abraham Christianson eyed the woman walking by his side. Sister Miriam looked like a proper polygamist wife (polygamist *widow,* he reminded himself), with her braided hair, high collar, sleeves to her wrist and dress to her ankles, and hands clasped demurely in front of her. But there was a glint in her eye, and he reminded himself that she'd been clever enough to fool the leader of the Church of the Last Days. He needed to be careful with this one.

He didn't know all the details of the business at the Zarahemla compound, but he knew enough. Miriam had been an FBI agent, infiltrated the compound, and dug around until she exposed the plot to kill a U.S. senator. Somewhere along the line, the lie had become truth, and she'd embraced the gospel. Or so she'd claimed. He didn't rule out the possibility that she was still deep undercover.

"Let me be clear, Brother Abraham," she said as they stepped across the sluice gates of the irrigation ditch. "I don't trust you, never have. I'm only here because of your son."

"I'm not asking you to trust me. You don't know me, so how could you? I don't trust you either, so there you go. Whatever happens, I do expect you to respect the priesthood."

"I respect the priesthood properly wielded. Now what do you want, and why are we out here instead of back at the house?"

"You know the answer to that. I can't have a bunch of gossiping hens eavesdropping on our conversation."

"Gossiping hens. Nice."

Abraham wasn't laboring under the delusion that women were inferior to men. Elder Kimball and his sons had made that mistake. One of Taylor's sons was dead, another missing, and the man himself had fourteen more years of a prison sentence to serve. Some of that had been Jacob's doing, of course, with some help from those rats with the FBI, but Eliza had been the one to crush Gideon Kimball's head.

And from the look in Sister Miriam's eye, he wondered if she was imagining *herself* with a large stone, standing over Abraham's prostrate body.

"No need to get worked up, it's just an expression."

"Fine," she said. "Then at least answer me this. Why are we keeping this a secret from Brother Jacob?"

"You know the answer to that, too."

A breeze kicked off the Ghost Cliffs. It smelled like sage and juniper. This would be so much better if he were having this conversation with Jacob, who felt at home here in Blister Creek. Zarahemla was too close to the cities controlled by the LDS, to the gentile influence in the hospital. Bring him out here, put him to work doctoring, or even just spiritual work, let him forget about the outside world. Unfortunately, Jacob was too stubborn, too persistent in his doubts.

Tactics. Be patient, persistent. He will come around in time.

They walked in silence along the irrigation ditches for a few more minutes before he tried again. "Sister Miriam, we don't have to be enemies. We both want the same thing."

"No, really we don't."

"We both want Jacob to reach his true potential, isn't that right?"

"I want Jacob to accept his role as the Lord's anointed," Miriam said, "to become the One Mighty and Strong prophesied to unite the saints."

And who the hell are you to talk about what the Lord wants?

Sister Miriam wasn't even a mainstream Mormon, let alone been raised in a community where plural marriage was still practiced and honored. She was born a gentile, had attached herself to Zarahemla after the FBI. And now she was preaching some pious vision. Jacob accepted her. Fine, but that wouldn't erase Abraham's suspicions.

"You make it sound so pure and selfless," he said, "but I know what you really want."

"Oh, you do? Why don't you enlighten me."

Abraham allowed himself a smile. "You want to marry my son. You were married to the prophet of the Church of the Last Days before he died, and now you want the new guy under your thumb. Of course, you know, he's already married to a strong woman. As first wife, Fernie won't be happy when you muscle in."

"Fernie and I are friends, and believe me, she wants nothing more than for Jacob to take a second wife."

"But you?"

"Would I marry him? I don't see why not. He's a kind man, intelligent. Handsome, too. But it's not my decision to make. Besides, what does that have to do with wanting Jacob to take his rightful place at the head of the church?" she asked. "I want *him* to lead. You want to control Jacob yourself, to groom him to take over your church, to unite the two churches under your leadership. Can you see how that's the opposite thing? If you control Jacob, how can he possibly be the Lord's prophet?"

"But we both want him to reach his spiritual potential. If he doesn't soften his heart to the Lord, how can that ever happen? He's only half a leader until he accepts that he *is* a leader."

"Jacob's doubts are more fundamental than that," Miriam said.

"He's my son, don't you think I know that? That kid has never fully believed in the Restoration. Even if he managed to fool everyone else, he never fooled me."

"And we're going to make Jacob a believer with secret meetings?"

"We're not going to make him do anything. Only the Lord can turn Jacob into a believer."

Miriam stopped and looked up at him. "Brother Abraham, that's the first thing you've said that I agree with. But that still doesn't explain why you asked me to come to Blister Creek."

"We can't make him believe, or give him a spiritual experience, but we can create the kind of painful, difficult situation that leads to a spiritual experience. And if the Lord is on our side, he will feel the spirit, whether he wants to or not."

"By creating a difficult situation, you mean something like the LDS who trek across Wyoming, pulling handcarts?" she asked.

"Never heard of that."

"They feed them short rations, put a few blisters on their hands, tell them how their ancestors suffered crossing the plains, and they come back with a testimony." Miriam shook her head. "It wouldn't work with Jacob."

"No, it wouldn't. What my son needs is a terrible trial. He needs his child to get sick, nearly die, and then be healed by the power of the priesthood."

"You can't be serious. What, are you going to poison them or something?"

"What? No! What kind of monster do you think I am?" He fought down his anger that she'd even think such a thing. "But I'll admit, I've prayed for the Lord to send my son some trial, to lay him low, humble his heart. He'd come out of it stronger, and with a belief that no man could break."

"Or woman."

"Or woman," he conceded. "But listen, there's someone he cares about who is already near death. I've seen it in my dreams. So has Sister Fernie. The Adversary has possessed him. If we do nothing, he will die. It could be the perfect way for the Lord to intervene."

"You mean David Christianson."

"You know him?"

"Never met him," Miriam said. "But Jacob and Eliza set off in a hurry a few days ago, and his wife told me they came to convince you to show mercy toward David before he died of a drug overdose."

"They confronted me, if you'll believe it. Made an ugly scene, and for what? David is just another wayward son. I've got a dozen of them," he added with a bitter note.

More than a dozen, if he were honest. Some of the younger ones were already gone, spiritually dead. It came upon a boy when he was a teenager, like a beast after prey, took hold of him and shook him in its mouth. And Abraham was the one to cut the boy off, drive him out of town with a few bucks and a promise he'd see the boy beaten to unconsciousness if he ever came back. It was ugly work. But if Abraham didn't, the boy would hang around, poisoning the younger ones, spreading sin through the community. Look at Taylor Kimball's sons.

"That's why Jacob is so important to me," he added. "There are a few others. Joshua is a pretty good kid, and so is Zeke, but nobody like Jacob."

"And you want to what?" Miriam said. "Use David as bait?"

"Yes, after a fashion."

Miriam was quiet for a long moment. Her foot kicked at the edge of the embankment, and a clod of dirt fell into the irrigation ditch, swirled into a muddy streak, and then disappeared. At last she looked up and shook her head. "Sounds like a corrupt and evil plan."

"No, not really."

"David is your son, too. Shouldn't you be helping him? What kind of man are you?"

Abraham grabbed her shoulders and spun her around. She tensed and for a moment looked like she was going to knee him in the groin. He'd almost forgotten her background in law enforcement.

"Listen to me. David is already damned. Jacob and Eliza aren't the only ones keeping an eye on the Lost Boys. I'd be a fool not to, after Elder Kimball's sons attacked us. David is way beyond drinking and smoking pot; he's hitting the hard stuff now. It's only a matter of time. We'll bring him back—that's a mercy!—and keep him supplied."

"Keep him supplied? You mean feed him drugs. That's not a mercy."

"He can't live without his drugs. If we don't give him drugs, he'll just run back to Las Vegas anyway, so yes, it is. Satan has him, there's nothing we can do. We'll let him kill himself, and when he's almost dead, we'll call Jacob."

"And then?" she asked.

"And then Jacob gives him a priesthood blessing to cast out Satan and the addiction to drugs. He'll be healed like that." Abraham snapped his fingers.

"Or not."

"Or not, if that is the will of the Lord. The Lord works a miracle, or He doesn't. If He doesn't, David will die, just like he's going to die if we do nothing. If the priesthood blessing works, not even Jacob will be able to deny that it's a miracle."

"Jacob will find a way to question it. Science yes, maybe even luck. But not a miracle, no, not necessarily. I can hear his voice, see the cynical glint in his eye."

Abraham shook his head. "Not this time. David will be too far gone to write it off that way. The miracle will be too instantaneous."

"Fine, let's say it works. Why do you need me?"

"You're former FBI, you'll know how to get all the worst drugs. And you're a pretty young woman, so David will trust you. And if trust doesn't work, lust will. David is overcome by carnal passions."

"Great, just wonderful."

"Think of it as going undercover."

"I've done worse. Doesn't mean I liked it." Miriam fell silent. She bent suddenly and fished what looked like a stone from the bottom of the irrigation ditch, but when she dried it off and held out her hand, Abraham saw it was an arrowhead.

He took it, turned it over, and then handed it back with a shrug. "They turn up sometimes. Probably washed out of the cliffs with the spring runoff. Better that than Indian bones."

She slipped it into the pocket of her dress with a thoughtful expression. He couldn't tell what she was thinking, maybe that the arrowhead was a sign of some kind, but how to take it? At last she nodded. "Okay, I'll do it, but if I see a way to help this boy, I'll do that, too."

"You'll see. It's hopeless." He smiled. "Except for the Lord. For Him, nothing is impossible. Not even softening Jacob's heart."

"True." A smile. "So we agree on two things, Brother Abraham."

"Apparently, we do."

"I'll leave first thing in the morning for Las Vegas," she said. "If David is as far gone as you say, I'd better get to him before it's too late."

"Don't worry so much about that. He's going to suffer, and that's okay. Remember, for our plan to work, David must be utterly destroyed."

* * *

Madeline lay on the filthy mattress at the bottom of the pit. She'd drifted in and out of sleep, dreaming about her mother. She came to in a cold sweat once, her fingernails tearing at her neck and breasts. She started in on the twenty-third Psalm, but before she reached the part about the Lord preparing a table in the presence of her enemies, the evil spirit left her.

In its place an overwhelming sense of guilt. She thought about her mother, heroically trying to keep it together after her father abandoned them. Madeline was twelve when he left, and adored her father. He was supposed to take her to see the Blazers play the Lakers at the Rose Garden that night. Her mother had come home early from work to get dinner on the table in time for Madeline and her father to make the game, but he simply never came home. Not that night, not ever. For two weeks, Madeline ran to her window every time she heard a car pull onto her cul-de-sac, sure he was returning.

He stopped by once on her seventeenth birthday, during that time of day when Madeline was home from school and her mother still at work. She'd stared at him from the front door with her hands on her hips, her heart pounding.

"Hi, Maddy."

"What do you want? Are you selling something?"

"It's me, don't you recognize me?"

"Nope. Sorry." She moved to shut the door, but he blocked it with his foot.

"Come on, Maddy. Can I come in and talk? At least let me explain."

"About what? My mother is at work and my father died, quite suddenly and tragically, so I'm alone. I've been told not to let strangers in the house, especially not lying, rat-bastard strangers. Now move your foot before I call 911 and tell them there's a strange man trying to break into my house."

He stepped back with a hurt expression, then let her close the door. But as she did, she saw him glance down to her arms. Madeline had come home, taken off her hoodie, and her forearms were bare and visible, and with them the gouges from the end of a bent paperclip. And she could see judgment in his eyes. The jerk, judging *her*.

She turned the lock, then leaned against the inside of the door and sobbed, not caring if he was still on the other side, listening. Let him.

That fall it was almost like there was a conspiracy to pump Madeline with self-esteem, as if she would fill up with happy, self-affirming thoughts until she floated above the street like a giant, grinning Mickey Mouse in the Macy's Thanksgiving Day Parade. At church, they claimed that Jesus loved her. Motivational speakers came to the school to insist that all the students were happy and popular, but if they were miserable losers they should get help. A little counseling and voila! Happy and popular again. Whenever she turned on the TV, there were self-affirming teen shows and self-affirming infomercials. It was going to be a wonderful, joyous, self-affirming holiday season.

Madeline's best friend killed herself on Christmas Eve.

After her parents went to bed, Ettie Spinoza went past the Christmas tree, surrounded by a mountain of presents, past the stockings hung by the mantle with care, and into the kitchen, where she broke into the liquor cabinet. Ettie locked herself in the downstairs bathroom, filled the tub and climbed in fully dressed, and proceeded to wash down sleeping pills with vodka until she passed out. They found her the next morning, face down in a tub filled with cold water. She'd scratched, "Send me to hell," on her forearm with a razor.

Somehow, Madeline survived until college. Midway through the first week after Christmas break, a black mood came over her and didn't leave. It was after she'd committed her darkest sin, and she couldn't stop thinking about it. She locked herself in her dorm room and ignored the pleas of her roommates until her mother showed up. Allison Caliari coaxed her daughter out, coaxed her to visit the campus psychiatrist, coaxed her to accept a prescription of smiley pills. Suggested, innocently, that she join a campus Christian organization, that maybe she could find her answers in the Bible. For some reason, that last suggestion had seemed almost reasonable.

And before she knew it, she had, in fact, found all her answers. If Madeline could survive this trial of purification, she'd be okay, she knew it. She just had to have faith. And stop thinking about home. About Mom, worrying, maybe even looking for her somewhere. Imagining how much pain she was causing her mother brought an ache to her gut very different than the hollow gnawing of hunger.

Someone banged on the refrigerator overhead to indicate that another day had passed. Madeline rose from the mattress, stopped to fight the lightheaded swoon, and then groped around the edge of the pit until she found the box. She pulled out a head of lettuce with shaking hands and ate.

CHAPTER ELEVEN

"*Eres de aquí, o nacíste en México?*" Eliza asked.

"Speak English," Benita said. "I have no idea what you're babbling about."

"Oh, sorry," Eliza said. "You just looked…I mean, I thought…"

"Well, you thought wrong."

Maybe it was partly exposure to so much sun, but Benita certainly *looked* Hispanic. Her skin tone, yes, but also the eyes and something about the facial structure.

"Your family isn't from Mexico originally?"

"My mom was born in Honduras, but my dad is from Idaho, and I never went back to the so-called old country. I probably speak like ten words of Spanish. Grab the other end of that tire."

Together, they dragged the tire, tipped it over to knock out some of the dust that had accumulated in the well over the years, and then rolled it around to the other side of the trailer, where two guys were stacking them. Others were stacking tires around back, just a few feet from the overturned sofa where Eliza had hidden the cell phone. The two women said nothing until they got back to the other side.

"So what are you trying to speak Spanish for anyway?" Benita asked.

"Just practicing, you know. It's a pain to learn a language, but you lose it if you don't pull it out whenever you've got the chance."

"Stick to English. The Disciple won't like it if he can't understand you."

Which was exactly why Eliza had tried the Spanish, not because it was a pain to learn (though it was), but because they'd be able to talk without anyone else listening in. She could ask casually about Madeline when the time came. No sign of the girl yet, but two people had left the dump that morning, one of them returning with three newcomers a few hours later. She had a feeling that if she were patient, Madeline would appear sooner rather than later.

"See that kid?" Benita asked.

"You mean Diego? Does he speak Spanish?"

"He doesn't speak anything. His mom was from the Philippines. She ran off a few weeks ago, when she couldn't hack it anymore. She used to speak Philippine to him."

"Tagalog, probably. That's the main language of the Philippines."

Benita frowned. They tipped over another tire. "Whatever. The Disciple told her to knock it off, speak English, and now the kid doesn't say much at all."

Eliza watched Diego work. He was filling coffee cans with sand and stacking them next to one of the teardrop campers. More busy, pointless stuff, like they were all doing. Moving tires around, shifting piles of garbage from one location to another, digging a pit in the hardpan. And in the middle of the day it seemed especially dumb. Diego's arms looked as thin as sagebrush branches, and she wondered how he managed to lift the cans high enough to stack.

"He looks hungry."

"We're all hungry," Benita said.

"Yeah, but he's just a boy. Look how skinny he is, and his face is pinched, like he's actually starving."

"You should drop that."

"Come on," Eliza said. "It's cruel not to give him food. He's too young; he doesn't even know what this is all about. When he's older, when he can decide for himself, I mean, then it wouldn't be so bad."

"I'm serious, Eliza, I wouldn't pursue that if I were you," Benita said. "Not unless you want to earn a rite of purification."

"A what?"

"Never mind. Come on, we have to move fifty tires. I don't want to be here all day, and you're just blabbering. We'll get in trouble."

They worked in silence for a while. It was Eliza's second day at the dump, and apart from the hunger, things had gone innocently enough. A cup of milk for breakfast, some stale bread for lunch, and a shared jar of peanut butter for dinner. Eliza had grown up with a monthly fast; she could handle a little hunger. And she started to wonder if maybe they were just a garden-variety sect. David was strung out on drugs, and Allison Caliari was desperate to find her daughter. Those two could have easily been wrong.

As for the doomsday part, she didn't find that particularly strange or alarming. Half the people she'd ever known thought that the world was about to end in fire, pestilence, and war. Her mother hoarded wheat in giant barrels, and an uncle had a stash of assault rifles in his cellar, plus enough ammo to fight a small war. Her father held thousands of acres of land in Alberta, Montana, and Utah, and before she was born, he had spent eighty thousand dollars building a bomb shelter. When the threat of nuclear war passed in the nineties, it had proven a good place for his wives to store their wheat.

"Have you done any rites yet?" Benita asked.

"What do you mean by rites?"

"If you don't know, that means no, you haven't. You're in for a treat."

Eliza didn't like the undercurrent in her voice. "You mentioned the rite of purification. How many are there?"

"Purification, sanctification, and the rite of cleansing."

"That all sounds like the same thing."

"No way," Benita said. "The only thing they have in common is that they're all hard. Cleansing is the worst, but you get numb to that. You never cleanse yourself, just other people. You just have to remind yourself that it's for your own good, that if you don't do it, you won't be ready and you'll be separated with the chaff."

"What about sanctification?"

Benita shrugged. "Not so fun at first. The first time is the worst, then you get used to it. Madeline even asks for extra rites of sanctification."

Eliza felt a thrill at the name. "Who?"

"Never mind, you've got me talking, and I'm too weak right now for another purification. Probably deserve it, though. You'll find out what the rites are about soon enough. Probably start with sanctification. Just don't fight it and you'll be fine. Come on, seventeen more tires to go."

Purification, sanctification, cleansing. Coming out of Benita's mouth, each one of them sounded more sinister than the last, and Eliza began to doubt her earlier confidence. Three dead cult members, a starved child, and the beating they'd delivered to her brother.

Eliza renewed her determination to find Madeline and get out.

* * *

That evening, the Chosen Ones ate their scavenged leftovers under an edict of silence. Eliza served stale saltines with peanut butter, and she made sure to give as much of both as she dared to Diego, who shoved the food in his mouth as if he was terrified someone would steal it from him.

And they might. Some people had ignored the boy during the day, while others gave him a pat or a kind word, but there were a few men and women who literally kicked Diego around the camp like he was a stray dog, covered in mange. The worst was a man named Christopher, who backhanded the boy three times in about ten minutes until Eliza and Benita told him to knock it off. Christopher had glared down at Eliza, and for a moment she thought he was going to hit her, too. She told him to go ahead and try. The Disciple came out of the trailer where he'd been meditating and told everyone to get back to work.

At dusk, the Disciple left in the truck and returned an hour later with three more women. They carried bags of scavenged food and five-gallon cans of diesel fuel for the generator that never seemed to run. Madeline Caliari wasn't with them.

Eliza held Diego's wrist when she gave him the third and last cracker at dinner. He met her eyes, and she tried to pass him an encouraging look. *I'm going to get you out of here.*

He snatched the cracker and scurried back to the corner to eat it. When she glanced over a minute later, he was watching her.

After dinner, they studied the Bible by the light of kerosene lanterns. It was mostly the Book of Revelation, together with anything eschatological out of the Old Testament, or anything to do with God's wrath: Sodom and Gomorrah, the plagues of Egypt, any verse that mentioned hellfire or brimstone. Eliza recited verses from memory, and this seemed to impress many of them.

"Very good, Eliza," the Disciple said. There was warmth in his voice, and she saw what looked like envy on Benita's face. "Do you know Revelation 13?"

She nodded and stood up and summoned her clearest, most articulate voice. "And I stood upon the sand of the sea, and saw a beast rise up out of the sea, having seven heads and ten horns, and upon his horns ten crowns, and upon his heads the name of blasphemy."

She recited all eighteen verses. When she finished, she could see the intensity in their eyes, and knew that she'd penetrated their defenses, and she felt an unusual stirring in return. *This is what Jacob feels—this is what he can do.*

The Disciple rose from where he'd been sitting cross-legged and took her arm. "You are one of us, Eliza. It's time for your first rite."

"Which rite?"

"The rite of sanctification."

* * *

Christopher had stripped Madeline naked and laid her down on a filthy mattress, and then Benita brought in a bowl of olive oil warmed over a kerosene stove. And then the Disciple put his hands all over her body. She tried to get up, but Christopher held her down and told her to be still or it would be worse, and when she cried out, nobody came to help.

Lying at the bottom of the pit with no sense of time, waiting for her next meal of lettuce, Madeline Caliari found herself obsessing over her first sanctification. It hadn't felt like sanctity at first. Anything but, in fact. It had felt like a violation. Benita had brought in more olive oil, and the hands over Madeline's body grew harder, more insistent.

You deserve this. Remember that football player you hooked up with at the frat party? And the kid in English class? How about junior year in high school? And all the impure thoughts, what about that?

And so Madeline had stopped screaming and clenched her eyes shut. She let the Disciple run his hands over her breasts, alongside her inner thighs, even slide his oil-soaked hands between her buttocks.

"Try to think pure thoughts," he said. "It is a rite, not carnal pleasures."

And yet when he'd disrobed, climbed on top of her, and rubbed his body against hers until he was also soaked with olive oil, he was hard enough for the task at hand and his breathing came in shallow gulps.

"Sanctify her," Christopher said, and the way he said it, the word *sanctify* came out like a vulgarity. "Harder, she needs it harder."

He'd kept talking until the Disciple finished. When Madeline opened her eyes, she could see Christopher watching with narrowed eyes and a flushed look. A bulge in his pants that he didn't try to hide. She expected the Disciple to tell Christopher to take his turn sanctifying, but instead, the Disciple took the other man's arm and pulled him from the room.

Benita knelt by her side, covered her with a sheet, and held her hand. "Was it bad?" she whispered.

"No worse than I deserved."

"I didn't want to watch, but it's my turn next, and he said I needed to see." She stroked Madeline's hand. "You seem like a good person. I don't think you needed to be sanctified. Not that way."

"Yes, I did."

"Other people need it more."

"Like you?" Madeline asked. "You don't want to do that."

"Of course not, but I need it. I need it all."

Madeline had a sudden image of two anorexic girls standing next to the mirror, praising each other for being so skinny, while finding their own bodies hideous and bulging.

To be honest, the sanctification had grown easier over time. Unlike this hunger that consumed her in the pit, the rite of purification. Starving, eating one head of lettuce every twenty-four hours and gnawing on her doubt and guilt and self-loathing. At least the sanctification ended quickly—at least it was one human being touching another. Shivering alone in the dark was worse.

A scraping sound from overhead startled Madeline from her thoughts. It sounded like someone pushing the fridge out of the way, and a wild hope rose in her chest. The twenty days were up. Somehow, she'd miscounted, maybe slept through the announcement of most passing days and left all those heads of lettuce uneaten. No wonder she was so hungry.

A cool breeze blew into the hole. She lifted her head and filled her lungs with the sweet, fresh air. At one edge she could see a shade of gray, a little lighter than the surrounding blackness, where the fridge had slid out of the way to reveal a sliver of the night sky.

Night. Not day, and not day twenty in the pit with lettuce and water. She hadn't miscounted at all, but was still near the beginning of her ordeal, with more than two full weeks of purification stretching ahead of her.

"Who is it?" she called. "Benita?"

No answer.

"Who is it?" she asked. "What do you want?"

No answer. Just a darker shadow, a head. Someone peered into the darkness and listened. A tight fear clenched her gut.

Please, Lord Jesus, save me. I'll be good, I promise. I won't whine or complain, I'll purify myself. Just don't destroy me. I promise.

Something dropped, bounced off the mattress. Madeline flinched. The fridge scraped again, and black replaced the sliver of gray. She tried to catch her breath, calm down. And then grew curious about whatever had fallen down.

She groped in the dark until she found it. Three bananas, soft and squishy and no doubt turned brown. It was the sort of thing the Chosen Ones scavenged from Dumpsters in the city. Someone had saved them for her, dropped them into the pit. Food to help her survive.

Unless it was a test. Unless the Disciple had told Christopher or Benita to drop the bananas to see if she'd break the purifying fast to eat them. And if the Disciple sent someone down in the morning to check and he found the banana peels, would that mean three more weeks of purification? It would be summer before she got out. If she got out. She'd probably die.

And you'll die if you don't eat the bananas.

She peeled open the first banana. Her fingers found the soft, mushy flesh, and she lifted it to her nose. Her senses filled with the rich, musty odor of overripe banana. Her stomach groaned in anticipation. She'd have to eat a little, maybe no more than half. Couldn't risk throwing it up again, and if she saved the rest, she could get half a banana a day and make them last almost a week.

It tasted like sin. She felt a sick feeling of guilt as it touched her tongue. She almost chewed and swallowed. Instead, she spit the bite into her hand. For a long moment, she sat with two and a half bananas in her lap, a mushy, partially chewed half banana in her hand and the delicious taste lingering on her tongue.

"You promised," she whispered. "You promised God that you wouldn't whine or complain, that you'd be good. This is Satan tempting you, lifting you up out of the desert during your fast and offering you bread. Get thee behind me, Satan."

Quickly, before she could change her mind, she groped for one of the gallon milk jugs that held urine and her thin, runny diarrhea, the result of a diet of lettuce. She would squat over a bucket every few days, then pour it into the gallon jug with extreme care and tighten down the lid. It cut down on the smell. She opened the lid, then forced the partially chewed banana through the narrow opening. She peeled the others and pushed them in, one after another, where they oozed through and plopped into the liquid at the bottom, and then she forced in the peels after them so she wouldn't be tempted to lick them later. Finally, she swished her mouth with water and spit it into the waste jug to get the bits of banana out of her mouth. She almost gagged at the smell when she lifted the waste jug to her mouth. She shoved it into the corner with a cry.

Madeline collapsed on the mattress and sobbed. So close. One second longer and it would have been too late. She squinted her eyes shut and thought about the Disciple with olive oil on his hands, rubbing them roughly over her body. And then, lying on top, sanctifying her.

No worse than I deserve.

CHAPTER TWELVE

David sat up in bed to find a woman standing over him. She held a gun in her hand. "Do not speak," she said, "just listen."

It was dark except for light from the hall. He must have slept the whole afternoon into the evening. His body ached and his head throbbed. He'd finally come down, and hard. And he felt curiously detached as he looked up at the gun.

"Go ahead, kill me." His voice came out flat.

"I'm not here to kill you." She pulled the chain on the lamp, and he squinted against the shards of light.

"Then why are you holding a gun?"

"It's for protection. Someone broke into your house during the day."

"I know she did," David said. He started to wake up and pulled himself upright and leaned against the headboard. "She's standing over me with a gun."

"Someone *else* broke into your house. The back door is forced, a bunch of broken stuff in the kitchen. You didn't hear anything?"

"No. I took a little something to help me sleep."

"In the middle of the day? Yeah, while you were sleeping off whatever crap you put in your body, someone broke in with a crowbar and could have caved in your skull. You're lucky to wake up."

"Too bad they didn't cave it in. I'd do it myself if I had any guts."

"Oh, you look to me like you're doing a great job of killing yourself. You're not wondering who I am, a strange woman in your bedroom with a gun?"

"I figure you'll tell me when you're ready." Under other circumstances he knew he'd be alarmed, terrified even, but he felt so miserable that he didn't care. "What time is it?"

"Dinner time."

He thought about Eliza, setting off into the desert. When had that been? Yesterday? The day before? Then the trip to visit Meth Guy. Needle, injection, a fantastic rush, and then a long, tapering euphoria. And a crash. Another injection, rush, crash. It was a fading stain in his memory, but now the drugs were gone, and he'd have to go back to Meth Guy. Except he had no more money.

The woman checked his closet, then slipped the gun into a bag she wore slung over one shoulder. He was paying attention now and recognized the prairie dress, the lack of makeup, the braided hair. His brain—what was left of it—started to work at last.

"So whose wife are you, my father's or my brother's?"

She turned with a smile. "Neither. My name is Sister Miriam, and I'm a widow. Has anyone told you that you look like Jacob?"

"Uhm...thanks, I guess."

"No worries, that's a compliment." She walked around the room with a look of concentration, and David had a sudden impression not of a polygamist wife, but law enforcement, studying every detail, looking for clues. She turned back to him with a hard look. "But you seem to lack his moral backbone. Unlike Jacob, you're adrift in the world, buffeted by whichever way the wind blows. That's why you're here and not back with your family and friends and why I'm guessing you'll end up dead sooner or later. My vote is on sooner. That, I'm afraid, is *not* a compliment."

"No, I guess not."

"Let me get to the point," Miriam said. "Before we waste any more of each other's time."

"Too late for that, but go ahead. Unless there's some way I can persuade you to go home and leave me alone."

"Alone with this, you mean?" She opened the top drawer of his dresser, tossed socks and underwear to the floor, and pulled out a Ziploc baggie filled with a dirty-brown powder.

"Hey, where did that come from?" It wasn't the heroin that shocked him, but the quantity.

"Oh, and look at all these pills. That's quite a stash."

"Those aren't mine."

"Of course not. If they were yours, you'd have taken them by now."

"Then what—?"

"I planted them," Miriam said. "What else? I'm going to call the police, tell them that you've got all these drugs, and they'll bust you as a dealer. You won't get rehab, you'll get twenty years."

He started to climb out of bed, alarmed and angry, but she reached into her bag where she'd put the gun. "Stay where you are."

"You're a cop, aren't you? Some sort of law enforcement. What's going on? I'll tell them you planted the drugs—there's no way I could get my hands on that much stuff, I haven't got the money."

"Right, you're out of money. That's why you've turned to dealing," Miriam said. "And there's enough legit crap in this place, not to mention the needle marks I'm sure we'll find on your arms or feet or wherever you've chosen to poison your body, that of course they'll think you're a dealer. So you're screwed." She gave a sad shake of her head. "Here's the way I see it. You've got two choices. You can come with me, or you can resist, I'll call the cops, and you'll go to prison."

"And what if I do come with you? What, you're going to take me to Zarahemla? I can't believe Jacob is behind this."

"No, I'll take you to Blister Creek. Your father and I have a little disagreement we want to settle."

The bitter feeling came up so fast he could taste bile. "I should have known that bastard was behind this."

"You should have gone with Eliza when she asked. You weren't so far gone then. What a difference a couple of weeks makes. From what I see, it's too late. Only the Lord can save you now. Your Father and I disagree about whether or not He cares enough to bother."

"And you think He does?"

"No, I think the Lord *doesn't* care, or at least He's got better things to worry about. Your father is expecting a miracle."

"A miracle? What is it to him? Why would he care? I'm supposed to believe that after all these years my father is hoping to save me?"

"It's not about you, David."

"Oh." His head pounded, he could feel every bruise, and his ribs throbbed. He sank back into the bed. "Why don't you go ahead and call the cops? I don't care."

He expected her to bluff—this whole thing was just a scam, he was sure of it—so it surprised him when she shrugged, walked to the phone, picked it up, and dialed 911. She lifted the receiver and then frowned.

"Your phone is dead."

"I forgot to pay the bill."

"Never mind, I've got a phone."

She fished in her bag, tossed the gun on the dresser, and pulled out a phone, waited a second for it to power on. "A drug dealer in Ely State Prison. Or maybe they'll send you to High Desert. I've heard some interesting stories. Not many skinny white kids there. Wonder how you'll do. I guess it depends on whether you survive the first week." She started to dial.

"Wait! You can't do that."

Miriam stopped and looked at him. "Brother David, you don't seem to understand that you're a dead man. If you stay here, some-one is going to break in again and kill you. You have no friends, and you owe a lot of people a lot of money, right? If I call the cops, a young guy like you with a smart mouth won't stand a chance in maximum security prison. If I bring you back to Blister Creek, you'll run away unless I keep you supplied with drugs."

"You could try to check me into rehab, how about that?"

"Right, and you'll listen to me when you blew off your sister? If Eliza couldn't wake you up, how could I?" She shook her head. "Any way I look at it, you're dead. And you don't seem to care. So I'm going to call the cops and get it over with."

"Can you hold on for one second and let me think?" He moved to the side of the bed and sat on the edge in his boxers, with his casted arm resting on his lap and his other hand gripping his hair by the roots. His eyes felt dry as ash when he finally lifted his head to look at her.

Miriam had deep, penetrating eyes, hazel with green flecks, and even through the prairie dress, he could see from her lean, athletic build and her alert posture that she'd have no trouble crushing him in his current condition. She was younger than he'd thought at first. Prettier, too.

"If you're bluffing," he said at last, "you're very good."

"I *am* good. I was the one they always sent undercover, to track down dirtbag drug dealers, pimps, and human traffickers. If I'd come in here pretending to be a pissed-off dealer, you would have believed it. I could have pretended to be one of the people who beat you up, and you'd have believed that, too." She shook her head. "But in this case, I'm not actually bluffing. Here's my offer. You get dressed and come with me. I'll bring you to Blister Creek and make it easy for you to get the crap you need to poison yourself. That's what your father wants. But if you decide to fight it, I'll be happy to be proven wrong."

Maybe he was just angry with Miriam, maybe he wanted to prove to that jerk of a father that he was wrong. Maybe the glimmer of hope Eliza and Jacob seemed to hold for him finally took spark. He made a sudden grab for his pants where they lay bunched on the floor.

"Fine. I'll come with you."

Miriam smiled. "Good. I don't hold out much hope, but who knows? The Lord does work miracles when it suits His purpose. Hurry up, I don't want to spend the night in this sin-infested cesspool."

David made an even more rash decision, and when he said it, he really meant it. "But leave that garbage behind, or flush it down the toilet. Whatever, I won't be needing that anymore."

A flicker of—what?—sadness, he thought, passed over her features, and then the hard look returned and Miriam shook her head. "I had to pull all kinds of favors to get my hands on this stuff. And you'll be begging me for some about the time we hit the state line. So if it's all the same to you, I think I'll keep hold of it."

It was only then that David was sure that Sister Miriam was not now, and had never been, bluffing.

* * *

"I don't know if she's ready," Benita said. Her fingers scratched at the scars on the inside of her arms. They were like tic-tac-toe games up and down her skin.

"Nobody is ever ready," the Disciple said. "It is God who makes us ready."

"You could sanctify me first, so Eliza could see what it was about. She wouldn't be so scared."

"Are you questioning me? Because if you are, you don't need sanctification, you need purification. Good, now bring in olive oil."

Benita nodded and hurried from the room, leaving Eliza alone with Christopher and the Disciple. Christopher gave her an unpleasant smile.

Eliza had lit the candles around the room at the Disciple's urging, then stood near the door with her arms crossed. She tried to give voice to her distrust rather than her fear. There were half a dozen people on the other side of the hollow wooden door, plus Benita, who would be back in a few moments. Whatever they had in mind for her back here, it couldn't be too horrific, not with so many witnesses at hand.

"What exactly do you mean by sanctification?" she asked.

"The problem is you've devoted yourself to impure things, and you need to be sanctified to the Lord. Only after you are sanctified will you be ready to survive the blood and fire that will sweep over the earth."

"And that means what, exactly?" she asked.

"It means you're a dirty slut, and he's going to remove your sluttiness," Christopher said.

"I'm nothing of the kind."

"You are, you filthy whore. I can see it on your face. You think about sex all the time; it's all you care about."

"Shut your mouth," she snapped. She turned to the Disciple. "Either he stops his lying insults, or I'm walking out of here right now."

The Disciple fixed Christopher with a hard look. "Keep quiet. You're here to witness the sanctification, not to do it yourself." He turned back to Eliza. "And it's too late to leave, you already agreed to this."

"No I didn't. I agreed to let you tell me about it, and then I'll decide. I'm still waiting for you to explain to me what the rite of sanctification is. Before I agree to anything."

"I don't have to explain it, I'll show it to you."

The tickle of alarm started to spread, and she forced herself to remain calm, reminded herself there were people in the other room and she could always scream if things got ugly.

Benita came back with a pan full of oil, which she put over a propane burner in the corner. Eliza had moved to let her back in, and now Christopher moved around until he stood between her and the front room of the trailer. The candles cast flickering light across the inside of the room, which Eliza found sinister, not calming.

"Benita, what's this all about?" she asked.

"It's easier if you just lie down and let it happen," the other woman said. "Nobody likes it at first, but it's really not so bad. And it's just what we deserve. It's what I deserve." She turned to the Disciple. "Sanctify me first. Then it won't be so bad for her, she'll see."

Eliza was still caught up on the first part of what she'd said. "What do you mean, lie down? I'm not going to do anything until someone explains what's going on here."

"Everybody gets nervous the first time they're touched," Benita said. "It's normal."

"Nobody is going to touch me."

"Why?" Christopher asked. "Because you'll like it too much?"

"I've heard enough." She reached for the doorknob, but he blocked the door and pushed her back toward the center of the room.

Eliza didn't hesitate. "Someone out there! Open this door and help me. I need help, now!"

"Shut up and get it over with," someone yelled back.

The Disciple grabbed her wrist. "It's the will of the Lord, and I am his disciple. He speaks through me. We are only the Chosen Ones because we obey His will, even when it is difficult. This is how you prove you are one of us."

She wrenched free. "Don't do this, I'm warning you."

"You are a pretty girl; I'm sure there are lustful thoughts in your head that you could purge. Think pure thoughts, think of God."

"Sanctify her," Christopher urged.

"Don't touch me."

"Think about it," the Disciple said. "If you don't sanctify yourself, men like that will come after you." He nodded to Christopher. "You don't want that."

Christopher pushed her from behind, and the Disciple grabbed her again. She struggled, but he was strong. "Benita, help me," she said. "Do something, I'm begging you."

Benita shook her head and backed into the corner, next to the propane stove. She closed her eyes. "Don't, Eliza, please. You're making it worse."

Christopher grabbed Eliza's shirt and tried to tear it over her head. She jerked her elbow back and hit him in the side of the face. He grabbed his jaw and stared at her in unmasked fury. "You slut! You whore!"

Together, the two men tore at her clothes while she struggled and screamed. Eliza hadn't grown up on a ranch to be weak and helpless. She fought and scratched and kicked and bit. But the two men didn't relent. The Disciple worked with grim determination, like he was doing an unpleasant task that he wanted to hurry and get over with.

They got off her shirt, had her bra over one shoulder and up around her neck, and tore off the temple garments that had been given to her when she'd gone through the LDS temple in Salt Lake, then started on her pants. She kicked and squirmed, but then they had her pants unbuttoned and were pulling them off. But when the Disciple had them almost to past her knees, she got one leg free and brought her knee up with a vicious thrust. It smacked him in the nose, and he fell back with a grunt. His hand flew to his nose. Blood squirted out.

"Bitch!" Christopher cried. "I'll do it myself."

He fumbled with his pants, and they came down. He was hard. But he had let go of Eliza while he did it, and she scrambled away. Benita stood cowering and helpless in the corner, her eyes still closed, her head down, shaking it with such violence that she looked like she was having an epileptic fit.

Eliza reached for the pan of olive oil. She had no idea what they'd meant to do with the oil, but during the struggle it had continued heating over the open flame, and now there was a smoky vapor coming off the surface. She grabbed the hot metal handle and swung it around just as Christopher reached her. He ducked, and most of the hot oil flew past his face. But a hot spray caught him on one side, narrowly missing his eyes. He screamed and pawed at his face.

The Disciple was regaining his feet, and Eliza didn't bother with her shirt, only pulled her pants up enough to be able to run. She grabbed for the door and burst into the front room of the trailer.

Half a dozen people sat on the worn linoleum floor, staring at open Bibles by the light of a single Coleman lantern. Eliza could tell by their glazed expressions that they were not actually reading, just staring at the pages while they listened to the horrific events in the next room. Faces jerked up and eyes widened in surprise. A young man named Kirk started to his feet, but she didn't wait to see if he was trying to help or meant to stop her.

Someone had installed locking bars to fall across the door and secure the trailer—some bit of paranoia about intruders—but thankfully, they weren't down now. She threw open the door.

Her mind was working at a feverish pace. She had to get to the cell phone she'd hidden in the abandoned sofa, call for help. But then what? Hide in the dump until the police showed up? Find the road and follow it all night? Locate the ravine? Maybe just find a broken two-by-four in the rubbish and use it to defend herself. Land a couple of good blows and drive some sense into them. Make them back off enough to explain she'd made a mistake, and could they just let her go? She'd forget all about them, they'd never hear from her again.

In her haste, she forgot that there were no steps, only a couple of cinder blocks stacked on top of each other so that you could get close enough to the doorway to stretch your leg, grab the frame, and hoist yourself up. Her foot groped at the empty air, and then she went flying into the darkness. Her arms windmilled. The landing drove the air out of her lungs. Her head smacked painfully against the ground. She wasn't injured, but it took a moment to recover.

By the time Eliza regained her feet, they were on her.

CHAPTER THIRTEEN

Miriam had been wrong about one thing. David didn't make it to the state line.

They were almost to I-15 when his legs started to twitch and he broke into a sweat. How long had it been, maybe fourteen hours since he'd last slammed a needle into the muscle on his leg?

Miriam glanced over as they pulled onto the freeway. "It's bad, isn't it?"

"I'll be fine."

"Sure, whatever you say."

She put a CD into the player and stayed in the right lane while faster traffic zipped past on their left. It was a choir singing "Praise to the Man."

"Please don't tell me this is the Mormon Tabernacle Choir."

"What do you expect, Metallica? Lady Gaga? Or do you object because it's apostate music?"

"I don't care about the LDS. Can you just turn it off?"

"Nah, I kind of like it. Besides, it will put you in the right frame of mind."

He gritted his teeth. "Fine, whatever. Just speed up, will you?"

"What?" she asked in a tone of faux concern. "You're not in a hurry, are you? I'm driving within the speed limit. Don't want to get a ticket."

He glanced over and saw that she was driving sixty. Seemed like forty. "Come on. I can't stand this. Drive faster."

"It's almost like you need something. I've got a baggie in the back, a spoon, candle and matches, syringe. Everything you need."

"You want me shooting up? And you're worried about a ticket?"

"The odds of a cop pulling up beside us are very low. Much better chance of a radar gun."

"The speed limit is seventy-five!"

"Okay, I'll speed up, if that's what you want."

Her speed crept up to about sixty-four, sixty-five. Five minutes later it was all the way to sixty-eight, and then she put it on cruise control. The headlights sliced into the darkness, illuminating the reflectors on the edges of the freeway. There was little traffic north of the city, heading for the spit of land in Arizona before I-15 cut north into St. George, Utah. An occasional semi barreled past on their left at about eighty, or even more rarely, a car, going even faster.

You are mine.

It was an audible voice inside David's head. The demon that had taken hold of him had crawled within and was now living in his head.

"Go away. Leave me alone."

Miriam glanced at him with a frown. "Excuse me?"

He closed his eyes and concentrated on his breathing. In, out, in, out. His heart raced, it pounded in his ears. His joints felt like they were pricked with red-hot needles.

You cannot escape. With every moment your chains grow thicker. Soon you will live with me in hell.

"Go away!"

"David?" Miriam asked. "Talk to me, tell me what's happening." She'd shed the snarky tone.

You will swim in a lake of fire. When you lift your head, you will see me standing above you, and you will worship me, beg for my mercy.

A shiver worked down his spine. His legs and feet burned, like acid was pouring into every needle track. He could hear the demon—or was it Lucifer himself?—chuckling. And a smell in his nostrils, like burning sulfur.

"Oh Lord, please, help me."

"Come on, David. Talk to me, talk it out."

He turned to beg her to stop, to get him something to take away this hell, shove the bloody needle into his neck, depress the plunger. Just make it stop. But he saw nothing but blackness. He was blind. He screamed.

"Stay with me, David, I'm pulling over. Hang on."

When you lift your head from the fire, my demons will tear open your throat and pour a bucket of acid into your gut. I will draw it from an ocean of acid, and every minute of the day I will pour another bucket down your throat. When all the ages of the earth have passed and I have emptied the ocean of acid, I will refill it with my malice and begin anew.

David could feel it now, taste the acid rising from his stomach. He writhed, groped for the door handle. The pavement would end his pain. Maybe one of the semis would crush him to a pulp. And then he could throw himself on the mercy of whoever waited on the other side of the veil. He shoved open the door and hurled himself into the darkness.

But he just fell straight to the blacktop, didn't even roll. Miriam had pulled off the road and stopped the car before he threw himself out. He lay on the ground with his face pressed to the pavement. Pain shot through his body, and he couldn't control the convulsions that seized his limbs.

You cannot escape and you cannot hide.

And then Miriam had him and was lifting him to a sitting position on a curb. His vision returned. They were at the rest stop outside Mesquite. Street lights illuminated the parking lot and the half a dozen cars and a pair of idling rigs. The smell of diesel gradually replaced the sulfur and acid. The shaking slowed, but didn't stop.

"I can't do this," he said. "Just fill the syringe and put me out of my misery."

"You're wrong. You can do this."

The look of sorrow and compassion on her face surprised him. It was an about-face from the disdain she'd shown him at the house, hard as the steel on the end of her handgun and just as merciless.

"You were right. I'm worse than worthless, I'm a blight on the earth and the sooner my soul flies to hell, the better for everyone. I deserve to roast for my sins."

"First of all, I never said that," Miriam said. "And I don't believe it. The worth of every soul is great in the eyes of the Lord. Second, there's no such place as hell, not like that, and you know it."

"Outer Darkness, then."

"Outer Darkness is for the elect who deny the Holy Spirit. You're just a lost soul. And lost souls can be found. Listen to me." She took his hand, and her touch was gentle. "Jacob saw something in you. He sent Eliza to bring you back, and he convinced your father to remove his edict. I believe there is something good in there somewhere, just like your brother. You even look a little like him."

"Like a hollow caricature. A bad photocopy. I'm nothing like him, except for a nose and a chin."

"David, please. I want to help, but you have to let me."

"Can you get me something?" he asked.

"Of course. What would you like? Water? A soda?"

"You know what I need."

"Oh." She hesitated. "David, you don't have to do this. You can make it to Blister Creek without drugs."

"No, you were right. I made it about to the state line, that's all."

"All that stuff I said at the house was an act," she said. "I'm good at it. It's how the FBI trained me, and I was a natural. Don't take it seriously, I was just trying to get you out of the house. Now that you're out of the house, I want to help."

"I don't believe you were acting. I believe you're acting now."

"You can do it, I'm telling you. For goodness sake, at least try. It's only a couple more hours."

"No."

"An hour, then."

"It's no use, Miriam."

"You can make it," she said. "One hour, then I'll pull over. Sixty minutes. I'm being sincere, I swear I am."

"You might be sincere, but you don't think I can make it. You *know* I can't." When she didn't say anything, he added, "Help me get the syringe ready. Then I'll be okay until we get to Blister Creek, you'll see."

A long moment of silence. "Okay, wait here."

A few minutes later, sitting in a toilet stall with a syringe in hand and the veins on his foot exposed, he hesitated. The shakes were gone for the moment, and the headache had subsided. He heard the flush of a toilet, the whirr of a hand dryer, smelled urine cakes and industrial-strength cleanser that only masked but didn't eliminate the smell of piss and shit. But he felt better than he had in hours.

Except for the longing, the desire so deep it felt almost like the burning need to breathe when you've been holding your breath underwater. It was stronger than ever. He shoved the needle in and depressed the plunger.

Almost instantly, all of it was gone. The whispering demon, the pain, the shakes, the desire, simply vanished. In its place a rising tide of euphoria that swept aside all other emotions.

David Christianson closed his eyes and sighed.

CHAPTER FOURTEEN

Eliza made them pay. She gouged eyes, bit, sent her knees and
elbows flying. Her forehead smashed someone across the bridge of
the nose. There was no crying out this time, no begging for mercy.
She knew what they meant to do and knew that nobody would
help her. And so she fought.

But eventually they had her arms pinned. Someone tore off
her bra and someone else her pants. Soon she lay naked, exhausted,
chest heaving, while they held her down. Christopher stood over
her with a kerosene lamp, the Disciple in the shadows to his left.

"Sanctify her," Christopher said. "Right here, in the dirt. Show
her, do it."

"You'd better get the rest of them," Eliza said through clenched
teeth. She tasted blood. It trickled down her lip. "You'll need every

one of them to hold me down. If you rape me, you'd better hold
me every second or I'll fight back."

And when you let me go, I'll come back in the night with a knife.

Her terror had gone. All that was left was a rage so pure that she
knew that if she held a gun in her hands at that very moment, she'd
shoot them all, one by one. Maybe even Benita, maybe even the
boy, though Diego was nowhere to be seen. It was a filthy, unholy
feeling that gripped her, unlike anything she'd ever felt.

The rest of them were already coming out, one by one. She
saw Benita, Kirk, even Diego.

"Sanctify her," Christopher said. He was almost pleading. "Do
it, hurry."

The Disciple started forward, then stopped. "No, she's not
ready."

"What do you mean she's not ready? Look at her, she needs it."

"Be quiet!"

He shut up, and Eliza felt a wild hope rising in her chest. They
were going to let her go, put it off until tomorrow. Well, there
wouldn't be a tomorrow—she would leave tonight, no matter what.

After a moment, the Disciple said, "She's not ready because she
hasn't been sufficiently purified. Once she has been purified, she'll
be ready to submit to God's will, and then we'll sanctify her. Get
her up. You and you, help."

They started to lift her up, but she jerked free and rose by herself. She stood naked in front of them. Eliza had grown up in an
environment of modesty where a woman didn't show her shoulders, where her mother shook her head at the thought of women
wearing pants because then you can see "where their legs come
together," which was her euphemism for "crotch." Eliza still felt

uncomfortable with anything that didn't go to the ankle and the wrist.

But she refused to cover herself or act ashamed. Instead she stood defiantly, with her hands on her hips. "I won't be purified or sanctified or anything else. Give me back my clothing. I'm leaving."

The Disciple looked through the group before his eyes settled on Benita. "Bring me thirty heads of lettuce."

Benita's eyes widened. "Thirty?"

"She's strong. She'll survive, if God wills it."

"Even Madeline only got twenty."

"Thirty!"

They dragged Eliza into the darkness of the abandoned dump. She fought back again, but by now she was exhausted and couldn't inflict the same damage she had earlier. Christopher set down the lantern, then pushed aside an overturned fridge, grunting and muttering. A black pit opened in the ground. A dank, foul smell oozed out, like an exposed cesspool, or something dead.

And a moan, a thin voice from the darkness below. "Please. I can't take it anymore. Please."

* * *

They lowered a ladder into the darkness. Immediately someone started to climb from below, but Christopher gave the ladder a shake and shouted down, "Get off there!"

Two people dragged Eliza to the edge. She was shivering from the thin night air, and her stomach twisted with fear and the stench wafting up from below.

"You don't have to do this. Any of you. It's wrong and you know it." Eliza fixed Benita with her gaze, but the girl looked

away. She found Kirk, the one she thought might have been trying to help her, but he wouldn't meet her eyes, so she looked at
the others, one by one. Some stared back in defiance, while others looked at their feet or let the darkness hide their faces. "You
say you're following Jesus, but these are the tactics of the enemy.
Listen, I made a mistake coming here, I thought you were something else. Now I just want to leave and never come back."

"It's too late for that," the Disciple said. "The only thing is to
find out if you're strong enough to survive, if you're one of us."

"I'm not one of you, and I don't care about your rites. Do the
right thing and let me go."

"You're broken, Eliza, like the rest of us. A sinner. You deserve
to die. God, in His mercy, has given you this one chance. Soon—
maybe even before you come back from purification—fire will
sweep over the earth. And then you'll see this is a kindness. It's
your only chance."

"No, you're wrong."

"The world hates us. They persecute us. Satan has penetrated
their hearts. They wish to tear us apart, stick their needles in us,
tie us to machinery and send electricity through our bodies. Only
God has led us here, and none of us will leave until the flames have
passed, until it has purified the whole world with holy fire. But first,
we need to purify you."

"You're insane."

"I'm the Disciple. My word is the word of the Lord."

She fought them as they took her to the edge, but when she
saw that she'd either have to be thrown down or take the ladder,
she finally relented. She climbed down, holding one hand over her

mouth against the smell. When she got to the bottom, she looked up at the light overhead, fuming.

Someone bent down with the box Benita had brought from the trailers. "Here, take your lettuce." It was Christopher.

"Go to hell."

"You'll be sorry if you don't," the Disciple said from the darkness at his back.

She wanted to tell them to choke on their lettuce, but if she wanted any hope of surviving, she had to take even the smallest advantage. And so she grabbed the box of lettuce and brought it down. The fridge scraped across the opening, and she was plunged into darkness.

Eliza stood on something springy, and as she sank down, she felt it was a mattress. It sagged beneath her weight, releasing the smell of human waste and body odor.

"Who is it?" a woman's voice asked from the darkness.

"Madeline?"

"Benita, is that you?" the woman asked.

"No. I'm not Benita." Compared to the flat, dead sound of her companion, Eliza's own voice sounded a defiant note. "My name is Eliza Christianson. Are you Madeline Caliari?"

"I am." A pause. "Do I know you?"

"Your mother sent me to find you."

A sharp intake of breath, then a sob. "My mother? How...how is she?"

"Worried sick. She's been doing nothing but searching for you."

Madeline broke down, sobbing. Eliza was too caught up in her own despair to think about going over to comfort her. She fought the horrid, sinking feeling of self-doubt, knowing she'd made a mistake, that she shouldn't have come here, that she'd underestimated them. And now she was going to die in a pit in the desert. It took a few minutes to give herself the mental slap needed to get her out of that destructive line of thinking. By then, Madeline's crying had faded to sniffles.

"Are you sure?" The voice edged closer in the darkness. "She's still looking for me? Are you sure?"

"Why is that surprising?" Eliza asked. "She loves you, and you're her only child. Of course she's going to keep searching. She was desperate. She even managed to convince me I could find you and get you out."

"How did she know where to find me? Nobody knows where we are."

"There's a group of parents who are sharing information and searching. She was watching some of you eating garbage, and then she tracked you to Las Vegas."

"Really? You're sure?"

"She's tall, right? Maybe five nine with heels. Brown hair with highlights, slender and athletic."

"What? No, that's not my mom."

Eliza frowned. "What do you mean? I met her myself, talked to her about you, and she told us how to find you."

"Did you say glamorous?" She sniffled. "I don't think so. My mom looks like someone with three kids and a minivan. A little frumpy. And her hair is darker, definitely no highlights. I guess she could have changed that part. But not the slender and athletic stuff. And she's maybe five-five. She wears pumps. You're just messing with me, aren't you? You don't know anything about her."

"I'm not messing with you." Eliza didn't know what to think. She had definite memories of Allison Caliari. She'd looked so out of place among the other women at Zarahemla, she may as well have been a model straight off the runway in Paris. There was no way Eliza had misremembered those details. "A woman found me, said she was Allison Caliari and needed help finding her daughter. She looked through some pictures we had, and we figured out you had to be out here. So I found you."

"Did she sound like she was from New Jersey?"

"No, not really." Eliza considered. "Sounded like she was from Utah or Idaho, now that I think about it."

"My parents moved to the Northwest from Jersey about twenty years ago. You can still hear it in Mom's voice, it's pretty obvious. I don't know who that woman is, but she isn't my mother."

"That doesn't make sense. My brother Jacob dug around online and found this group of parents who are sharing information about the Chosen Ones. They really exist. Your mother is really the head, so I don't...well, it doesn't matter," Eliza said, though she was sure that it did matter, somehow. Who was that woman, then, and how had she known so much? What did she want? And her story about Madeline's descent into the cult had been detailed and told with emotion.

There was a moment, though. When Allison Caliari warned her to be careful, when Eliza had gotten the impression of hearing the voice of an actress speaking offstage in an unguarded moment. Who was that woman?

"But you really came out here just to find me?" Madeline asked.

"That's exactly what I did. I tracked down the cult just to get you out."

"It's not a cult."

"Fine, your religious movement," Eliza said. "The problem is, my sheltered life, with all its religious weirdness, still wasn't enough to prepare me for this."

"What do you mean by that?" Madeline asked.

"Usually, they're more subtle when they try to subject you in the name of the Lord." Eliza fought a choking sense of panic, tried to force a glib tone that she didn't feel to keep from breaking down. "I didn't expect them to toss me down and try to publicly rape me. Seems kind of dumb now, but I thought I'd stroll in, find you, and get you out of here. I guess you could say oops."

Madeline said nothing. Eliza felt around the room while she tried to catch her breath. She had to get working, do something. There were two mattresses on the floor, one of which held a number of gallon jugs. Water, she guessed, or maybe Madeline's waste. Dirt walls let a seeping chill into the room. A second box with wilting lettuce. Her hand found Madeline's arm, and the girl flinched.

"Sorry," Eliza said. "Just getting my bearings."

"It's okay, you startled me is all. It has been so long since anyone touched me."

"Not much down here, is there?"

"No. It's a hole in the desert. Water, these crappy old mattresses, lettuce, and your own filth. I'd say it's like hell, except it's cold. I've got fifteen more days to go. How about you?"

"Thirty."

Madeline drew in her breath. "Thirty? Nobody can live thirty days without food. You'll die."

Eliza wanted to grab the other woman and shake her. *Don't you think I know that? Wake up, we're both going to die!*

She forced calm into her voice. "Madeline, I'm not going to die, not like this. And I'm not going to stay down here starving to death only so they can drag me up and rape me when I'm too weak to fight back."

"Does that mean the Disciple already sanctified you?"

"He tried," Eliza said. "He won't get another chance. I'm going to find a way out."

"How are you going to do that?"

"I'll figure out something. And if I don't, it won't be because I sat here doing nothing. Can you help me?" When Madeline didn't answer, Eliza added, "Or are you going to sit there waiting to die?"

"Could you reach out your hand again? Just touch my arm like you did?"

Eliza touched Madeline on the arm, and the other woman grabbed her and held on. Eliza moved over to her side and held her. She was naked, her shoulders sharp and bony. She began to sob again.

"I'm sorry," Eliza said. "I'm afraid and angry and I didn't mean to take it out on you." She stroked Madeline's face, then her arm. Eliza felt thin, parallel lines marking the other woman's forearm.

"Don't touch my scars."

"I'm sorry."

"It's no use, is it?"

"You've got to have faith that we'll find a way out."

"I don't think so," Madeline said between sniffles. "No way to escape, and they won't relent until we're purified. And even if I could, it would be wrong. I *need* to be purified. The Disciple said so."

"He's no disciple. He's a nutcase, that's all. Whatever possessed you to join them?"

"They're not crazy."

"You're wrong. They're crazy and they're evil."

"They're not evil!"

"Madeline, they raped you, they threw you in a pit to starve to death."

"That's for my own good. Seriously, don't you understand? I'm unclean, I'm a filthy sinner, and I need to be purified and sanctified."

"Stop using those words. They're lies. Purified means starved and sanctified means raped. That's all. What have you done, what could you *possibly* do that would make you deserve all of this?"

Madeline pulled away and shuffled backward across the mattresses. "You don't know anything about me. You have no idea the horrible things I'm capable of doing."

"Tell me. Maybe I can help."

"I had a boyfriend. Lots of them, actually, but one in particular. I got pregnant, halfway through my freshman year, can you believe it? I was going to get an abortion."

Eliza tried to keep her tone neutral. "And did you?"

"I would have. I had an appointment. God gave me a miscarriage instead, but I was going to."

"So you didn't actually do anything."

"I had the intent, that's the same thing. I'm a horrible, bad person, and Satan keeps trying to get me." She sighed. "Don't you ever feel that life itself is too painful to bear? Sometimes, suffering feels like an escape."

"Is that why you cut your arms? Is that what caused the scars?"

"I don't want to talk about that," Madeline said.

"You're doing it because you think you *deserve* to suffer? That's what this is all about, isn't it? You've found a new way to punish yourself, and you're telling yourself it's about God."

"Yes, I was cutting," she snapped. "It only made things worse. Can't you see? That's why I need this, it's why I need these people. Only after I'm purified and sanctified am I good enough to go out and cleanse the world. Right now I just have to watch."

"By cleanse, do you mean the part where you go out and assault people?"

Madeline hesitated for a moment before saying, "We only attack the worst, most unrepentant people. Drug dealers and murderers."

"Let me tell you about one of those people. Do you remember the guy with the produce truck, down past the ravine? Where you stole all this lettuce?"

"How did you know about that?"

"I know because that guy is my brother. I found him in bed, lucky to be alive the way you beat him nearly to death. And what did he ever do to you?"

"David was Benita's old boyfriend," she said.

"Really? So that's how they singled him out?"

"He was leading her into a lifestyle of sin and addiction. We had to cleanse him in order to help her."

"It was a cruel thing you did," Eliza said. "He didn't deserve it, whatever you think. You don't know anything about my brother, and I swear he'd have never led anyone into any sort of lifestyle. That's just another lie they told you." When Madeline didn't answer, she added, "Let me tell you about my brother. I have seen David teaching young children to read. I saw him carry spiders

outside because he didn't want to kill them, saw him sit all night
with an old dog who was about to die. He was a good kid, maybe a
little distracted and maybe didn't take things seriously enough, but
he would never hurt anyone. I come from…well, a religious family,
and my father kicked him out for not being good enough. That's
when things went bad for David, when he started abusing drugs and
living a fast lifestyle. But whatever he's done, I can tell you that he
didn't deserve what you did to him."

Eliza took a deep breath, tried to fight down her anger, and
then crawled through the darkness to Madeline's side again. "And
you don't deserve what you're doing to yourself."

"It's the only way. Otherwise I'm going to burn."

"No, you're not."

"The world is coming to an end. Everything will burn up."

"You know what? I've met a dozen guys who claimed the
world was coming to an end on this day or that. Nobody knows
when it will happen. It could be tomorrow or a thousand years
from now. The Bible says, 'like a thief in the night.'" She put her
arm around Madeline. "The Disciple is a fraud. You can tell by the
things he's doing. That's not from God. He can't help, he can only
hurt you."

"No, you're wrong. I've felt Satan, he's real. I've awakened in
the night to find him sitting on my chest, I've heard him whispering. I cut myself to make him go away, just for a few seconds. Only
the Disciple can make him leave me alone."

"Madeline, I don't know what that was. Maybe it was Satan, or
maybe, I don't know, you just need counseling and medication."

"That's not true. You don't know what you're talking about.
It was Satan, I swear it!"

"Listen to me," Eliza said in a hard voice. "I don't care. Forget about the Disciple for a moment. What if a friend came to you and said she wanted to join a religious group. And when she did, she could never speak to you again, or to anyone in her family. The leader would make her sleep in Dumpsters and eat garbage. Then she'd go live in the desert and be thrown naked into a pit for weeks at a time, with nothing to eat except for lettuce. When they dragged her out, they'd rape her. Then they'd take her into the city where she'd join a mob and beat strangers, break their bones, and leave them a bruised, bloody mess. Two people in this group would freeze to death in a back alley, and another one would jump from the Hoover Dam to her death. And your friend told you this was the will of the Lord. What would you tell her?"

"You make it sound so wrong. But it's not like that."

"It's exactly like that." Eliza wanted to scream, to shake Madeline until the girl woke up. But that would be absolutely the wrong tactic. "How about you promise me one thing?"

"What is that?" Madeline asked.

"Promise me that as soon as we get out of here, you'll sit down and talk to your mother. It's the least you can do."

"I don't know if I can do it. I'm afraid she'll talk me out of it."

"Shouldn't that be telling you something? She loves you—she at least needs to know that you're alive."

"That wasn't even my mom you talked to, remember?"

"It doesn't matter. Your mother is still the leader of a group of parents trying to find their children. That part is real, that's what you need to hold onto. All I'm asking is that you talk to her. Can't you promise that much?"

"I'll tell you what. If you still feel the same way when we get out, I'll talk to her. But I don't think you will. I think you'll change your mind."

Eliza was taken aback. "After everything I just said, you think I'm going to change my mind?"

"You don't get it, do you? We're trapped down here. Fifteen days for me. Thirty for you. One head of lettuce a day, that's all. When you've been here a few days, you'll see. Fasting weakens you, it makes you humble. You don't know that yet, but you will."

"I know what fasting is. This isn't fasting, it's forced starvation." Eliza groped around the room until she found the box with Madeline's wilted lettuce, then her own box. "And I'm not going to play that game."

"What are you doing?"

"Getting you some of my lettuce—it's fresher than yours. It's barely even food, but it's all we've got. Here, eat as much as you can. We'll wait an hour and you can eat another head."

"You can't do that," Madeline said. "You'll never make it if I eat your lettuce."

"I don't plan to *make* it. I plan to get out of here. I'm going to do something, and I need you strong enough to help."

Madeline hesitated for a long time, and it seemed she was going to refuse, that nothing Eliza said had penetrated. That she would crawl back into her corner to suffer in silence until she somehow survived fifteen more days in this hole. Or didn't.

But at last, she took the lettuce. "Okay. I'll try."

CHAPTER FIFTEEN

When he was seventeen, Abraham Christianson was ordered to kill a dissident. His uncle, an elder in the Church of the Anointing, took him to the Ghost Cliffs, put a deer rifle in his hand, and told him to shoot the man through the heart.

Abraham's childhood in the fifties and sixties had a hard element. He'd grown up castrating lambs with his teeth. He was eight when his father showed him how to pin the lamb by the back legs, shove his face forward and grab its balls with his teeth, and then slice them off with a knife and spit them to the ground. The lamb would scream and stagger away in dazed terror and pain while Abraham moved on to the next animal. He could castrate the entire flock of spring lambs in an afternoon by the time he was twelve.

He'd winched pigs off the ground by their hind feet, while they fought like hell to get free of the chains. Nothing smarter than a pig on the farm, not even a dog, and they damn well knew what was coming. It was no easy thing to forget the screaming as you brought the knife to its neck, the gush of blood, an endless river of it. Abraham had also put down old dogs, drowned unwanted kittens, and whacked off the heads of hundreds of chickens, ducks, geese, and turkeys over the years.

When he was nine, he sat by his grandmother's bed, holding her thin, papery hand while she suffocated on her failing lungs. Pneumonia. Probably curable, but there wouldn't be a doctor in Blister Creek for another twenty years. Everyone knew that penicillin was toxic, the smallpox vaccine sterilized those dumb enough to get the shot, and fluoridated water would cause dementia over time.

But Abraham was unprepared for what his uncle dragged out from under a tarp in the back of his 1947 Ford pickup that summer morning. It was a man, blindfolded, hands and feet taped together. Elder Tomlinson, Abraham could tell from his hair. He was about thirty and had just taken his second wife. He was already mostly bald, with a few strands of hair in an optimistic comb-over, and the bushy remnants around his sideburns and above his ears turning prematurely gray. When he sat behind the pulpit, nodding sagely at Elder Kimball's sacrament meeting talks, he had a serious, distinguished appearance. His wives sat in the front row, knitting, feeding babies, calming toddlers.

Uncle Heber hauled Elder Tomlinson out of the truck and pulled off the blindfold. The man's eyes were wild. Heber pushed him, and he flailed, sprawled to the dirt.

It hadn't rained for weeks, and wind scoured dust off the Colorado Plateau and swept it across the Ghost Cliffs. There were few plants near the edge of the gorge, just low, scrubby brush, cactus, and a pair of bristlecone pines growing from the hard ground, their branches twisted by hundreds of years of winds howling over the plateau. That wind kicked up now, knifing through Abraham's jacket and making his eyes sting.

Heber dragged Tomlinson to his feet and ripped away the electrical tape over his mouth. The man started pleading. "Please, don't do it. It isn't true, I wasn't going to do it. I was just talking, don't you see? My big mouth got away from me. I should have shut up, I know it, but it was just talk, there was nothing serious."

Heber pinned him against the truck with his forearm, then released him to reach into the backseat and grabbed the rifle. He checked to make sure it was loaded, then shoved it into Abraham's hands. The boy looked down at the gun as if he'd been handed a snake.

"Listen to me," Elder Tomlinson said. "I was mad about the Luskey girl, that's all, so I started running off my mouth. It won't happen again."

Heber slapped him across the face, so hard his head rocked and he nearly fell. Abraham swung the rifle away with one hand and grabbed the shoulder strap of Tomlinson's overalls with the other to keep him from falling. The man regained his balance.

"It's not about the girl," Uncle Heber said. He spoke in that slow, rural Utah twang, where everything was "Is this fer me?" or "Givit tuh them." Wolves became "wooves," and a greeting came across as, "How yuh doon?" It gave the impression of a harmless rancher, still young enough to dig an irrigation ditch by hand, but with skin tanned to leather by decades in the sun. There was nothing harmless about the edge to his voice now.

"You asked," Heber continued, "the quorum met, and we decided it wasn't time. You're only thirty; you've got two wives already. You were there, you bowed your head and said, 'Thou sayest.' And then you walked out of the temple and the evil began. You gossiped, you complained. Back-biting, evil speaking of the Lord's anointed. Even then, when you were warned, if you had simply bowed your head and said, 'Thou sayest' again, and meant it this time, it would have ended."

"I know, I—"

Heber grabbed the man by the throat. "If this man says one more word," he said to Abraham, "shoot him. Do you understand?"

"I understand." Abraham held the rifle against the man's chest. He could feel Tomlinson trembling through the barrel.

"You didn't say those words; you kept talking. You poisoned the minds of your family against the prophet, and you whispered in the ears of the young men of the quorum. You schemed with your friends to move your wives and families to Wayne County. To divide Zion. If it had been just you, we would have stripped you of your blessings, taken your wives and children to give to the faithful. But it wasn't just you. We need to be sure that you won't come back in the night and whisper in the ears of the saints."

Tomlinson's eyes widened, but wisely, he said nothing.

Uncle Heber looked around. The wind howled across the cliff, blowing a talcum-fine mist of dust over the edge, like a waterfall. He told Abraham what to do, and the two dragged Elder Tomlinson toward the edge. When they got there, Heber fisted the front of Tomlinson's overalls and shoved him backward toward the cliff as if he were simply going to push him to his death. Hands and feet taped, the man heaved back and screamed. At the last moment,

Heber tightened his grip and jerked Tomlinson back upright, a few inches from the cliff. A dark spot spread down the man's pant leg. Abraham's heart felt like it would hammer out of his chest.

"Brother Tomlinson," Heber said in a loud voice. "Thou art guilty of the blood and sins of this generation. By the power of the Holy Melchizedek Priesthood, we now seal thee unto death."

"No," Tomlinson whispered.

"Come with me," Heber told his nephew. "If he moves from that spot, shoot him."

"I understand."

They walked slowly away from the cliff's edge. Heber clamped a hand on Abraham's shoulder. "You're a good boy. Like your father, but he might be a little soft. Certainly, he doesn't have the stomach for this, and anyway, we can't bother the prophet with this sort of thing. He has to be above the conflict, a leader of all men, and that means we have to take the hard measures."

"Are we just trying to scare him? You're not really going to kill him, right?"

"No, I'm not going to kill him. You are."

Abraham swallowed and looked down at the rifle. Shoot a man like a coyote among the sheep? He couldn't.

Uncle Heber studied his face. "It is better for one man to perish than a nation to dwindle in unbelief."

They were the words of the Lord in the Book of Mormon, when Nephi went back to Jerusalem to retrieve the Brass Plates. When Laban had refused to surrender the plates, the Lord ordered Nephi to cut off the man's head. Nephi had initially balked, and now Abraham did, too.

"He's just one man with a few weak followers," Abraham said. "If they're stupid enough to follow Tomlinson, they deserve to be cut off."

"And their wives, too? And their children? Why, that's fifty people. Isn't it better that one man die than lose fifty souls to the adversary? And it's a mercy for Elder Tomlinson. You'll shoot him through the heart, and his own blood shall atone for his sins. It will give him a chance to be forgiven on the other side. Now quick, lift the gun, do what needs to be done."

Abraham lifted the rifle but had a hard time steadying it in his hands. His mouth was dry. He looked down the sight. It was only twenty yards. His Great-grandmother Cowley, ninety-six years old and born on the plains of Wyoming in the back of a Conestoga wagon, could have made the shot without standing from her rocking chair. But the way the gun shook in his hands, he'd be lucky not to blow off his own kneecap.

Elder Tomlinson found his voice. "Please, I know I was wrong. It was a terrible sin, but I'm sorry. Have mercy, I beg you."

"He is suffering the regrets of the damned," Heber said in a low voice. "It is not true contrition."

"Uncle Heber, please. I don't know if I can do it. How about a warning?"

A sigh. "And what would be a sufficient warning? A wound?"

"Yes, that's a good idea." Abraham's words spilled out, one on top of the next. "Just a wound, maybe on the thigh. It wouldn't kill him. We could take him back to Blister Creek, and he'd know that next time would be it, there wouldn't be another chance, he'd die if he defied the prophet a second time. What do you think?"

"Maybe." Heber was quiet for a moment. "Not his thigh, though, that's too easy. How about his shoulder? Can you hold your gun steady enough not to miss low?"

Abraham let out his breath. "I can do it. But he's too close to the edge. He'll fall back, and he might go over the side."

"Hmm. Good point. Wait here."

Uncle Heber walked back to Elder Tomlinson on the edge of the cliff, while Abraham tried to steady his nerves. He'd been breaking a horse just two hours earlier when Uncle Heber had pulled up in his truck. Abraham's original plan for the day had been to join the survey team working at the edge of federal land on the west side of town. He wanted to teach himself how to use the theodolite. He couldn't remember why he'd changed his mind and stayed at the ranch. If he'd stuck with the original plan, maybe he wouldn't be standing here with a rifle, getting ready to shoot a man.

His uncle said something to Tomlinson, who whimpered and begged. When he slumped down to his knees, Heber dragged him back up and said, "Do this with honor and there may be mercy. Here or on the other side, the Lord will decide." This stiffened him a little, and Heber moved him to a new spot.

Heber walked back toward Abraham. "There, that's better. Remember, the shoulder."

The boy lifted the gun, his hands steady now. He said a silent prayer that the Lord would guide his shot. It had to be clean. Through the shoulder and the man would be okay. If he missed low, he'd kill Tomlinson. If he missed high, Uncle Heber might grab the gun and finish the job.

"Ready?"

"I'm ready."

"Vengeance is mine, sayeth the Lord," Heber whispered.

Abraham pulled the trigger. A crack from the rifle. His shot was perfect. It struck Elder Tomlinson in the perfect spot on the shoulder. A shot that would slice clean through with painful, but not crippling, damage to muscle and bone. It would miss vital organs and leave a clean exit wound. He would recover, maybe with an old twinge to remind him of the time he'd defied the Lord. He'd never do it again.

Except Uncle Heber had lied. The bullet slammed into Elder Tomlinson's shoulder, throwing him back. He staggered, as if trying to keep his feet, and then he disappeared over the edge of the cliff. He screamed as he fell. It was four hundred feet; the fall couldn't have lasted more than a few seconds, a terrible, wailing sound that seemed to go on forever, falling in pitch like the whistle of a train as it passes. And then it stopped, but the echo reverberated through the canyon, together with the last, fading echo of an echo of the whip-crack retort of the rifle.

"No," Abraham whispered. The gun fell to his feet.

He followed Uncle Heber to the edge of the cliff. Elder Tomlinson hadn't fallen all the way. Instead, he'd caught on a ledge maybe a hundred feet down. His legs lay at a strange angle, the tape ripped off, and his back looked odd, like it was bending the wrong direction. And then, most horribly of all, his head moved.

No, dear Lord, don't let him be alive.

But before he had a chance to see if Elder Tomlinson had somehow survived the fall, Uncle Heber led him way. The boy imagined Tomlinson conscious, trying to move to relieve the pain, his back broken, his organs ruptured, lungs punctured by broken ribs. Abraham pulled away and threw up.

Heber patted him on the back. "There, now. I know, it wasn't easy. But it was a trial. You passed."

Abraham wiped his mouth with the back of his hand and looked at his uncle. "You said...you *told* me..."

"The path is not always easy for the Lord's chosen people. I'm afraid this won't be the last time you'll be called on to do difficult work in His name."

Yes, over the years Abraham Christianson had been confronted with other difficult decisions. Driving his boys out of town, for instance. He still remembered the way Enoch had pleaded for mercy, how David had stared at him with that hurt expression, and how Abraham had remembered that same expression from when David was five years old. It was enough to tear out his heart.

But sending Eliza to her death was another thing entirely.

The woman met him in the Ghost Cliffs, near the reservoir. It was only a mile from where Elder Tomlinson had fallen to his death. And for a moment, Abraham Christianson was a boy of seventeen and could see Uncle Heber giving him that look of mixed pity and pride. Heber had later become prophet for fifteen years before dying of a brain tumor that first caused terrible headaches and later led him to paranoid speeches about "wooves" in sheep's clothing.

Few of the old men were alive, and some of the stronger ones of Abraham's own generation had fallen from the church, or, like Taylor Kimball, were serving time in federal prison. And so Abraham found himself scheming with women.

First Sister Miriam, brought from Zarahemla to bring back Jacob, and now this one. She called herself Allison Caliari this time.

They both knew this was not her real name. She had played other parts in the past: a polygamist wife, a reporter for *USA Today*, a social worker from the DCFS.

She drove up in a BMW convertible, its top down. The wind had swept her hair from her face. She wore red lipstick that gave her mouth a hungry, sensuous look. A bit of liner made her eyes wide pools, and she'd plucked her eyebrows. She wore a sleeveless dress, and he had to pull his eyes from the muscles in her shoulders and the scoop in front that showed a hint of her swelling breasts. He had wives, some young and beautiful, others matronly, and others of the homely type known as sweet spirits. He enjoyed them all, and time had only dulled, not ended, his love of feeling a woman's curves under his hands. He was not an indifferent lover, who spread his seed and then rolled away to tend to the stock.

Even though his experience had been limited to women of a certain background, Abraham Christianson was no fool. He didn't take this woman's appearance at face value, and he fought against the pull of her sexuality. She would not be his Salome.

She stepped out of the convertible, leaving the engine running. "It's beautiful, isn't it?" He followed her gaze as it swept across the reservoir to the cliffs, then lingered on the valley below—green pastures and fields, surrounded by red rock and distant bluffs. "Nothing like it anywhere in the world."

"Well?" he demanded. "What did you find?"

She continued as if he hadn't said anything. "The air, can you smell that? Juniper and sage. Wildflowers because of the spring rain. And I love looking at the red rock cliffs. I like to walk along the plateaus and look over the edge. You can see forever, the curvature of the earth and then look down thousands of feet."

"People have fallen to their deaths that way."

"They have? I wouldn't know anything about that."

There was an ironic tone to her voice, and for a moment he imagined that she could read his thoughts, knew about the death of Elder Tomlinson.

"And what about the stars?" she asked. "You come out at night and lie on your back and they're so close it feels like you're clinging to the skin of the earth. It's impossible not to wonder about your place in the cosmos."

Abraham had felt those moments, too. And he would hear the scripture, *Worlds without number have I created.*

"We're not here for chitchat. Tell me what you've discovered or leave and don't trouble me again."

"I love listening to you talk, Abraham. It's like a time warp to the fifties. Yes, she's there."

"And? Is she alive?"

"For now. They put Eliza in the pit. She might have been raped, I don't know for sure. If they haven't done it yet, they will."

He felt his mouth go dry. Hopefully, she'd fought to protect her virtue. Yes, she would have, she was a fighter. "She's not finished."

"She has a chance. You know and I know that Eliza is cut from the same cloth as Jacob."

"Not exactly the same cloth. Jacob has the priesthood."

"If by that you mean that people give him deference he hasn't earned, because of what dangles between his legs, then yes, I suppose so."

Abraham said, "Why is it that whenever people live with gentiles, they come back spewing crudities?"

"That's not crude, that's a euphemism. Nowhere did I say penis, dick, or cock."

He winced. "Okay, fine. Whatever the reason, God decreed that men hold the priesthood, not women. That gives them power and authority."

"It hasn't always been that way," Allison said. "And in the temple, women wield that power, too."

"True or not, it *is* that way now. We're not in the temple, and the Lord has withheld the priesthood from women for His own purpose. Eliza has the spirit to guide her, but the forces of hell are arrayed against her. What chance does she have?"

"Not a good one. But she's as smart as her brother—smarter than you, Abraham—and she's got the same force of will as any Christianson. The Lord has chosen her for this task, and if He wants her to survive, she will."

Says the woman who has shed her temple garments to live a gentile life, he thought. *What could you possibly know about the will of the Lord?*

"Speaking of Jacob," she continued. "How long do we have before he goes looking for her?"

"Not long. I'll bet he sent Eliza with a phone and made her promise to call in. They'll have taken her phone, or maybe she'll have been smart enough to hide it first, but I don't think she'll be able to make a call." He considered. "Let's say a few days to miss her first call, another day or two for Jacob to get worried and go looking for her."

"Does he call the police or go after her himself?" she asked.

"I don't know, but I don't think it will take that long. She's there now. Our prey should reveal himself."

"And that prey is valuable enough to sacrifice one young woman," she said, "as much as it pains each of us to admit it."

"Yes. It is necessary." His voice turned bitter. "But don't, for one moment, compare your pain to mine. She is *my* daughter—it is *my* heart being torn out of my chest."

"She's just a girl." The sarcasm in her voice sounded filthy to his ears. "What is one girl worth? You've got dozens of them. And if you lose one, you can use that dangly thing you're so proud of to make another."

"How dare you?"

"Me? You're the one pretending he cares about his daughter, when you and I both know she's just an object to you. I may be willing to take the hard steps, but at least I'm not a hypocrite."

He stared. "I can't believe I'm standing here listening to this garbage."

"You don't have a choice. You couldn't get to Senator McKay without me, and you can't do this, either."

"You know, someday Jacob's ex-FBI agent will come around to my point of view, and then I won't need you anymore. She could do everything you do, but better. I'll bet she could infiltrate Caleb's cult herself, she's almost young enough."

"Good luck with that, Abraham."

"We're done here. Will you please leave?"

She put her hands on her hips and stared at him for a long moment, as if daring him to raise his right hand to the square, rebuke her, and cast her out. He fought the urge. At last she shrugged and turned back to her car. She climbed behind the wheel of the BMW, a car with lines and curves that only enhanced the sexuality of its driver. She pulled onto the road, then blew a kiss over her shoulder as she accelerated rapidly. The engine growled and leaped forward.

As soon as she was gone, Abraham fell to his knees. "Dear Heavenly Father, I submit myself to thy will. But if it please thee, if it will not thwart thy plan, I beg thee to strengthen thy daughter, allow Eliza to escape the den of vipers. In the name of the Holy One of Israel, even Jesus Christ, amen."

He rose, dismayed to find that prayer had not banished the unsettled feeling. If anything, he felt worse, a claustrophobic sensation, like walls crushing in on him. As many children as he'd lost over the years, this one would be the hardest.

It occurred to Abraham that while Uncle Heber may have compared him to Nephi that day when he'd shot Elder Tomlinson, he wasn't Nephi now. He was his namesake from the Bible. But instead of the Lord asking him to take his son into the mountains to offer as a sacrifice, it was his daughter he threw onto the altar.

The only question was whether or not the Lord would show mercy or require Abraham to burn her.

CHAPTER SIXTEEN

"Are you ready to die?" the Disciple asked.

"I will die for the glory of God," Christopher said. "If I have to."

Christopher stood close enough that their noses were almost touching. They were almost the same height, and once, in a BART station restroom in San Francisco, the Disciple had glanced in the mirror to see Christopher watching him, and for a moment he'd seen himself reflected in the other man's eyes. A prophet, a visionary. The man worshiped him, honored his every word and edict. If only they all felt this way, things would be different. He could stand on the wall overlooking the quad at the universities, proclaim the will of God, and they would listen.

"They mock us," he said. Behind him, the double-wide lay quiet. Only the two of them stood overlooking their domain, the three square miles of the dump, surrounded by wilderness.

"Yes, Master."

"They laugh, spit on us, throw beer in our faces, egg us from cars."

"You warned us it would happen," Christopher said. "And it came true. You speak for God."

"In Seattle, the police arrested us for vagrancy. In Los Angeles, they dragged us in for questioning." The whispering in his head grew louder. He closed his eyes, trying not to listen.

"They always persecute the righteous," Christopher said. "But still His holy work continues. Nothing can stop it."

"Well spoken, my servant. That is all."

Christopher handed him the nettles cut from the far side of the dump, then picked his way through the piles of tires toward the trailer. The Disciple felt the sting on his hands, reveled in it. He would sit naked in the sanctifying room and rub nettles over his nude body until he had clarified his thoughts. They needed to be very clear today if he was to have the strength to accomplish the horrific tasks that lay before him. He couldn't have the angels and demons whispering, arguing, fighting in his head.

The Disciple couldn't remember a time when he didn't hear the voices of the damned and the elect. And sometimes one of the demons would go a step further and try to possess him entirely. He remembered once when he was a boy, waking with his limbs paralyzed and a terrifying presence sitting on his chest. The voices were screaming, and only after he'd prayed silently for several minutes did the evil being leave him alone. He'd crept down the hall in the darkness to the bathroom, thinking that if he splashed water on his face he could shake the urge to hurl himself from the second floor window.

The hall in the children's wing was maybe fifty feet long, with half a dozen bedroom doors on his left. Twenty children slept in these rooms, most of them set up like dorms, with three or four children per room. His older brothers Gideon and Taylor Junior shared the room next to his. He heard them arguing as he crept past.

"Do it, T.J. You know you want to."

And Taylor Junior's whining voice. "I don't want to. Come on, please, just go back to bed."

Caleb—that was his name in those days—stopped, amazed at the cowardly tone in T.J.'s voice. Both boys were bullies, but Gideon was older and seemed content to torment T.J. and two of his teenage half sisters, one older, one younger. Taylor Junior, on the other hand, directed his nastiness to anyone younger than him. He'd stick out his leg to trip a younger child walking by, or reach into the shower while you were in it to turn the water scalding hot. Caleb had even seen him loosen the nipple of a bottle so that it would dump milk over a baby's face and clothes.

Caleb had fallen prey to a combination of pranks, random punches, sabotaged chores (Father never believed the explanations), and other nasty behavior, so it hadn't occurred to him that T.J. might be equally oppressed by his own older brother.

One of the demons overheard his thoughts and whispered, *And you could do the same thing. You can't get back at T.J., but Vera is helpless, and Phillip is a sissy.* Two of the angels immediately chimed in with a rebuttal.

But Caleb wasn't paying attention to the arguing voices, not now. Gone too was the Satanic visitor who had sat on his chest and paralyzed his arms and legs just minutes earlier. He cracked the door and peered in at his brothers.

Taylor Junior sat on the floor, naked. He was just hitting puberty, and a few hairs sprouted around his groin. Gideon stood over him, fully clothed. In his hands, a pair of girls' panties, pink, with frills. They looked like they'd fit a child no older than seven or eight, but where they'd come from, Caleb couldn't guess. Nothing so worldly would be allowed in Blister Creek.

"Put them on."

"Come on, Gideon. Please, just let me go to bed."

Gideon shook his head. "Not until you put them on. Or do you want me to tell Father what I found? That you're hiding girl panties to rub on yourself."

"They're not mine! You put them there!"

"Why would I do that?" Gideon asked in a faux injured tone. "I don't want to tell Father that you're a girly boy, that you want to stick your thing in boys' bums, but I might not be able to help myself."

"Liar!"

Gideon's tone turned nasty. "You have five seconds. One... two..."

Taylor Junior snatched up the panties and struggled into them. When he had them up, they stuck to him, too tight, ridiculous looking. Watching from the doorway, Caleb fought down a giggle that was part nervousness, part delight to see T.J. humiliated like this, when he was usually the one doing the humiliating. T.J.'s back was turned, and Caleb couldn't see the expression on the boy's face, but he could imagine it.

"Just like a girl," Gideon said. "I can't wait until you start to grow titties."

Caleb meant to slip away, but just then Gideon turned and fixed him with a half smile and a raised eyebrow. A look that said, *Do you like it? Do you want to wear panties, too?*

He fled. In the bathroom, he locked the door and made faces in the mirror that alternated between the sneers the demons told him to make and the gentle, beatific expressions that reflected the sweet things whispered to him by the angels.

The next day he was walking by the shed nearest the greenhouses when he heard Taylor Junior inside, trying to start a weed whacker. T.J. pulled the cord, the motor coughed and died, and then he'd do it again. Caleb watched through the glass window, delighted to see his brother sweating and fighting with the tool. He pulled and pulled. At breakfast, Father had told T.J. to hack down the weeds in the north irrigation ditch, and Father wasn't the type to accept weak excuses about faulty equipment.

T.J. stopped and panted, then gave another pull. It sputtered and refused to start. "Damn it! Start, you son of a bitch."

Father would stick hot pepper sauce on the tongue of anyone caught swearing, and some of the sister wives would split your lip with a backhand without a second thought. Few things brought on a quicker expression of righteous fury in the Kimball household than any curse stronger than a damn or a hell.

He should be punished.

It was a strong, clear voice. He didn't know at first if it was an angel or an evil spirit, but the thought struck him as so right, so *righteous*, that he decided it must have been an angel.

"How?"

Use your gift of discernment.

There was a can of gas mixture for the weed whacker outside, together with a damp spot on the brick threshold where T.J. must have spilled some on the gravel while filling the tank. It was a chilly morning, and unlike Caleb, T.J. wasn't wearing a jacket, just a T-shirt, as he'd anticipated working in the sun as it rose. And so he'd apparently gone into the shed where it was warmer instead of staying outside to fight the weed whacker. Caleb unscrewed the lid off the gas can.

Inside, T.J. started yanking at the cord again and shouting at the weed whacker when it refused to cooperate. He didn't glance over his shoulder as Caleb hefted the can and sloshed some against the door. He spilled more on and around the wooden siding that surrounded it, then emptied the rest in a puddle on the brick outside. There was no lock on the door—little petty theft in Blister Creek—but the door did have a latch higher up on the outside where you could shut it so the wind wouldn't drive it open or a small child wouldn't come in and fool around with tools and garden machinery. He stood on his tiptoes and flipped the latch. It locked Taylor Junior inside. Caleb reached into his pocket, lit a match, and dropped it into the pool of gasoline. Then ran.

He raced up the stairs to his room, then looked out his bedroom window. Flames already engulfed that side of the shed, consuming shingles that had been dried to husks by the desiccating winds that blew off the Ghost Cliffs. The shed door was still closed.

T.J. is going to die.

He realized this with a mixture of horror and delight. The fire would consume him like it was consuming the building. He would scream as the flames roasted his skin until it was crackling and oozing fat like pork at a pig roast.

But to Caleb's disappointment, Taylor Junior didn't die in the fire. By the time someone from the house spotted the flames, it was too late to save the shed, but T.J. had managed to kick out the window on the far side and climb to safety. But Caleb didn't know that at first. He had watched as thick smoke curled into the sky, as a dozen women scrambled about with hoses and shovels and sent children running for the fields to find Father.

Caleb wasn't sure, but he thought that both Father and Taylor Junior blamed Gideon for the fire. That was about the time that Gideon started falling out with Father. A few years later, when Gideon was home from college, someone caught him with some dirty magazines, drove him into St. George, and dumped him in the parking lot of a 7-Eleven.

Caleb's turn to be driven from home and from the Church of the Anointing would come a few years later. The angels told him it was God's will, that the Mormon fundamentalists practiced a corrupt form of Christianity, that they would show him the pure faith and teach him how to announce the coming of the Great and Dreadful Day of the Lord. And proclaim the fall of Wormwood from the sky.

"Master?" Christopher asked, shaking him from his thoughts.

"I have to go to Blister Creek," the Disciple said. "To finish what I started."

"What do you mean?"

"The cleansing. If it is to sweep over the earth, it must begin there, where everything started."

After Gideon died, Taylor Junior disappeared, and Elder Kimball was sentenced to prison, Abraham Christianson had swept in to take over the Church of the Anointing, moved most of the Christianson family from Alberta to Blister Creek. The Disciple wasn't so isolated that he didn't know this already.

"I don't understand," Christopher said.

"You don't have to understand. You're staying here."

"Master?"

"I'm taking the boy with me. Nobody else."

"What? No, please. Diego can stay here, I'll go. Kirk and Benita could do what needs to be done."

The Disciple fixed Christopher with a hard look. "I need someone here I can trust. Someone who is not afraid to die. Benita is afraid. Kirk is afraid—so are the rest. You said you'd die for the glory of God. Do you mean it?"

Christopher looked down for a long moment, then raised his eyes to meet the Disciple's. "I'll do it. But what about Madeline and Eliza? They need to be sanctified."

"I don't have time; I have to leave for Blister Creek. But don't worry, if we can't manage, the fire will take care of everything."

"But you said they'd be sanctified," Christopher said. He licked his lips. "Maybe I could do it."

He had a gleam in his eyes, and the Disciple worried it would be a distraction, that if he said no, Christopher would do it anyway and the work here wouldn't get done.

"Listen to me. First, prepare for the fall of Wormwood. Tomorrow night, when you're done, you may sanctify them both."

CHAPTER SEVENTEEN

"So the worm crawls home," Father said.

Abraham Christianson possessed a withering sense of righteous anger, and David felt the weight of it now, as Father clumped up the stairs to the porch that overlooked the ranch.

"You've sold your birthright for a mess of pottage. You let go of the iron rod, and now you're wandering in mists of darkness. You're like the idle workers in the vineyard, and now you want to be paid."

"You're mixing your parables," David said.

But Father was just winding up. "I gave you a talent of silver and you buried it in the ground, just like a slothful servant. You're the prodigal son, who collected his inheritance and wasted it on fine clothing, rich food, women, and wine. And now you're stealing food from pigs."

"Food from pigs? That's not very nice. One of your wives made me breakfast this morning."

Abraham narrowed his eyes. "Oh, is that supposed to be a joke? Do you think you're funny? Would your loser friends think you're clever?"

"I don't know, would yours?"

David had dragged himself outside, where he settled into an Adirondack chair on the veranda with a pair of sunglasses, squinting at the sun. He could use a cup of coffee—to start. In truth he was craving harder chemicals—but he had as much chance of finding coffee in Blister Creek as a pulled pork sandwich in Mecca.

It couldn't be later than eight, but when his father stomped onto the porch, he was already covered with dust, with sweat rings under his arms, and the hair peeking out from beneath his hat was damp with sweat. He'd peeled off his gloves and tossed them to his feet with disgust before jumping into the first of what would no doubt prove many tirades.

David leaned back, closed his eyes, and tried to concentrate on the morning sun that warmed his face, the sound of the single cricket still chirping from beneath the porch. Twenty minutes earlier, there had been several.

"So you're going to take a nap? You've put in a long day, walking out to the porch and letting some hard-working woman cook you breakfast, and now you're going to sleep it off. Is that it?"

"I can't help it. Droning lectures always put me to sleep."

"I don't know why I listened to Jacob. I told him you were worthless, but he didn't believe me. He seemed to think you could be redeemed. He seemed to think that all I'd have to do is tell you to come back and here you'd be, repentant, ready to change, to admit your mistakes and do what it takes to get back into the good graces of the Lord. Can you believe Jacob actually thought that?"

"If you see him, be sure to tell him thanks," David said. "It's working out great. So peaceful, so relaxing. It's great to be home in Blister Creek, where everyone loves me and wants only the best. Who could ask for more?"

"Too bad he's not here to see you himself. It's obvious just looking at you that you're hopeless."

"That was meant to be sarcastic, by the way. You seemed to have missed that."

"And this is intended to tell you I don't give a damn," Abraham said. "David, I don't give a damn."

He opened his eyes and propped his sunglasses on top of his head so Father could look him in the eye. "Where's Miriam? Don't tell me she's gone back to Zarahemla. I understand the two of you have a little wager to settle."

"She's coming, don't worry. Getting your drugs ready, so you can inject yourself with pot or crack or whatever it is that you're using to kill yourself."

"You smoke pot and crack. You shoot up heroin."

"Ah, well if you say so. You're the expert. Look, here she is now, right on time."

Miriam came out of the house with a clatter of the screen door. She'd washed up and braided her hair. No makeup, although she was still surprisingly pretty, and there was no disguising the cunning look on her face. She'd managed to pry him out of Las Vegas where Eliza had failed, dragged him to the edge of the wilderness. The Ghost Cliffs stretched along the northern horizon, with the wide sweep of the ranch in front of them, and a glimpse of the sandstone walls and spires of the temple to the right. Behind the temple and stretching toward the cliffs, the red rock fins and hoodoos of the Witch's Warts. He felt like he stood on the edge of the nineteenth century, with a glimpse back to pioneer times.

And yet here was this pioneer woman, in a pioneer outpost, holding a syringe in her hand. David's mouth felt dry, and a tremble seized his right hand.

"How are you doing?" she asked in a voice that was surprisingly tender. "Did you sleep okay?"

"Yes, those pills helped, thanks."

"I can give you some other stuff that will help even more."

He didn't take his eyes off the syringe. "What other stuff?"

"Methadone."

"Ah, I see."

"It binds to the receptors in the brain, can stabilize your addiction, help wean you off the harder stuff. Give you a fighting chance."

"You've got methadone now?" David asked.

"No, but I made some calls. I can get it. All you have to do is hold out for today, fight through it, and then I'll have it by tonight."

"You're wasting your time," Abraham said. He turned to David. "You want it, don't you? I wish you could see yourself, that look of lust on your face. You can't stand it. Now I know what a true addict looks like."

"Why don't you get the hell out of here?" David snapped.

In his head, a whispering voice. *Take it. Don't think about it, just grab the syringe and shove it in your leg. Hurry, it will only take a second.*

Miriam held the syringe just out of reach. He'd have to get up and grab for it. "You don't have to," she said. "You know that, right? Say the word and I'll crush this with my foot and go upstairs right now and flush the rest of these poisons down the drain."

"You know I can't make it, you know I can't say no."

"I don't know anything of the sort."

Abraham let out a snort. "Like I said, you're wasting your time." He stood with his thumbs hooked in his belt, with a look on his face like he'd just licked a wet cow pie.

"Can you make him go away?" David asked.

"I think he should stay."

"He's only making it worse."

"Exactly. See that look on his face? That's not being harsh, that's a reflection of reality. Nobody does you any favors by dolling up the truth with makeup and lipstick. This addiction is ugly, and getting uglier every time you give in to it. At some point—and I mean soon—you've got to stand up, give it a hard kick in the crotch, and walk away. The longer you wait, the harder it will be, and then it will be too late. This horrible, ugly thing will consume you entirely. You'll be a walking corpse, and then you won't be walking anymore."

"Don't you think I know that?"

Stop talking! Just grab the syringe and get it over with. The demon sounded…what? Maybe a little desperate. David felt a twinge of hope.

"Are you actually trying to talk him out of it?" Father asked. "What's the point of that?"

Miriam ignored him and continued to address David. "Of course you know it, but you're trying to forget it. I'm not doing you any favors if I let you."

David's whole body began to shake. He scratched his fingernails into the armrests of the chair, trying to hold down his hands, keep from grabbing the syringe. Just a moment with that syringe and the pain would be gone.

"Please, just…just…"

"What?" she asked. An eager hope in her voice. "Do you want me to throw it away? Just say the word, David! Say a prayer, ask the Lord for help. Do *something*, please. You can fight this. I'll help you, I promise. You won't be alone."

"Just give it to me," he said with a gasp.

David let go of the armrests, and when Miriam tried to step back, he clamped a hand over her wrist. She dropped the syringe. He caught it with his other hand. He sank back into the chair, then rammed the syringe through his pants, straight into his right thigh.

There was a split second before the drug hit his bloodstream, and in that moment he caught a look in Miriam's eyes. Sorrow, regret. And he knew that in spite of her hard words, she'd actually held out hope that he would resist. And David felt a terrible longing to be the type of person to earn the respect and admiration of someone like Miriam. That instead of disappointing her, he could have been the kind of man people could count on, the kind of man who made people proud, who made them want to be better people.

And then the heroin slammed him with the force of a tsunami, washing everything else away. The rush was stronger than he'd ever felt; it pulsed through his body, made his eyes roll back in their sockets.

"Ahhhh…" He opened his eyes and stared out across the desert.

"David?" Miriam asked. She sounded worried. "Is it too much? Did I mess up? Please, talk to me."

"Shhh, I'm looking."

The landscape that had looked so harsh moments earlier was the most beautiful thing he'd ever seen. How had he not noticed before? He felt like he was floating above it all, that the red colors were hot air lifting a bird on thermals above the desert. He could feel it stretch out in all directions, thirty thousand square miles of the Colorado Plateau. The smell of desert with pansies from the beds around the porch filled his head.

Abraham Christianson's voice sounded from a distance. "Disgusting. Almost obscene. Did you hear that sound? Like a copulating bull. He's so far gone, look at that expression on his face."

"Leave him alone," Miriam said. "You got your way. Just don't say anything more—I can't stand the sound of your voice."

"Hah! You thought he'd actually turn you down? What a fool you are, Sister Miriam. He's too far gone, I told you that. Lucifer owns him now. Only a miracle could save him."

David could hear all of this, but he didn't care. Father could have taken a pair of garden shears and clipped off his fingers, one by one, and it wouldn't bother him. His droning voice didn't even rise to the level of annoyance.

He heard a crow somewhere to the left, the chirping cricket, and a breeze that tickled his eardrum, and David felt like he was a part of them all.

It's beautiful. This is the true spirit of the Lord.

It was the demon speaking, he knew that, but he didn't care.

"Call Jacob," Father said. "David is farther gone than I thought. It is time."

CHAPTER EIGHTEEN

Eliza tried the obvious first: climb out. She groped along the walls of the pit. Most of the sides were smooth, but after about twenty minutes, she discovered that one corner had a pair of boulders spaced at intervals that served as shelves. Whoever had excavated the pit had just dug around them instead of working to dislodge them completely from the soil. Using these as steps, she climbed maybe three feet off the ground, then felt nothing. Carefully, she felt every inch and, just when she was about to give up, touched a thin lip of rock at the edge of her reach.

"Are you okay?"

"Fine. Stand up, let me try something else." Eliza came back down. "Here, put your hands on my shoulders. Now step up—I'm going to make a stair. There's a rock sticking out just out of my reach, but I might be able to hoist you up."

She clenched her hands together and got them under Madeline's foot. But even though the woman had lost a lot of weight through months of semi-starvation and enforced fasts, Eliza couldn't lift Madeline past the height of her own waist. They struggled with different combinations of this method for about ten minutes before giving up. For a long moment there was no sound in the pit but their heavy breaths.

"How tall was that ladder anyway?" Eliza asked.

"I don't know, maybe twelve feet."

"That's what I thought. Help me move these jugs."

"What are you thinking?"

"When I stretch out, I'm a few inches shorter than the mattresses. I'm guessing they're six feet each. We can lift them upright, then stack one on top of the other in the corner. You hold the mattresses in place while I climb up. I should be able to reach the top pretty easily."

That was if they could keep the mattresses in place, which proved simpler in the plan she sketched in her head than in practice. It was easy enough to get the two mattresses stacked one on top of the other, and though the topmost mattress didn't reach the surface, Eliza guessed it was close.

Unfortunately, the same thing that made the mattresses so easy to stack made them unsuitable for climbing. They put the heavier mattress with springs on the bottom and the flatter, springless mattress above. Madeline held them in place, but when Eliza reached the second mattress, it sagged and bent back on itself. She almost fell when she tried to climb from the first to the second.

Eliza said, "Lean your body into the bottom one to hold it, then hold your hands up and keep this one from falling."

"I'm trying that already."

The problem was putting her weight on that mattress. If she could make it in one scramble, she could grab the edge of the pit and use it to support most of her weight. She tried to catch her breath with her face pressed in the dank, urine-soaked mattress.

"Okay," Eliza said. "Here I go—don't let me fall."

She dug her toes into the sewn buttons and scrambled up. The top mattress bent back when she was halfway up, but then her outstretched fingers grabbed the edge of the pit. Below, Madeline pushed and grunted against the slumping mattresses.

Eliza had it—she got most of her weight off the mattress, and Madeline wrestled it into place. She swung her other arm up and pushed on the edge of the fridge. It didn't budge; she couldn't get enough leverage. Her arms ached. Below her, the mattress buckled and Madeline let out a cry.

One moment Eliza was clinging to the edge of the pit and the next the whole unstable pile was collapsing. She fell, crashed into Madeline, bounced off the mattresses, and then slammed into the ground. Pain stabbed through her shoulder.

Madeline found her in the darkness. "Are you okay?"

Eliza tested everything, found she was all right. Her shoulder ached, but it didn't seem serious. "Yeah, I'm okay. Ugh, what's that smell?"

She'd crashed into the waste buckets. At least one had lost its top, and the stench of urine and fecal matter and something rotten—was that bananas?—mixed in the enclosed space. She put her hand over her mouth. Madeline made little gulping sounds.

"Don't throw up!" Eliza cried.

She wasn't just worried about the added smell, but her own stomach roiled and she thought she might lose it herself. And then Madeline retched, three times, and it was all Eliza could do to keep her own reflexes from following. Somehow, she managed.

"I'm sorry," Madeline said. "Please don't be mad."

Eliza waited one more long moment to make sure she had the gag reflex under control, then said, "Don't worry about it, you couldn't help it."

"There wasn't much there, anyway. Mostly water."

"Come on, let's get this cleaned up."

It was only one gallon overturned, thank goodness. The other two gallons of waste still had their caps on. It could have been worse. Eliza screwed on the lid with half of it still inside, then rinsed her hands with some of the drinking water. She threw the thinner mattress over the top of the mess. The smell was still overpowering.

"That didn't exactly work out," Madeline said. "Unless you can think of some other way to use the mattresses."

"I'm tempted to make a joke about illegally removing mattress tags," Eliza said.

"Please don't, aren't we suffering enough already?"

Eliza laughed and felt a spark of encouragement that the other woman seemed to be waking from her stupor. "Okay, let's get this other one down. We'll keep thinking."

Her resolve stiffened. She had to get out of this cesspool.

They were dragging the mattress with the springs back into place when someone started pushing the fridge from above. Both women froze.

A shaft of light stabbed into the darkness. Eliza had to look away it was so bright. She caught a glimpse of Madeline cringing.

Her hair was a matted, dirty tangle, and dirt and tears stained her face. The bones of her face were sharp over her pale skin, her eyes brilliant blue. Her breasts tiny, her hips angular. She looked like a filthy mannequin, stripped of clothes, impossibly slender. Only the ribs and the heaving chest spoiled the effect.

Eliza looked back up at the light. Someone looked back at her, but the light was so glaring behind the person's head that it left the face dark. With the light came a flood of fresh air. It was the sweetest thing she'd ever tasted.

"Let us go, please," she said.

Something dropped from above, and she ducked as it flew past her head. And then whoever it was pulled back and started to push the fridge back over the hole.

"What kind of person are you?" she shouted. "This is inhuman, it's monstrous!"

The hole closed. They returned to darkness. To her side, Madeline sank to the ground, sobbing.

"Stop it," Eliza said. "You're wasting energy. Now pull yourself together."

"I can't."

"You were with me a second ago, and I need you back."

"It's no use."

Eliza wanted to grab Madeline, shake her, work out her own anger and frustration. She couldn't get back at the monsters who'd thrown her down here, but the urge to punish Madeline was overwhelming. What kind of idiot came down willingly into this hell? What kind of weak, pathetic fool was she that she thought she deserved this, sat back and passively let them starve and rape her in turns. No wonder that other girl had thrown herself off the Hoover

Dam bridge. If you're going to give up, you may as well get it over with.

Stop it, Eliza told herself. *You're just as bad as she is. Stay calm, stop feeling sorry for yourself, and figure this out.*

Eliza made her way over to Madeline. The rage had passed, and she meant to grab the other woman and hold her for a few minutes, maybe share some of her own strength so they could make another attempt. Suddenly curious, she groped on the floor until she found the object tossed down at their heads. It was a plastic bag. She untwisted it to discover several pieces of bread and a jar. Eliza opened the jar and lifted it to her nose. Peanut butter, maybe a quarter jar full.

"What are you doing?" Madeline asked. "What's that rustling?"

"It's food. That person just dropped it. Bread and a jar with a little peanut butter."

"It's a trick, don't eat it."

"What do you mean, poisoned?"

"No, like a test. Whoever it was dropped me some bananas, to see if I was strong enough to resist. I almost ate them, stopped myself just in time."

"You mean you didn't? Where are they?" And then Eliza remembered the smell of rotting bananas that had come out of the spilled gallon of human waste. "Wait, you didn't. Are you out of your mind?"

Again, she had to fight down her anger. The woman had been in the pit for days, starved, sexually abused, convinced that only strict obedience would get her out of this hell.

She made her way to Madeline's side, holding the bag of food. She groped until she touched the other woman's face. "I need you to listen to me. Maybe someone dropped this to test us, and maybe it's someone trying to help. Either way, it doesn't matter. You can eat this food, and then we'll rest a little and try again."

"How can you be sure?"

"You need to stop this. There's no way to think clearly when you're starving in a dark, filthy hole. We need to get out of here and away from these people, and then there will be time to figure things out."

"But—"

Eliza needed a new tactic. "Did you know that my family has known Caleb's family for many years?"

"Caleb?" Madeline asked.

"The Disciple. That was his name before he started recruiting people to his sect. I didn't know Caleb, but I knew his family." She thought about Gideon, lying facedown and dead in the sinkhole, about Taylor Junior trying to sexually assault her before her brother Jacob came in and rescued her, and she shuddered. "I knew them too well. My father once got a young golden Lab that had been housebroken by Caleb's family. I think it belonged to his older brother, Taylor Junior. They said it was defective, a biter, and were going to shoot it. My father heard and brought it home. He said, 'Whoever heard of a Lab that's a biter? Liz, see what you can do with him.'"

"And was it a biter?" Madeline asked, sounding interested, with the black mood lifting from her voice. "Or was your dad right?"

"It bit my hand the first time I tried to feed it."

"So you had to kill it in the end, anyway."

"Not at all. My brother Jacob found me with the dog in the mud room. It was growling with its tail between its legs, and I was frozen about five feet away, holding my hand where the dog had bit me. It hadn't broken the skin, but I was too afraid to move. My brother looked at my hand and when he saw it wasn't serious said, 'He's scared. Look at the poor guy.' And then I saw that the dog was trembling, that he'd dribbled pee on the floor. His tail was between his legs. I felt sorry for him. 'Be kind and patient,' Jacob told me, 'and that dog will be your best friend in the world.'

"It took a week until I could come close to Lubby without him snarling and snapping his teeth. The Kimballs had given him the kind of training that means a beating for getting in the way, or shoving a dog's nose in its poop when it makes a mess in the house. Poor thing had scars from all the bite marks of the other Kimball dogs. They'd been treated the same way, and of course Lubby turned mean like all the rest. The only difference was that Lubby was dumb enough to snap at humans, too, so Elder Kimball was going to shoot him.

"Jacob was right, there was nothing wrong with him. Too much energy, of course, like a typical Lab. Eventually he got fat and lazy, also like a Lab. But he wasn't mean or defective. Lubby turned into the biggest sweetheart you can imagine."

Eliza reached into the bag and pulled out a piece of bread. It was dry and stale. She pressed the bread into Madeline's hand. "The problem is, Elder Kimball treated his sons like he treated his dogs. And just like the dogs, they turned on each other and anyone else who got too close. You take one of those bullied kids, someone like Caleb who suffers from mental illness, and he becomes a neurotic, dangerous lunatic. They were a religious family, so his insanity comes out through rants about God."

Madeline ate the bread. Eliza gave her a minute, then said, "See, all you need is a little food and you'll be fine, too."

"Oh, so now I'm one of the dogs in your story?"

"You've got a lot of eating until you're as fat and lazy as Lubby. Here, have some peanut butter."

Eliza ate a piece of bread herself but didn't want to stick a finger into the peanut butter, not after she'd been messing around with the spilled gallon of waste. Madeline ate until Eliza took the jar away. Eat too much and she'd make herself sick.

After about twenty minutes, when Eliza felt a little stronger and the smell in the pit had either diminished or she'd simply grown used to it, her mind started working again. She ran through the possibilities until she came up with something that might actually work. She roused Madeline, who had fallen asleep.

"Wake up, we have work to do."

"Work?"

"We've got to get busy. Here, have some more peanut butter. Lettuce, too, if you can stomach it."

"What are you thinking?"

"I'm thinking of ways to escape, of course."

"You still think that's possible?" There was an edge of determination in her voice. Good.

"Of course I do. I know this sounds incredible, but I'm not discouraged."

"We're naked and starving at the bottom of a pit," Madeline said. "You've got to be at least a little discouraged."

"I'm sure that's what your so-called Disciple is counting on. He thinks he'll be rid of me, that by the time I'm done, I'll be either dead or starved into submission. Sorry, that's not going to work. I've been through worse."

"Worse? You can't be serious."

"It's true," Eliza said. "And I learned something about myself. They can only destroy me if I submit. And I'll never submit. You need to ask yourself the same question. Are you going to submit? Or are you going to fight?"

Madeline was quiet for a long moment, but when she spoke, there was strength in her voice. "I'm going to fight."

"Good, now here's what we do. First thing, we're going to tear open this mattress. We need to get at the springs. Those will be our tools."

CHAPTER NINETEEN

The Disciple and the boy entered Blister Creek through Witch's Warts. Arriving in late afternoon, the Disciple stashed the truck in a dry irrigation ditch near the McCormick ranch. He didn't know if McCormick had been caught up in the fraud investigation or if he'd simply taken his wives and children and fled the Church of the Anointing, but the ranch house was abandoned, the yard and fields returning to sagebrush. Tumbleweeds had blown into the porch and filled it, then stacked in front and halfway down the sidewalk to the road.

"All the better," he said to the boy. Diego looked up at him with round eyes, impossibly large in his pinched, hungry face.

The Disciple snapped his fingers for the boy to follow, and they crossed the dirt road and entered Witch's Warts on foot. He carried few possessions. No food, no water, no map. Children had become lost for days inside Witch's Warts, turned around, disoriented. Once, in the 1940s, a woman tried to flee Blister Creek by escaping through the maze of sandstone hoodoos, fins, and spires. Nobody saw her go, though it had been no secret that she wanted to escape her abusive husband. They found her coyote-gnawed body several months later, just thirty feet from the road, inside the last row of sandstone fins.

A racer lizard sprinted away from them, leaving a set of parallel prints, bisected by a tail track like a pencil lead dragged across the sand. A moment later, a jackrabbit tore across their path. Diego flinched, and the Disciple put a quick hand on his shoulder to steady him.

The Disciple fished out his compass, oriented himself, and then figured out his bearing.

Voices whispered in his head. *Put the compass away; you won't need it. Let us guide you, trust us.*

"I need to be sure."

You'll be sure. We'll tell you where to go.

His brother Gideon had died in here. This was just a few months after the man had tracked Caleb down at the trailer park in Barstow, California, west of the Mojave. Caleb—he hadn't yet thought of himself as the Disciple—had been working at a truck stop diner, flipping pancakes and burgers for ten bucks an hour. One day, he'd come home to find Gideon sitting on the porch. An unpleasant smile crossed his face when he saw Caleb.

"There he is, the prodigal son."

Caleb hadn't been happy to see his brother. He stopped about ten feet away. "No more prodigal than you. What are you doing here?"

"I've come to welcome you back to the fold."

"What fold? You're not part of any fold."

"Of course I am. Father and I have reconciled. I've even come to terms with Taylor Junior."

"What are you talking about?" Caleb asked. Lost Boys did not reconcile with church elders. Once Elder Kimball drove his sons to St. George, that was it. You didn't come back.

"And now it is your turn. Father said he would forget the kitchen fire, and how you diddled your little sister."

"I never touched her."

The accusation outraged him, as it had when Father had suggested, not that he'd "diddled" anyone, but that he'd been *thinking about* diddling his half sisters. When Caleb had protested, vigorously, Father had given a grave nod and said, "See, this is how I know you're unrepentant. You didn't come with the idea of atoning for your sins, only to deny and justify."

"You don't care, you've already decided. If I'd come to you to confess first, it still wouldn't make any difference."

"So you do? You *do* admit that you've thought about incestuous fornication with your sisters?"

"No!"

"Like I said, your attitude is poor. It's a sign that you don't belong in Zion."

The problem wasn't the alleged lustful feelings. He could deny those. It was harder to deny that Charity Kimball, Father's senior wife, had caught him pouring lighter fluid on the stove burners.

He glared at Gideon. "You don't believe me, do you? You think I actually did that stuff to my sisters?"

"Oh, who cares?" Gideon asked. "None of that matters anymore. Don't you see, this is your chance to get back in."

Inside, over a pair of Sprites reluctantly taken from the fridge and offered, Gideon explained the bones of his plan. Father had decided that the Church of the Anointing was weak and corrupt and needed to be cleansed if they were to have any hope of filling the earth with their righteous seed. The details of the plan were hazy, but apparently Gideon was gathering Lost Boys to take over Blister Creek.

But Caleb had succumbed to the voices by then and couldn't be fooled.

That is not God's way. Listen to us. We are Legion, and we have wisdom beyond that of your pitiful brother. In due time, God will show you the path. Do not follow the Wicked.

Gideon had left shortly after, sputtering and condemning him, and shaking the dust from his shoes to damn Caleb's soul. The younger brother had watched this rant with growing certainty that he was doing the right thing.

Well done. You shall be the chosen of the Lord. You shall be his disciple.

And what had happened to Gideon? He'd died right here in Witch's Warts. The Disciple didn't know the exact details, but apparently he'd tried to kidnap a wife while fleeing from the police, and then the girl had bashed in his brains with a hunk of sandstone.

"No woman can be tamed before she has been purified and sanctified," he said out loud.

Diego stopped and looked up at him.

"Keep going. We have two, maybe three miles to go."

So why was he going through Witch's Warts? Why not just drive into town after dark and park on a side street, then walk a few blocks to the Kimball house? He wasn't Gideon, fleeing into the wilderness in a desperate attempt to escape his enemies. Nobody was expecting Caleb Kimball to return, if they even knew that he'd become God's chosen one. He could complete his holy vengeance and go back to Nevada to be with the others when Wormwood fell. But the voices had told him to come this way, and there must have been a good reason.

Tonight you will send your enemies to hell.

And rid himself of every injustice, every cruelty, every sin against his body and person. The ridicule, the abuse, the ejection from his family and home.

They continued in silence for about twenty minutes before Diego wobbled and fell. He looked like he was going to get up, then lay down in the sand, as if he were going to take a nap.

"Get up." The boy tried to rise, but failed. The Disciple hauled him to his feet. "I said get up!"

"Please." The boy's voice came out in a whisper.

The Disciple stopped, surprised. How long since he'd heard Diego speak? "Please? What do you mean, please?"

But Diego simply shook his head.

"You are ready, child. I have anointed your head with oil and prepared a table before you in the presence of your enemies. Tonight you will atone for the blood and sins of this generation."

Still, he couldn't have the child fainting. He searched the stretch of sand between two fins of red rock and discovered a prickly pear cactus sprouting in a stretch of hardpan. He carefully plucked off several fruits, then found a place to roll them in gravel to remove the small, hairy prickles. He peeled them and fed them to the boy, one by one, as they continued.

"It's only a few more minutes; you've got the strength," the Disciple said. "And then we'll do what we came to do, and you can rest."

His rest will be eternal.

It grew dark among the rocks, long shadows stretching like hands as the sun dropped. Wind blew down from the Ghost Cliffs, kicking up sand so fine it was almost dust. It coated nostrils and eyelashes. They squinted and pressed on. The last of the lizards had fled to their holes, and even the insects fell silent. There was something in the air that made him think of a storm, but it was too dry and the clouds overhead didn't look dense enough to hold rain. Minutes later, he heard a low rumble from the west. A dry thunderstorm.

"It was you, wasn't it?" the Disciple asked a few minutes later. "You were the one violating the rite of purification."

The boy said nothing, just kept trudging ahead. His limbs, thin and spindly as chair legs, shambled one after the other.

"I knew that Madeline was taking extra food. She's weak, and I thought I could purify her and sanctify her until she was strong enough to resist her sinful urges. But she gave you extra food, and I couldn't let that go. You took it—that makes you guilty as well. But you didn't stop there, did you? You managed to convince Benita that you needed help. Don't think I didn't see her slipping you extra food when you didn't need it."

The boy looked up at him and spoke a second time. "Please."

"Please, what?" He stopped, spun the boy around, and brought his own face down until it was eye-to-eye with the boy's. "There is no please. There is only obeying the will of God. The will of God was that you become His pure vessel." He grabbed the boy's shirt and pushed him along. "But what is worse is that you hid food and gave it to Benita, and then she violated the rites, didn't she? One small, helpless boy—or so everyone kept saying—and you managed to pollute the other Chosen Ones."

He wanted to keep talking, to explain to the boy that not everyone was meant to survive the purification. That was for God to decide. But if Benita dropped food into the hole, and the people below were weak enough to take it, then they would all feel God's wrath.

But before he could, the voices in his head started clamoring for his attention. It was all he could do to focus on the path.

At last they broke through the other side of Witch's Warts. The Disciple was more to the south than he'd expected, a few blocks from the temple, but his instincts—or the angels and demons—had carried him through without a compass. He stopped and sat the boy by his side, then waited while the light failed. When it was fully dark, they crossed the street and made their way toward his old home. His feet traced the steps almost independently, and the smells and sights took him back, instantly, to the eighties and nineties, and the hell that had been his childhood.

He found the Kimball ranch, and to his surprise, there were lights in most of the rooms. He'd expected to find it abandoned and boarded up. Taylor Kimball was in prison, his wives and children scattered. Taylor Junior had disappeared. So who was living in the house?

Brother Joseph is dead. Another man is running the Church of the Anointing.

Of course. Elder Abraham Christianson had become the new leader of the sect. And since the Kimball house was the largest, and Christianson had many wives and children, it was only natural that he take over the house when he moved down from Alberta.

All the better. You can cleanse them at the same time you cleanse the house.

The Disciple reached into his pocket and rubbed the glossy cardboard under his fingers. The matchbook read, "Welcome to the Glorious Excalibur," and showed a Merlin-like figure with a magic wand.

"I'll cleanse them all," he whispered.

CHAPTER TWENTY

Jacob Christianson knew when a man was going to die. He'd seen it a dozen times at the hospital. There was a glassy look in the eyes, a hollow expression, like the soul was already tugging free, ready to leave the body for the other side. Once the soul left, the body would collapse, be nothing more than a glove without a hand.

His brother David had that look.

He sat on the veranda, deeply sedated. A heavy dose of heroin, according to Sister Miriam. She confessed that it might have been too much and stood to one side, chewing on her lip. David stared into the distance, in the direction of the Ghost Cliffs, but his eyes didn't seem to focus on anything in particular. A smile played across his face, but it was a deceptive look that didn't mask the dead expression in the eyes. A soul pulling free of a dying body.

Jacob checked his pulse. It was sluggish. He felt his brother's forehead, then rolled up his sleeve and attached the blood pressure cuff. He didn't like the numbers: 90/50.

"He doesn't need science," Father said. "It's too late for that."

"And you want me to do what? Give him a blessing?"

Miriam touched his arm. "Yes. We want you to heal David with the power of the priesthood."

He looked at her, wondering if this was some kind of trick. It was no secret that Miriam thought the Lord had chosen her for Jacob's second wife, that she was ordained by her patriarchal blessing to be the wife of the prophet and that Jacob was the rightful prophet since the death of her first husband. Never mind that his wife, Fernie, was willing to consider the idea, or that Miriam was a smart, attractive woman, he didn't want anything to do with polygamy.

So what was the trick? Get him down here, find David dangerously sedated with some opiate. Give him a blessing and...what? He wasn't sure, exactly, but it couldn't be coincidence that brought his father and Sister Miriam together.

But she wasn't looking at Jacob now. Instead, she rolled down David's sleeve and tucked the blanket back around his body against the evening breeze that swept in from the desert. She put her hand against his forehead and frowned. Miriam was more than a concerned bystander; there was something in that touch that was gentle, like a worried mother with a sick child.

Dry thunder sounded to the west. The storm would be over them in a few minutes, but it didn't feel like it was going to rain. Still, he wanted to get David inside and lying down, do something about that sluggish respiration.

"Is anyone in Blister Creek on oxygen?" he asked.

"Forget the oxygen," Father said. "I've got consecrated oil. The power of the holy priesthood will heal him."

"Why don't you give him a blessing yourself while I track down oxygen? Just tell me where."

"It needs to be both of us. One to anoint, the other to bless. The Lord is calling on you to bless."

"Father, please, this isn't the time."

"It *is* the time."

Jacob considered. "Fine, if I give him a blessing, will you tell me how to get some oxygen? His pulse and blood pressure are too low. It's worrying me."

"Give a good blessing, and I'll get you the oxygen."

"A good blessing, great."

"I mean, be serious. Don't mock."

"I'd never give a mocking blessing," Jacob said. "You know that."

Abraham pulled out his keys. Attached to one loop was a small brass vial. He unscrewed the lid and dripped some of the oil onto David's head.

Miriam squeezed Jacob's arm. "This is the time," she whispered. "I can feel it. The spirit will be with you and you will command the power of the Lord."

"If you say so."

Jacob had given hundreds of blessings. He gave them almost daily at the Zarahemla compound. Every sick child, every worried mother, every elderly person with an ache or injury came to him for a priesthood blessing. He healed most of them…with medical science. Of course they trusted him as a doctor, and thanked him for prescriptions, examinations, set bones, and the like, but they gave credit to the priesthood and to God. He nodded and agreed, while thinking, *You want to thank someone for saving lives? Thank Jonas Salk, thank Louis Pasteur.*

"Jacob," Father said sternly. "Remember, I said a *good* blessing. Summon your faith. Your power is there, but you have to tap it."

"Okay, I'll do it."

Of course it would be good. It was wrong, it was hypocritical, but he knew the right things to say, the right tone of voice. He could fool almost anyone, and if he threw himself into it he guessed he could fool his father and Miriam, too.

Abraham put his hands on first, with Jacob's on top. The two men bowed their heads. Abraham said, "David Brigham Christianson, by the authority of the Melchizedek Priesthood, we anoint thy head with oil which has been consecrated for the healing of the sick and do so in the name of Jesus Christ, amen."

They lifted their hands, and then Jacob put his down first, with his father's on top, to do the actual blessing. Jacob scrolled through the standard blessings in his head, thinking he'd ad-lib something about fighting the addiction, together with an exhortation to live righteously, and a few choice scriptural phrases. Give his voice a veneer of command, and voila! A blessing good enough to get Father to cough up the location of the oxygen tanks.

Too bad you're stoned out of your gourd, he thought as he adjusted his hands on his brother's head, his palms slick from too much olive oil. *It might actually do you some good to pay attention.*

"David Brigham Christianson," he said in a commanding voice, "by the authority of the Melchizedek Priesthood, we lay our hands upon thy head to give thee a blessing."

And then Jacob's mind went blank. All the prepared, oft-repeated words simply fled his mind, and all he could think were scattered thoughts. *Why did lightning crack out of a dry sky, anyway? Who named the town Blister Creek? Systolic and diastolic blood pressure, measured at the brachial artery, were really a mean arterial pressure over a single arterial cycle.*

His father cleared his throat. "Jacob?"

"I…uhm…the blessing is…"

In the first year in Blister Creek, three settlers suffered rattlesnake bites, but only one died. Oil in Spanish was aceite, which was derived from aceituna, olive. Or was it the other way around?

What was going on? Why couldn't he speak?

Lord, are you out there? I'm mute. What's wrong with me?

Something had gone wrong. Was this a stroke? It was as if a thrombosis had formed in his brain, choking blood from his Broca's area and crippling his ability to speak. He tried again. Nothing. Panic rose from his gut.

And then the words came. "David, thou art healed. Rise and cast the demon from thy soul. Thus sayeth the Lord."

Jacob ended, lifted his hands, blinking, without bothering to close the prayer properly. Behind him, Miriam murmured, "Thou sayest."

He stepped back from David to see that his father had drawn back and wore a deep frown.

Thus sayeth the Lord? Had those words ever come out of his mouth? What was wrong with him? He'd never blanked like that before.

David opened his eyes and rose to his feet, blinked, and looked around at the three of them with a look on his face like he'd just awakened from sleepwalking.

Alarmed, Jacob grabbed his arm. "Sit down, your blood pressure is through the floor."

David pulled free. "No, I feel okay. Let go, I'm all right."

Miriam came to David's side. "Listen to your brother. He's a doctor, he knows what he's talking about."

"Okay, I'm sitting." He returned to the Adirondack chair.

He still didn't sound entirely there, and Jacob immediately turned to logical explanations for what had happened. That was how people built testimonies of the truthfulness of supernatural events. Take two unrelated oddities and mix them together in a spiritual context and it suddenly became a miracle. Jacob had blanked out on the blessing. Big deal; even professional speakers sometimes coughed up a hairball on stage. And then, just when the blessing ended, David woke from a drug-induced stupor. Two random events that came together at once. So what? Give it an hour and David would be begging to shoot up, snort up, or smoke up whatever poison was most readily available.

Jacob could almost convince himself that it meant nothing, except for the weird blessing that came out of his mouth. *Thus sayeth the Lord?*

Hard to say what the others were thinking, but a glance at Miriam confirmed one suspicion. There were tears in her eyes, but she didn't pay him any attention. Instead, she had a hand on David's face and looked him in the eyes with a tender expression. And that's when he knew. Jacob's aspiring second wife had fallen in love with his brother.

David, for his part, wasn't looking at Miriam, but stared into the darkness beyond the porch. "Yes, I was right. I *thought* I heard something, but I was too stoned to care."

"Heard what?" Jacob asked.

"Shh, listen."

There was a flash of light, then thunder, then nothing but the sound of the wind. And then Jacob heard it, too. Someone's boots crunching across the gravel that led down to the shed.

"We have an intruder," David said.

* * *

Eliza set down the bent, worn-out spring and felt her work. A mound of dirt and rocks gouged from the walls lay packed against the side of the pit, maybe twenty inches high. It was wider than the thickness of the mattress, standing on its end, and stable. On top of this, they put the two lettuce crates, stacked lengthwise for stability, which added another ten inches.

"That's all," she said. "It will have to be enough."

Madeline panted at her side. "Well, at least we're warm now."

"Give it a minute, gather your strength. Then we'll go for it." Eliza reached out until she found the other woman's arm. It was trembling. "See, you're stronger than you thought."

"I just hope it's enough."

"It'll be enough."

"What do you think they're doing up there?" Madeline asked.

"No idea, but we can't worry about that until we're out of here."

A couple of hours earlier, Madeline had hissed a warning. Eliza had been so engrossed in her work, scraping with a coiled spring around the edge of a boulder that she was trying to dislodge from the walls of the pit, that she hadn't heard it at first. And then, from above, the sound of metal clanking, like two drums knocking

against each other. Someone sat on or put something on the overturned refrigerator. She heard voices, a shouted argument between
a man and a woman. Hard to say for sure, but the man sounded like
Christopher. They'd waited until the noise passed before resuming
the blind scraping, digging, stacking.

Together, the two women wrestled the first mattress into a
standing position atop the mound of dirt and rocks. They'd only
torn out a couple of the springs, and it still held most of its shape.
They lifted the thinner mattress into place.

"You got it?" Eliza asked. "Here I go, don't let me fall."

She scaled the mattresses. They wobbled, but she didn't need to
go as high this time, since the hill of dirt and rocks gave her a critical boost. She reached the top and stretched her arm to get some
leverage against the fridge that blocked the entrance. And stopped.
Her hand felt dirt.

"No," she said, in a low voice. "Please, no."

"What is it?" came Madeline's voice from the darkness below
her.

She almost didn't have the heart to share the crushing news.
"We built the mound on the wrong side. This isn't the opening.
The fridge isn't up here, it's just dirt. Somehow, we must have got
turned around when we brought the mattresses down and moved
everything into the wrong place."

"Then it's over." Madeline's voice was flat, dead. "We tried
and failed."

Eliza slid back down, groped until she found the other woman's
shoulders, and grabbed her to make her listen. "It's not over, only a
setback. We'll move the dirt to the other side, that's all."

"I can't do it. I'm wiped out."

"An hour, tops, and we'll be done. Think about it—the dirt is already loose, the rocks are dug out. All the hard work is done. It's just a few minutes to loosen up our mound, and then we'll carry it over in scoops."

"I gave everything I had," Madeline said. "It's all I can do to stand up."

"You've got a little more." Eliza fought to keep her voice from giving away her disappointment and her growing fear that the other woman was right, that they didn't have enough left to make another attempt.

"And how can we be sure, anyway? There are four sides to this blasted pit, and the fridge is only over one corner. What if we do it again?"

But Eliza had already worked that out. She groped in the mound until she found several small pebbles, then tossed them up, one by one, until she heard a plink instead of a thud. "Come stand over here. I'll roll the big rock to you, and then we can start."

They worked in silence. Eliza was too tired and discouraged to offer much to her companion. The good news was that it seemed to take much less than an hour to move the pile to the other side, but unfortunately, the mound was shorter when they finished. It was either packed down more firmly or they'd lost some of the dirt transporting it across the pit. And so they spent another twenty minutes scraping more dirt from the walls of their prison, until Eliza felt satisfied with the height.

"Okay, let's try again."

But Madeline was too weak to be much help, and Eliza had to get the crates and the mattresses in place herself. When she finished, she said, "I know your tank is empty, but you've got to hold these in place while I climb."

Madeline answered in a thin, quavering voice. "I don't know if I can."

"There's got to be something left in there." She kept her voice even, confident, and encouraging. "We're almost out. You know that and you can do what it takes."

"But Eliza, I—"

"No excuses. You're not a child, Madeline, you're a grown woman, and you can find the strength."

"As in, I am woman, hear me roar?" There was a scraping sound as Madeline regained her feet and groped her way over.

"Sorry, I have no idea what that means."

"Jeez, you really did lead a sheltered life. It's just something my mom used to say, ironically, I think. I guess it means that I'll do my best."

"I'll take whatever you can give. Lean into it, I'm going up."

Eliza's own arms were exhausted and shaking from hours of work. Hunger made her lightheaded. But no way was she staying down here to die. She was too close.

She reached the midway point of the thinner mattress, then lifted her hand and was relieved to find the fridge overhead. Maneuvering so her lower foot wedged in the gap between the two mattresses and the toes of her upper foot curled around one of the oversized mattress buttons, she leaned her shoulder against the wall and dug her fingers under the edge of the fridge.

The mattresses wobbled, threatening to tip over. "Don't let them fall!"

She heaved. Getting it to budge was the hardest, and then she got the fridge to slide a fraction of an inch. Cool, clean night air rushed in on her face. She stopped, trying to stabilize herself while giving her arms a rest and taking in gulps of the clean air. After a moment, she caught a whiff of diesel fuel, but she couldn't hear the generator running. Maybe when she got it open wider she could figure out what was going on.

"Are you okay up there?" Madeline asked.

"Yes. Going to give it another heave. Hang on."

Eliza counted to three, then thrust her weight into the fridge. It slid out of the way, but her changing position on the mattresses threw off her balance. The mattresses bucked, and Madeline grunted and struggled to keep them in place. Eliza grabbed for the top of the pit. Her hands caught the edge just as Madeline lost her struggle below and the mattresses fell. Pushing off the side with her toes, Eliza scrambled to get her arms up. Dirt and rocks crumbled from the side of the pit, but she didn't let go.

A moment later she was squirming through the hole on her belly. It was night, with a full moon overhead, casting the tire mounds into dark shadow. A breeze prickled across her naked skin. It was the most wonderful thing she'd ever felt. Her spirits rose with every breath of fresh air. She could be at the overturned sofa, fishing out the cell phone, in two minutes. Call Jacob, tell him to send the police. But first, she had to get Madeline out. How was she going to do it? Maybe lower down tires until there were enough to climb out? Quickly, Eliza bent and put all her weight into sliding the refrigerator all the way off.

She bent over the hole. "Okay, here's what we're going to do."

"You're not going to do anything, you filthy bitch," a low voice said.

Eliza whirled around, heart pounding.

Christopher stood a few feet away. He carried the ladder, and as he approached, she smelled diesel fuel, as if he'd spilled some on his clothes. He was a big man, and even in the moonlight she could see the crazed look on his face.

Eliza stood her ground. "Get away from me."

"I should have done it before, should have done it first. I knew it. It's the only thing that will teach you a lesson."

Christopher swung the end of the ladder around, intending to catch her across the body and knock her down. She tried to back out of the way, but the fridge blocked her path to the rear.

"Get ready to be sanctified, bitch."

CHAPTER TWENTY-ONE

The Disciple had found the shed without difficulty. It was in the same spot where he'd almost burned his brother Taylor Junior alive. His father had rebuilt it within a few weeks, and there it had stood for the last fifteen years. Mocking him.

Be careful. Do not alert the enemy.

He sent Diego into the shed first, but that apparently wasn't what the voices had been warning, because nobody was inside. Fortunately, the new owners used it for the same purpose as Taylor Kimball, as there were mowers, hedgers, and other tools. And a five-gallon can of gas. He heard the boy clanking around with the can, trying to get it to budge, then finally decided to go in and get it himself.

"No, you stay in here. You don't want to get in the way. The rest of this I can do myself."

The Disciple closed the door with Diego still in the shed, then reached to flip the latch and lock the boy inside. He opened the gas can—nearly full, as it turned out—and sloshed some on the doorframe and around the foundation of the shed. He reached into his pocket and retrieved the book of matches from the Excalibur Hotel.

Not yet. The house first.

And so he moved around the porch and the back edge of the house, spreading the rest of the gasoline. Tumbleweeds had piled against the house and the porch on the north side, and he made sure to soak these with gasoline.

Thunder rumbled in the distance, offsetting the occasional flash of light. No rain, just as he'd guessed. Between the thunder, he heard voices from the front porch. Someone said something about oxygen, but he couldn't figure out what that could be about.

He emptied the rest of the can at a spot where the end of the porch connected with the house. The spruce railing had started to split, and paint flaked from the shingles on the side of the house. In the dry air of the Colorado Plateau, both the porch and the shingles would be dry as kindling. He pulled out a match and lit it. The wind blew it out.

Stay focused. You are almost done, and then you can return to Nevada for the falling of Wormwood and the end of the world.

He turned his back to the desert and sheltered the matchbook between his body and the house. This time it stayed lit. He touched it to the railing, and a tongue of fire licked along the top where he'd poured the gasoline, up to the edge of the house. The heat and smell radiated toward him, and he had to resist the urge to reach out and bathe his hand in the flames.

Quickly now, he hurried to the pile of tumbleweeds around back and lit that on fire, then permitted himself a moment to watch the tumbleweeds ignite. They burst into flames all at once, like marshmallows thrust too far into a campfire. The Disciple turned to go. One more task and then he would be done. The shed. It had to burn.

But as he crossed back toward the shed, he stumbled across a path of crushed stone. In the dark, he hadn't seen it and couldn't remember there having been a path on this side of the house, just hard-packed dirt. In fact, he was sure there hadn't been one the way he'd come before. He must have come around the front this time. There wasn't enough light cast off from the porch to differentiate the path, and when he tried to cross, he found instead that he was following its course. His feet crunched again. He could see the shadow of the shed to his left, and presumably the path curved toward it. It took several more steps across the crushed rock before he found his way off the path.

The Disciple heard the voices again, but there was a sudden change in their tone. A flashlight cut through the night, waving in his direction.

The voices all clamored at once. *Go! Now!*

He ran.

* * *

For one moment, David had felt a peaceful wave flow over him.

That feeling was nothing like the euphoria of the too-heavy dose of heroin Miriam had given him. That was a sedating feeling, like floating above his body. In the moment when the drug had him in its claws, he lost all feeling for the world, cared about nothing.

The others could have taken hacksaws to his legs and he would have sat there with a vacant smile.

But when Jacob spoke the words, "David, thou art healed. Rise and cast out the demon from thy soul. Thus sayeth the Lord," it was over. He was instantly alert. Like pulling a stopper, the euphoria of the drug swirled around the drain and was gone. Without the drug, he expected the shakes to return, to hear the demon howling for him to shoot up again, for his veins to catch fire.

Only this time it was different. He felt his soul, a thinning of the veil, with angels and the Lord on the other side. He felt a connection to the others on the porch, and an outpouring of love from his own dry, withered heart that brought tears to his eyes. These people—his brother, Sister Miriam, even his father—they seemed to him the most wonderful people he'd ever known, and hope radiated from them.

You are home, brother. Take this chance, it is a miracle.

David stood up, ready to tell them that he was healed, that it was over, that he would never touch drugs again. Jacob looked stunned. Normally, he wore a mask of confidence, an intelligence and charisma that other people could only envy. But that was stripped away. In its place was confusion and self-doubt. It was apparent to David that Jacob had not prepared those words, had even tried to fight them as they came out of his mouth.

And then a flash of lightning, and when the rumble stopped, he heard crunching feet on the gravel. He'd heard it at the beginning of the prayer, still semi-catatonic from the heroin. A dark warning passed through his soul.

"We have an intruder."

Sister Miriam and Father moved at once. Sister Miriam stiffened and reached across her body to a spot just under her left armpit—expecting to find a gun in a shoulder holster, David realized. But she wore a prairie dress and there was nothing there. She turned toward the door.

Father grabbed for something behind the other Adirondack chairs on the porch and came up with a flashlight. He swung it back and forth over the yard. More crunching. The light caught a figure, running toward the shed.

It took Jacob a moment longer, but then he said, "I smell a fire."

David could smell it too. There was a hint of campfire, but also a chemical tang, like burning plastic or paint. "Father, you need to wake up the house."

"But what about the intruder?"

Jacob took the flashlight. "We'll take care of him, you get people out."

Miriam burst out of the house, almost colliding with Abraham, headed the other direction. This time she did have a gun. She and Jacob started down the stairs from the porch, and David came after them. Jacob held out his hand. "Sit down, you're too weak."

"No, I'm not. I feel fine, and I'm coming." He felt stronger than he had in years. Even the aching ribs had stopped complaining.

The three of them made their way down the crushed stone path toward the shed. As they approached, flames licked the edges and climbed the door. He smelled burning gasoline, which explained why the fire was spreading so quickly. At the house itself, the end of the porch was on fire, and there was a second, even larger fire around back. But lights were already flipping on throughout the house, and he heard the shouts of women and children. The people, at least, would be okay. David started toward the shed.

Jacob grabbed him. "It's just tools and junk, it can burn. We need to find the firebug before he burns down the whole town."

But he wasn't sure. Why light a small outbuilding on fire? As Jacob and Miriam—one armed with a flashlight, the other a gun—searched in the direction of the greenhouses, David continued toward the shed. The whole side was on fire now, and it had reached the shingle roof. He could see a latch up high on the door, but there was no way to reach it through the fire.

He got as close as he dared. "Is anyone in there? Hello?"

No answer. That feeling must have been wrong. David turned to catch up with the others.

And then, so quiet that he had to listen carefully to be sure over the crackling, smoking fire, he thought he heard a sob, like a small child. A moment later, another sob. A hot lump of fear lodged itself in David's gut.

"Jacob!" he shouted. "There's a child in here."

The other two came running. David took off his shirt, wrapped it around his good hand, and tried to get to the latch, but the fire was too hot and forced him to retreat.

"Around here!" Miriam cried. "There's a back window."

The two men followed her to the back side of the shed. There was a small window at chest height, and David pushed the others away so he could smash at it with his shirt-wrapped hand. Together, they pulled away the shards of glass, and then David leaned halfway in to see who it was.

It was dark inside, but the fire through the window on the opposite door gave enough light that he could see a boy standing, facing the window. He wore a T-shirt and jeans and looked impossibly thin, almost like he'd been sick or starved.

David leaned in. "Come on, hurry. I'll get you out."

The boy's eyes were deep, liquid pools on a face so thin that the skin looked stretched, like a too-small glove on a too-big hand. He shook his head.

"Come on!" Miriam shouted from behind David's shoulder. "Hurry, we'll pull you out."

The boy simply stared at him.

"Come on, kid," David muttered. He turned to Miriam. "He's in shock—I've got to go after him. Help me in."

Jacob grabbed his arm. "What about your broken arm? Let me do it."

"It's fine, it doesn't hurt. Come on, we don't have time, and I'm skinnier than you. Help me up."

The other two lifted him to the window. He got halfway in and realized his mistake. It was too narrow. All he'd managed was to wedge himself in the window frame, where he'd die in the fire. The frame was too tight around his shoulders, and the more he tried to force himself in, the more stuck he got. But then, just as panic started to take him, he was in and spilling to the floor. It was hot inside, and filling with smoke. He grabbed the boy, who struggled to free himself from David's grasp.

"It's a lie," David said. "Whatever they told you, it's not true. Please, we're here to help."

And then the boy went limp in his arms. David lifted him to the window, and the other two pulled him through. The smoke filled the room now, and fire was on the inside, roasting hot. He coughed, tried to lift himself into the window, but couldn't get high enough to get his arms through. The stupid broken arm—it didn't hurt until he got it up and tried to put weight on it. He coughed again, feeling light-headed. His eyes burned and watered. He tried again and still couldn't get up.

"David!" Miriam said.

"It's no use."

"No use? You jerk!" Miriam shouted. "We didn't go to all that trouble so you could just die. Now get up here!"

The lawnmower sat just to his side, and he wheeled it in front of the window and then climbed onto the motor. The mower started to roll, but he caught the window frame and steadied himself. Standing on the mower gave him just enough height to hook his arms over the window, and then Jacob and Miriam had him by the shoulders and were yanking him through. Or at least until he got wedged again. He'd turned his hips somehow, or maybe his pants had caught on something—he couldn't exactly see what.

"Come on, come on," Miriam said.

"I'm trying." He hacked and coughed. The fire at his back felt like the flames of hell, and whatever he'd felt moments earlier—an inevitable feeling of one's impending death—was long gone. Terror remained. "Just get me out of here."

"Suck it in," Jacob said. "We're going to yank you out if we have to pull down the whole shed. Ready? One…two…three!"

There was a sharp pain in his left shoulder, and *now* he felt his bruised ribs. He cried out at the pain. Through he came, and then he was out, lying on the gravel and breathing the air. The shed blazed behind him, the fire crackling and roaring. Smoke poured into the sky. David crawled away from the shed and regained his feet. Miriam grabbed the boy and pulled him clear.

The Christianson family worked around the edge of the house. Two women had hoses, while women and children knocked flaming piles of tumbleweeds away from the house with shovels or batted at flames with brooms. Father stood to one side, shouting instructions, like a general directing troops.

They were slowly bringing the fire under control. The house would be saved. The shed, on the other hand, was a total loss. It burned like a torch, illuminating the yard and gardens surrounding the ranch house. David clutched his ribs and winced.

"What about the firebug?" Jacob asked. "Should we go after him?"

Miriam shook her head. "We can raise a search party, but I bet it's too late."

David scanned the desert side of town. The Ghost Cliffs were a darker gash against the horizon, and in the moonlight he could see the edge of Witch's Warts beyond the temple. No flashlights or other lights in that direction, but house lights flickered on to the south and east. Word of the fire would be spreading through town, and soon all of Blister Creek would be on their way to help with the fire and to search for the enemy who'd dared attack their community. He guessed Miriam was right; they could search, but they wouldn't find anything. Whoever it was had known the area.

He put a hand on the boy's head. "I'm guessing this one knows something. Look at these rags. He's not from Blister Creek."

The boy looked up at him with those deep eyes, and something stirred in David's heart. What kind of monster would starve and then immolate a child?

And then, suddenly, he knew.

CHAPTER TWENTY-TWO

Even in the moonlight, Eliza could see the sneer on Christopher's face, the lust and the crazed fervor in his eyes as he swung the ladder. He was going to knock her over, then rape her, and every moment he would think he was doing the Lord's holy work, sanctifying her for the Disciple. She remembered his words and his ugly tone.

Sanctify her. Right here, in the dirt. Show her, do it.

Eliza stood naked, 135 pounds before the last few days of forced starvation. He had to weigh two hundred pounds, and the heavy ladder whooshed through the air, picking up speed as it came around. It caught her on the chest and drove her into the overturned fridge.

But instead of pushing back, Eliza grabbed the ladder and pulled. She slid over the fridge and let her momentum pull her back. He grunted as he lost his balance. She heaved, and then the ladder lost its propelling force as Christopher let go, trying to recover.

Too late. Christopher had staggered toward the hole. For a moment, he teetered on the edge, trying to catch his balance, and then he fell with a cry. Madeline screamed. There was a sickening crunch. Madeline continued to scream.

"Madeline!"

The other woman seemed to catch herself. "I'm okay. He didn't hit me, not directly. Oh no, he's alive. Eliza!"

"Move out of the way. Over to the side."

Christopher groaned, muttered something. There wasn't a second to spare. Eliza grabbed the ladder, swung it around, looked for the darker patch next to the outline of the fridge, and then tilted it up so it would slide down into the pit.

"It's the ladder, grab it."

She hadn't got the ladder level on the ground below, and it wobbled as Madeline started to climb. Eliza hooked her leg around the edge and braced it against the fridge. Madeline's head had just appeared above the ground when she screamed again. "He's got my leg."

"You filthy bitch, I'll show you."

Eliza grabbed her arms while Christopher tugged on her feet and Madeline kicked and fought. And then Madeline freed herself and was on the surface. Christopher was coming up after them. They shook the ladder, trying to dislodge him, and it seemed that he'd injured himself in the fall because he only gradually emerged from the ground, but they couldn't shake him loose. He was cursing and snarling as he came up, threatening them, not just with sanctification, but swearing he would kill them and drink their blood.

As he began to emerge, Madeline kicked at his face, while he tried to fend her off with one arm. His other, Eliza now saw, dangled uselessly by his side. The elbow was bent at a bad angle. He should be lying on the ground, in shock, but something propelled him forward. She had no doubt that he'd find a way to make good on his threats if they let him escape from the hole.

There was garbage all around her, so much that she tripped over it. She bent and groped, and her hands found something hard. It was a ripped shred of a tire, about as heavy as a leather belt, and she wrenched it free from the dirt and other garbage around it. She swung from the shoulder and caught him across the side of the head.

Christopher snarled, a feral, animal sound. "Oh, you just made a big mistake." He hooked his good arm over the top of the ladder and began to lever himself out of the pit.

But she wasn't done. She beat him again and again on the face, until she forced him to let go and try to protect himself. "Get the ladder!" she cried.

Madeline grabbed the edge of the ladder and shook it, while Eliza kept beating. For a moment it looked like he'd get out, and Eliza braced herself to grab Madeline and make a run for it, but then he started to slip. She redoubled her attack. Her arm ached. He tried to regain his grip.

Eliza dropped the piece of tire and rushed him. She shoved her hands into his face and threw her body into the ladder. It flopped back against the other side of the narrow opening. Christopher fell with a cry.

"Get the ladder."

The two women pulled it up. Even now, he didn't give up. He'd caught a foot or arm on the bottom rung of the ladder. They shook it back and forth and finally wrenched it free. Moments later, they had it out of the pit and dragged it away from the opening. Christopher found his voice and started in again on his shouts and threats. But he was at the bottom of the pit now. There was nothing he could do.

Eliza couldn't help herself. She bent over and said, "Hope you like lettuce, jerk. And you can think about how two naked girls gave you a beating." She turned to Madeline. "Get the fridge."

The fridge was easier to move from above, and they shortly had it maneuvered back over the hole. It muted Christopher's rants. Soon, they died altogether, leaving only the sound of the breeze flowing over the desert.

Eliza doubled over, panting. When she caught her breath, she said, "Looks like he's ready to purify *himself*, see how he likes it. Or is that only for women?"

"Uhm…Eliza?"

Eliza followed Madeline's gaze. She turned to find a dozen others standing a few feet away in a half circle around them. One young woman held a lantern. Their faces were grim.

* * *

David drew Jacob and Miriam aside, into the shadows behind the house, where the fire had never taken hold. The sharp smell of burning paint and gasoline filled his nostrils. He had the boy by the hand and could feel him trembling. Miriam put a hand on the child's shoulder and whispered encouraging words.

"What are we doing?" Jacob asked. "We should help put out the fire."

"We can't do anything about the shed," David said, "and they've got the house fire under control. I don't want the old man to hear this."

"What, exactly, don't you want him to hear?" Jacob asked. His tone had changed, and David could tell his brother shared his suspicions about Abraham Christianson.

"I don't know what this is all about, you coming down here and giving me a blessing, Miriam and her drugs."

"I'm so sorry, David," she said. "It was the only way, and—"

"It doesn't matter, not right now. I don't trust my father, and neither should you. If you listen to me about anything, trust me on that."

"I don't trust him," she said. "Not a bit. It's just that—"

"Please, I'm serious. You don't have to explain anything. Later, maybe, but not now. We don't have time. I know who the arsonist is."

"It's got to be a Lost Boy," Jacob said. "Who else would try to burn down the prophet's house? And who else would know Blister Creek well enough to come in at night?"

"Yes, but not *just* a Lost Boy. Look how skinny this boy is, the rags."

Jacob was a smart man, and it only took him a second to put the pieces together. First, the light of understanding, then a look of horror. "Oh no. Eliza." He reached for his phone and started dialing. A moment later, he said, "Dammit, no answer."

David thought about the reference to the Book of Revelation on the side of the produce truck, and his mind filled in the rest.

And the name of the star is called Wormwood. "I don't think we have a lot of time."

"Could someone please fill me in," Miriam said.

"The thing about millenialist cults is they can sit around doing nothing for a long time," Jacob said as he dialed again. "The instant they start killing people, you know they're serious. That's when they think the world really is coming to an ènd." He stopped and said into the phone, "Liz, if you get this, call me right away. Immediately, it can't wait." He hung up and let out his breath.

David squatted until he was eye-to-eye with the boy, while Jacob dialed again. "Can you tell me your name?"

No answer.

"Who brought you here? You know they're not your friends, right? Whoever put you in that shed was going to burn you alive. You don't have to protect them."

The boy shook his head. David didn't know what that meant, that he *did* have to protect them? That he *wasn't* trying to protect them? That he didn't understand any of it?

"Can you tell me anything about what happened?"

Another shake of the head.

"It's no use," Jacob said as he hung up his phone again. "He's too traumatized to help, and we're wasting valuable time."

"But *you* know something," Miriam said to David. "Any idea how to find these people?"

David nodded. "It'd be easier if this kid would help, but I think so. Or I could find it with a little mental effort. They came in off the desert behind my subdivision. Problem is, the arsonist has a head start on us, and maybe they're already drinking their Kool-Aid, or whatever they're planning."

"Fire, I think," Jacob said. "Based on the evidence."

"Fire sounds right," Miriam said. "The problem is, we'll get there too late. Maybe the best thing is to call the Las Vegas police."

"I don't think that will work," David said. "We don't have much evidence, and we'd have to make it an anonymous call. And I don't have an exact location to send them, anyway. They'll spend about five minutes driving around, and then they'll go back to their speed traps and prostitution stings."

Jacob turned to Miriam. "What about your FBI buddies?"

"They're hardly my buddies anymore, not after I left in such an…awkward way. Krantz is a good guy, he'd probably help, but I haven't talked to him in months and he might even be in Central Asia somewhere. They offered him a position as a legal attaché overseas, but I don't know if he took it. Fayer, maybe? She's never quite forgiven me for what happened at the Zarahemla compound. I don't know if it's the religious thing or the abuse she suffered, but I think that somehow, she blames me for what happened. But she's a professional, and I think she'll believe me. I'd still have to get ahold of her, which might not be easy."

"Whatever we do, we're not waiting here," Jacob said. "Not while Eliza is facing heaven knows what." He pressed his hands to his temples. "I never should have let her go. What was I thinking?"

Miriam put a hand on his shoulder. "You were thinking she's a strong, intelligent woman who can take care of herself. Whatever else is happening out there, none of that has changed. Now let's get out of here before we get sucked into another one of Abraham Christianson's schemes."

"And the boy?" David asked.

Jacob said, "We'll leave the child with one of Father's wives. It's too dangerous out there."

* * *

Eliza stood naked in front of the half circle of men and women closing in on them. The light from a pair of lanterns cast their faces in ghostly hues. She forced a confidence into her voice that she didn't feel. "This is all wrong, and every one of you knows it. Look at you, starving, abused. Some of you raped. Where are your families? What about school and jobs and college? You gave all that up for this?"

"We didn't give up anything, we left the Lone and Dreary World," one young man said. His head had been shaved to a stubble, and a beard sprouted in tufts from his chin. He couldn't have been more than nineteen. It was Kirk, the boy who'd sprang to his feet when she'd fled from the trailer door. "Who needs that? Now we've got the Word of God to show us."

"The Lone and Dreary World?" She felt the ground under her feet solidify. It was fundamentalist Mormon speak; she'd heard it before. And there was no sign of the Disciple. These others had been bullied for so long that maybe they couldn't move without their two leaders. "And the world is less dreary living in the dump, eating garbage? Less dreary how, exactly?" She spotted Benita, who held one of the lanterns. Eliza went to her, grabbed the girl's arm, and turned it over to reveal the scars. "This stuff can heal. What they do to you in the desert doesn't scab over so easily."

Benita pulled away. Madeline seemed to wake up as she came to Eliza's side. "Nita, it's okay. It's over. We can get out of here. Listen to Eliza, she makes so much sense."

"Why, because she's whispering the words of the devil in your ear?" Kirk asked. A few of the others murmured. "If you listen to the devil long enough, of course he starts to make sense. We're the Chosen Ones, and we only listen to God."

"It's not God who starves people in pits and rapes them while twisting scriptures to make it sound holy and righteous," Eliza said. "It's not God who tells people to find helpless strangers and beat them half to death. You think that's God?" They weren't listening, she could see their faces hardening, but they no longer looked like they were going to attack Eliza and Madeline, either. "Now listen to me. Madeline and I are leaving tonight. Anyone who wants can come with us."

"You won't get far," Kirk said. "The world is ending tonight."

"Tonight?" Madeline said, her voice strangled.

Benita nodded. "The Disciple left several hours ago to prepare the way. He'll be back soon. It will happen just before dawn. Wormwood will fall from the sky and burn the wicked from the face of the earth."

"But...tonight?" Madeline repeated.

"The world isn't ending," Eliza said, more for Madeline's benefit than anyone else's. "Morning will come and the sun will rise like it does every day. And either the Disciple isn't bothering to come back—having taken everything he wanted—or he'll come back with some excuse as to why the world didn't actually end at dawn. There was some slight miscalculation, or the Lord said it would be another year or two so you could finish the work."

"You're wrong," Kirk said.

"Fine, if I'm wrong, I'll be burned up when Wormwood falls. If I'm right, will you admit it? Will you say, 'I was wrong, the world isn't coming to an end'?"

Eliza didn't just say this last part with confidence, she felt it. In the past, she might have suffered a twinge of superstitious worry. Not tonight. She'd seen nothing to indicate that the Disciple was anything more than a fraud or insane or some combination of the two.

Kirk had no answer, and she could see doubt on his face. In spite of giving up everything, surrendering everything they had to wait for Wormwood to fall from the sky and burn up the wicked, a tiny seed of doubt remained. And a little doubt was all she needed to get herself and Madeline—as well as anyone else who would come—out of there.

Nevertheless, there was a flaw in her plan, she could now see. If the Disciple had taken the truck, they'd have to walk out of the desert. Even if she could get clothing and water, there was no way she could walk out by dawn. And what if she came down the road and the Disciple came back from the other direction? Meanwhile, as soon as she left, they'd no doubt fish Christopher out of the hole. She couldn't let that happen. Eliza thought she could handle the Disciple alone, maybe with some help from Madeline, and possibly Benita and a couple of the others. But Christopher scared her. And he would scare the others, too.

"Can someone bring us some clothes? I'm getting tired of standing here naked."

"Come inside," Benita said. "I've got a couple of things that should fit."

Eliza eyed Kirk. "If it's all the same, I'll stay right here." She sat down on the edge of the fridge. The pit below her was quiet, but she wasn't fooled. There was a monster down there, and he would be plotting. She'd left him the same tools she'd used to get herself out. Would he figure it out? Would his injured arm allow him to make a try?

Madeline came to sit by her while Benita went for the clothes. "Are we leaving?" she asked Eliza in a low voice.

"We can't leave until morning, we won't make it."

"I don't want to stay here."

"Me either, but we can't make it out on foot, not after starving in the pit. We have to hold out until morning, see if the world comes to an end. And no, I don't think it will. I think the Disciple will come back with some lame story, and we can work that to our advantage. We'll take his truck."

"It would help if some of these people didn't want to toss us back into the pit. And this time we'd have company."

"Give me a few minutes," Eliza said. "I'll work on that."

When Benita came out with the clothes, she exchanged a glance with Madeline that Eliza tried to decipher. Some of the others returned to the trailers. A few, including Kirk, kept their distance but watched the two women as they dressed. The clothes were torn, dirty shirts and pants with missing buttons. No underwear. Still, a huge improvement over being naked. Benita watched them dress, then turned to leave.

"Stay here for a moment," Eliza said. "We want to talk to you."

"About what?"

"We want you to come with us," Madeline said.

Benita shifted the lamp from one hand to the other and glanced back at Kirk, who now turned back toward the trailer. "I don't know. I…I just don't know."

"They can't hurt you if you leave," Eliza said.

"Maybe not, but other things can."

"Of course, you're right, but there are people who can help, too. Do you have family? I know people who can help if you don't."

"You don't understand."

"Explain it to me," Eliza urged. "I want to help, that's why I came here. For Madeline, but for you, too. If I can help, it will all be worth it, but you have to talk to me."

"I…I just can't."

Madeline wrapped her arm around Benita's shoulder and sat the woman between herself and Eliza atop the overturned fridge. "You can talk to her, she's like us. She understands."

"No, not now. I really can't. It's…too much."

Eliza tried to keep her voice reassuring. "It's okay. There will be plenty of time for that later. Just come out with us, get away from the Disciple and the Chosen Ones for a few days and see how you feel." She smiled. "Unless the world ends tonight, of course. Then I'll admit I'm wrong and join up, if it's not too late."

Benita tensed and Eliza thought she would pull away, but then she nodded. "Okay, I'll come with you."

Eliza felt things turning her way. She thought about the pre-paid cell phone. "Don't move. I'll be back in a minute." She took Benita's lamp and left the two women in the darkness.

But when she walked around the back of the trailers, she had a shock. They'd moved more tires, spreading them in piles on the back side of the compound until they overran and buried the sofa where she'd hidden the phone. Maybe she could have found it in daylight, but it was too dark to see more than shadows and deeper shadows. She walked through the tires, bending and holding out the lamp, but it was no use. Everything was overturned, buried, or moved, and she couldn't remember exactly where she'd put it.

Eliza fought down her worry as she made her way back to the others. Even without the phone, she was in better shape than she had been a few minutes earlier. She and Madeline had escaped, put Christopher in the pit where he couldn't hurt anyone, and the Disciple was out of the picture. She could figure this out.

"What was that about?" Madeline asked when she came back.

"Nothing," she lied, "just clearing my head so I can think of a way out of here."

"Do you have a plan?"

Eliza considered. She didn't need all of them, and she didn't need full cooperation. Kirk still worried her, and she couldn't stop imagining Christopher in the pit below them, plotting. She handed Benita the lamp. "I'm going to talk to Kirk. Don't either of you get off the fridge, whatever you do. If he figures out how we got out, he might try it, too."

Eliza made her way to the double-wide where Kirk and a few of the others had disappeared. What was the best way to approach him? With all the abuse of women she'd witnessed, she had to remind herself that these men suffered, too. Not all of them could be monsters like Christopher. And yet they had assaulted strangers, so there was something dark in every one of them.

Voices raised as she climbed the cinder blocks that served as stairs. "Let him out!" a woman shouted. "The Disciple left him in charge!" A man—Kirk?—told her to keep it down. They should wait to see what God meant to happen. It might be a test.

Eliza was tempted to eavesdrop, see who stood where, but it was a dangerous moment and she needed to be part of the conversation.

She stepped inside, and the conversation died as all eyes turned in her direction. They squatted around the edge of the room.

"For every prophet called of the Lord, there's a second man sent by Satan to betray him," Eliza said. "A snake came to deceive Adam. Satan whispered in Cain's ear until he murdered his brother, Abel. Even one of Jesus's apostles betrayed him."

"What are you saying?" one of the women asked.

Eliza looked at Kirk, who met her gaze for a moment before looking away. "I'm saying that Christopher is the Disciple's Judas. He's the one who is trying to corrupt this group, and until he's taken care of, the Chosen Ones are in danger."

The woman stood up. She was tall, and looked Eliza in the eye. "The Disciple left him in charge. He left you in the pit to be purified. And somehow you're out and Christopher is down. That's a problem."

"It doesn't matter," someone said. "The world is ending tonight. What's the point in arguing about who is where?"

"Let him out," another woman said. "He belongs with the elect. He needs to see Wormwood fall from the sky."

"Yes, let him out."

"Kirk," Eliza said. "Think about what is happening here. You know it's not right. And you know who is responsible, too. Who is the one who goes back with the Disciple to sanctify people? And I'll bet he's the one who chooses who to cleanse, as well. It doesn't matter if the world ends tonight or not. If it does end, you don't want to be standing next to someone like that. If it doesn't, then you've got to think about how to get the Disciple away from that man."

Kirk was quiet. He glanced up at her, then looked away. Eliza couldn't tell if he was buying it. She didn't buy it herself. The Disciple was just the other side of an evil coin, as far as she could tell. If Christopher hadn't joined the Chosen Ones, the Disciple would have kept searching until he found someone else to be his sadistic second in command.

At last, Kirk rose to his feet. "She's right. Christopher stays in the pit."

"Until the Disciple gets back," the woman with the strident voice said. "And then he'll decide."

"No," Kirk said. "Not even then. I'm going to get Benita and Madeline. Everyone will come inside. I don't want any of you to leave the trailer until morning. We need to make sure nobody does anything stupid."

"What are you saying?" the woman asked.

"I'm saying it's over. We're all going into the city tomorrow to turn ourselves in, tell the police what we've done. The cops can get Christopher out and decide what to do with him."

The room erupted in shouts, and Kirk had to pull two women apart who immediately came to blows. One of the young men started screaming at him, and Kirk told him in a sharp voice to shut up. Once he'd settled people down, he met Eliza's gaze.

She stared back. A feeling of triumph rose inside her. It was more than she'd hoped. She'd hoped only to preserve a stalemate until morning, then escape with whatever cult members she could bring with her. And now, thanks to one member with a conscience, or perhaps just waking up from a nightmare, she could see the whole sect breaking apart before her eyes. The two leaders would go to prison—or a mental hospital—where they belonged. The rest of these people could get help.

But lurking below the surface, Eliza could almost hear Jacob's warning. Eliza had avoided getting sucked into the shootout with the FBI at the Zarahemla compound. She was one step removed from the mentality of the people who'd abandoned everything to follow a prophet into the desert.

He might have reminded Eliza that there was a common thread between a person who would willingly enter a pit and a junkie's need to fill his veins with heroin. But for the moment, she didn't allow these thoughts to rise to full consideration.

That would prove to be a deadly mistake.

CHAPTER TWENTY-THREE

David thought he'd defeated his enemy, but five miles outside of Blister Creek, the demon returned to the battlefield.

At first, he dismissed it as motion sickness. The road flattened out west of town, but Jacob was driving too fast for the buckled, ill-kept asphalt, and he took turns as if he were driving a race car. Outside the window, sagebrush crowded the road. Bugs hurled themselves against the windshield. The headlights caught a startled jackrabbit, which froze until the last minute before bounding into the dark. The moon cast the distant buttes into silhouette. Lightning still flashed over the Ghost Cliffs to their rear, but none of the sound reached the car.

Within another five minutes, it became clear that David wasn't fighting garden-variety motion sickness. A tremble took his left hand, and then he felt the need to kick his feet. His broken arm itched, and he wanted to break off the cast and scratch his skin until it bled. Finally, the veins on his feet began to burn. It felt like he'd walked barefoot through a bed of desert ants, the kind that form a mound, clear every twig or plant within ten feet, and attack any creature bold enough to step within the dead zone. He could feel them climbing his legs, biting.

You can't live without me. You need me. Don't fight it.

"No," he whispered.

Sister Miriam watched with brow furrowed, chewing on her lower lip. She sat in the back with him, while Jacob sat alone up front. "David, you can do this," she said in a quiet voice, meant only for his ears. She took his hand and squeezed. Her hand felt cool.

He opened his mouth to tell her he couldn't make it, that he was an addict who could never give it up, but she shook her head, as if anticipating his response. "Not anymore, you're not."

"Are you okay back there?" Jacob asked.

"We're fine," Miriam said. "Pay attention to the road."

If Jacob didn't see David's struggles, it was because he seemed to be wrestling with demons of his own. He was brooding, David initially believed, about what would await them outside of Las Vegas and why he couldn't reach Eliza on the cell phone. When they stopped for gas in St. George, he spent a few minutes poring over the MapQuest and Google Maps pages he'd printed before leaving the house. They'd narrowed the access point to the Chosen Ones' sanctuary to one of two dirt roads leaving the northwest edge of Las Vegas, near the abandoned subdivisions where David lived.

But when they set off again, Jacob started muttering to himself. Once, David caught something about Doubting Thomas. It sounded like self-recrimination.

"Jacob, you need to stop this," Miriam said.

He started. "Stop what?"

"You're eating yourself alive up there. Can't you let go of the doubt for one minute and admit what happened? The Lord gave you His power and He worked a miracle. Accept it, glory in it."

"If it was such a miracle, why is David going through withdrawal?"

He'd apparently been more alert to the struggles in the backseat than David had thought.

"So David isn't suddenly cured. Maybe that's not the way the Lord works. Maybe He strengthens us after we've done everything we can do. Your priesthood blessing stripped the heroin out of David's body. It gave him the tools to defeat this, made him strong enough to do it. But he still needs to make that final effort on his own."

"We'll see how strong he is soon enough, won't we?" Jacob stopped and seemed to realize what he'd said. "I'm sorry, David, I didn't mean that."

"Yes, you did," David said. "I can hardly blame you. I'm a junkie, why wouldn't you think that?"

"It was wrong to say it though. You know I want you back—I want you out of that destructive lifestyle, and I want you whole and healthy. I just have a hard time believing I had anything to do with what happened. It was you, me, Miriam, and Father, all throwing our wishful thinking into the ring, and we wanted it so badly, it became a self-fulfilling prophesy. At least in the short term."

"You can justify it away," Miriam said. "But it doesn't change the facts."

"See, I'm not sure we can agree on the facts," Jacob said.

"I think we can. David sat on that chair on your father's porch a hardcore drug addict."

"And I'm still a drug addict," David said.

She continued as if she hadn't heard him. "He was stoned. I didn't know what I was doing, and I gave him too much. He was barely conscious. Am I right?"

"That's true," David admitted. His brother said nothing.

"You put your hands on David's head and promptly lost your ability to speak. I've heard you give dozens of blessings and never seen you blank out like that. We could ask your wife, but I'll bet Fernie's never seen it happen before, either. It never has, has it?"

"A coincidence, bound to happen sooner or later."

"Maybe, except you have to add another coincidence that when you started to speak, you didn't just go back to the old, confident-sounding flowery style you use. The one that convinces everyone you're speaking for God, when it's just theatrics. Someone else was speaking through your mouth."

"Except that David isn't healed yet, is he? That's the flaw."

"Back to the facts. What happened after you gave your blessing?"

"Okay, fine. What happened?" Jacob asked. "I can't quite figure it out."

"You have an idea; let's hear it."

"I'm too much of a mess to engage in this conversation," David said, "but I like that you're using his own tactics against him."

"He seemed to make a temporary recovery," Jacob said. "The power of suggestion."

"You can't *suggest* heroin out of the bloodstream," Miriam said.

"Maybe he wasn't as drugged as we thought."

"Come on, that's the best you've got? You're like a drowning man, clawing for air."

At this point David lost track of the conversation. He turned in on himself to fight the pain and need tormenting his body.

Sometime later, he felt Miriam's hand on the back of his neck. "Lie down," she said. "It will help."

She unbuckled his seat belt and laid him down until his head was on her lap. Then she brushed her cool fingers against his face, ran them through his hair. A tiny spark penetrated the dense feeling of hopelessness.

He looked up and met her gaze. "You were so disgusted with me before. What happened? Why are you being so kind? I don't understand."

"More than one person's eyes were opened tonight, David."

* * *

"Oh, Christopher. What a disappointment you've been."

The man's face looked up from the pit, a shadow within a shadow. "Forgive me, Master."

"I can't forgive you," the Disciple said. "Only the one who is great and terrible can do that, and right now, He is displeased."

"I tried, I did what you asked, but the two girls overpowered me."

"Two naked, starving girls overpowered you? I find myself wondering about that."

"They weren't alone. They had Satan's help. Somehow, he helped them get out of the pit."

"I don't think so."

It was about an hour before dawn, and the first hint of gray had begun to erode the eastern horizon. It was almost time. The Disciple had driven to Las Vegas in silence. No radio, no conversation, just the sound of tires on the road and the voices in his head. He imagined Blister Creek burning, consuming his enemies, imagined Wormwood falling from the heavens. The earth would burn, the wicked consumed by God's wrath, screaming, skin melting from their faces. They would beg for mercy. Too late, they'd had their chance.

He thought about the boy in the shed, looking up at him as the Disciple locked the door. In his memory, it wasn't Diego who looked back, but a young Caleb Kimball. The boy who heard the voices at night, who suffered the torment of older brothers and a callous, indifferent father. A father with dozens of children, who sometimes struggled to remember each of their names. There was no place for them in the church. The oldest few brothers stood a chance, and the girls had value. But the younger boys? May as well lock every one of them in a shed and set it on fire. The adults would shake their heads in sorrow. All those boys burned to death. Wasn't that a terrible tragedy? But it was unavoidable. Boys will be boys.

You are wrong. That is how you became strong. That is how you became the Chosen of God. The one to call Wormwood from the sky to cleanse the earth with fire. You suffered and you learned and eventually it became your turn to rule.

Something quivered in his senses as he turned onto the old ranch road and the access to the abandoned dump. His tires crunched over the gravel, and he drove slower and slower until he came to a stop maybe a mile from the compound. He stepped out of the car, looked in the direction of the trailers, and frowned. Something had gone wrong. He wasn't sure what or how, but he could sense it.

Beware your enemies.

Christopher should have been on the road, waiting for him with one of the kerosene lanterns hissing in his hand. The man would be anxious to explain how he'd carried out the Disciple's commands, would be justifying the extra-zealous steps he'd taken to fulfill not just the exact words of command, but the true intent. This sometimes meant harsh measures. No doubt Christopher would have hurried through his tasks, eager to get to the part where he sanctified the pretty young woman from Blister Creek.

So where was he? Down in the pit, still working on Eliza?

As he approached the trailers, he expected to see the others gathered outside, waiting. The world was about to come to an end, and they would help him prepare for that moment. That was the instruction, that was the command. So where were they? Why were they inside with the lights on?

He started toward the door, ready to barge in and shake them with his wrath, to stiffen their courage. Yes, it was a hard thing they had to do, but that's why they'd been selected. They were the Chosen Ones. He was at the cinder block stairs when he stopped, listened. A woman was speaking inside. He didn't recognize the voice, but he recognized the tone and the accent.

"…important to remember…"

And then a male voice. The Disciple thought it might be Kirk, a weak young man, easily swayed. "I think we get the picture. It's just words, he'll just talk. He'll be alone, remember."

Her response was quieter, and the Disciple couldn't quite pick up her answer, but her strong, confident tone came through. It was the girl from Blister Creek. He'd made a mistake with Eliza, should have watched over her. Somehow, she'd talked someone into letting her out and was now poisoning them against him. A terrible, overpowering anger burned inside him, rising until he felt it straining at his eyeballs.

So where was Christopher, and why wasn't he standing up to her? That was his job, to enforce discipline while the Disciple was out looking for converts or on other missions from God. The only answer was that somehow Eliza had overpowered him. She must have had help. Madeline, and maybe Benita and Kirk. The weakest of the Chosen Ones. Had they killed Christopher? That seemed unlikely. Subdued him, then, perhaps. Where would they have put him? Probably had him tied up in the back room where the Disciple sanctified the girls.

The others had holed up in the center trailer. They were waiting for the Disciple to come, so they could subdue him, too. No doubt they expected him to stroll into their midst, be caught unaware.

It was then that he heard the faint sounds of shouting to his rear. He turned around, made his way back into the deeper darkness that surrounded the piles of tires and abandoned, fading appliances, the half-buried black plastic bags of garbage. The noise came from the purification pit beneath the fridge. He made his way through the piles of tires, smelled diesel where Christopher had poured it in and around the trash.

A moment later, he was looking down at the man's face in the blackness, fighting the disappointment and disgust at seeing how badly the other man had failed.

"It was Satan," Christopher insisted. "They never could have done it themselves."

"Today is the day of reckoning, Christopher. The day when the Lord lifts the Chosen Ones and thrusts the wicked into hell. So when I come back to find you in a pit, defeated by two girls, having disobeyed my simple instructions, where do you think I classify you?"

"I didn't disobey, I—"

"I'm not interested in excuses. I'm only interested in knowing whether you will obey me with exactitude. That when I tell you what to do, you will do it immediately, with no questions. Do you understand?"

"Yes, Master."

"And will you?"

"Yes, Master. I'll do anything you ask. Immediately, and without hesitation."

"Very good. Are you injured?"

"My elbow. It's broken, or maybe dislocated. So I don't have any use of my left arm."

The Disciple frowned. "Two girls did this? You're lucky they didn't kill you."

Still, Christopher appeared clear-headed, in spite of his injury. And dead to the pain.

"Please, Master, get me out of here. It won't happen again."

"It's odd," the Disciple said. "All this time and you've never once been purified. Others have gone down three, four times, sometimes for as long as a week. You haven't even eaten one head of lettuce."

"I can't stand it anymore. It's the stench; it's going to drive me crazy."

"Maybe it was God who put you down there. He saw my oversight and decided to put you in the pit to be purified. I wonder what would happen if Wormwood fell and you were still in the pit. Would the fire sweep over the earth and leave you alive down there? You've got a few dozen heads of lettuce and plenty of water. You might live on for several weeks."

"No, not that. I'd rather die."

"You might still do that, too," the Disciple said. "Only God knows what will happen this day."

"Please, forgive me. I was weak, I made a mistake. I'll do anything you want."

"Your path to repentance will be difficult. You must obey me exactly."

"I'll do anything!"

The Disciple looked around for a way to get the man out of the pit and stumbled over the ladder. He tried to imagine how they'd lured Christopher to the pit with the ladder, then somehow broken his arm, climbed out, and fished the ladder out before the man could challenge them. What a fool.

That is why they obey you. God chose the humble and malleable as your followers.

Yes, well, humble and malleable was one thing, but gullible was another. Or maybe Christopher, in his weakness, had gone down into the pit to sanctify Eliza down there and then been overpowered. But by two naked, starving girls? It was hard to imagine.

The Disciple lowered the ladder. Moments later, Christopher appeared, climbing with his good hand. His other arm dangled by his side, and when he reached the top, the Disciple reached down, grabbed him by the waist of his pants, and hauled him onto the ground.

Christopher lay panting for a moment, then rolled over and sat up. "You're strong."

"Of course I'm strong. I have the power of God within me. And because you're with me, God will strengthen you, too. He will deliver the wicked into our hands. And then they will burn."

"Yes, Master. They will all burn."

The Disciple helped the other man to his feet. "Now, listen carefully. Eliza has poisoned their minds, and we have to imagine they are turned against us. We have to show that God is in charge, not this girl."

The Disciple bent and felt along the edge of the pile of garbage and tires behind the overturned fridge. His fingers closed around a piece of metal not much bigger around than his thumb. He dug it out of the garbage and discovered it was a piece of rebar, rough and slightly bent, maybe thirty inches long. He handed it to Christopher. "A rod, with which thou may correct thine enemies."

Christopher hefted it in his good hand. "Good enough. What do you want me to do?"

"As soon as they come out, I expect Eliza to argue with me. When the moment is ready, I'll say, 'Justice is mine, sayeth the Lord.' At that moment, you will attack. Strike her in the face first, then, when she is down, keep hitting her in the head until she stops moving. It will be messy, it will be terrible. Can you do it?"

"Of course I can, Master. But what about the others?"

"I shall command them while you fulfill God's justice. None of them will lift a finger. And when she is dead, they shall all follow us. We shall call Wormwood to the earth. Now hurry, dawn is almost here."

CHAPTER TWENTY-FOUR

The voice outside the trailer was like one of the trumpets of Revelation, loud and brassy in the thin desert air. "The Great and Dreadful Day of the Lord is at hand! Come and let us separate the wicked from the righteous."

Inside the trailer, all conversation stopped at once. People who had been arguing moments earlier stopped with mouths agape or hands raised in mid gesture. Eliza started at the sound, but as she glanced around the room, she could see stunned expressions on the faces of the others, glassy, terrified looks, as if they had just been shown a photograph of the exact moment of their death. It was that look of shared insanity that scared Eliza, not the braying of the self-proclaimed prophet outside.

The argument had raged through the trailer for the past two or three hours. Eliza was content to let Madeline and Kirk carry her side, that they should wait until dawn and then, if the Disciple hadn't returned with the truck, gather water and walk out of the desert. These two, plus two others, reminded her of sleepwalkers, awakened from a nightmare, opening one door after another until they finally emerged from the dream. As they rubbed sleep from their eyes, they grew more and more alert until at last they realized just what had been done to them.

Others had remained locked in their nightmares. They defended the Disciple and shouted angrily whenever Madeline or Kirk suggested that the Disciple's rants about the end of the world were pure fantasy. They grew even more angry when Eliza said, at one point, "Let's call it what it is. The Disciple didn't *sanctify* anyone. He raped them."

A woman screamed, threw her shoe at Eliza, and tried to storm out of the trailer. Kirk stopped her, ordered her to sit back down.

Eliza remembered the chilling story of a thirteen-year-old girl who'd been abducted from her home in Boise to be forced into polygamy by her kidnapper. The girl had several chances to escape, and when she was in a mall, alone, about eighteen months later, an alert security guard had recognized her and asked her point blank if she was the missing girl he'd seen on TV. She'd denied it, and when the guard tried to stop her, she'd run. They'd eventually found the girl, but Eliza and Jacob had argued about why the girl hadn't tried to escape. Had she come to believe the brainwashing? Was she just frozen in terror?

Some of these people reminded her of the kidnapped girl. Were they blind? Couldn't they see what the Disciple had done to them? But by the time he returned, these supporters had either come reluctantly to their side or fallen silent. The last few holdouts sat in the corners, wrapping their arms around their knees and listening with sullen expressions on their faces.

And now Caleb Kimball was outside, shouting. "Come out, one and all. Face the judgment of the Lord!"

Benita sprang to her feet. Eliza grabbed for her hand but didn't get her before she reached the door. Kirk was closer and could have stopped her, but he looked as stunned as anyone else. By the time he moved, it was too late, and Benita was throwing the door open. Others followed.

"Wait!" Eliza said. "Not yet, we need to—"

But nobody was listening. They spilled out of the trailer and down the cinder block stairs. Eliza rushed to the door and looked out after them. The Disciple stood in front of the trailer, his robe open and revealing his bare chest, his eyes wild, arms outstretched. Behind him, the horizon glowed with the fire of a coming dawn. Christopher stood to one side. A dark expression clouded his face. There was a gash on one cheek, and he tucked in his left arm, which bent the wrong way at the elbow.

The people pouring out of the trailer dropped to their knees in front of the Disciple, or grabbed his robes or hands. One of the last holdouts from inside buried her face in his robes and wept. A young man begged for forgiveness.

"Stop, all of you!" Eliza cried as she came down after them.

Madeline and Kirk stopped a few feet away from the Disciple, visibly torn between following the others and the arguments of the past few hours. Eliza grabbed their arms and they turned, and she could see them shake off whatever strange compulsion had taken hold of them.

The Disciple lifted his arms. "Wormwood is falling from the sky. Before the sun rises this day the burning shall come. The wicked shall perish. But you! You are the Chosen Ones. Those who stand by my side shall survive to see the coming of the Lord."

"Listen to me, all of you," Eliza said. "It's a trick—it's just a voice and flowery biblical crap." A few faces turned toward her. "The world isn't going to end today. If you want, you can stay here and find out. The rest of us are going into Las Vegas. Now who else is coming with me?"

A smile lifted the Disciple's face, and he said, "Justice is mine, sayeth the Lord." Christopher stepped forward. The dark expression had become something twisted and evil. "Do it now," the Disciple said in a low voice. "Cleanse Eliza Christianson from the earth."

He lifted his right arm, and now she saw that it carried a length of rebar. She'd been distracted by his broken arm and the rants of the Disciple. He stepped toward her with the rebar pulled back like a club. By the time she saw him coming, it was too late to react, only to lift her hands against the blow.

Kirk stepped between them, grabbing for his arm. "No! Not like this."

Christopher swung the rebar at Kirk's arm and connected. The other man cried out and fell back, clutching at his arm. Christopher pulled back and swung again, this time at Kirk's head.

Eliza regained her senses before the second blow fell. She lowered her shoulder and rammed it into Christopher to knock him off balance, but didn't make it in time. The rebar slammed into the side of Kirk's head, just above the ear. He fell face down. Eliza knocked into Christopher. He snarled and turned on her.

As he pulled back the rebar, she grabbed with both hands for his bad arm. She seized him by the wrist and wrenched his arm around. Christopher screamed and flipped himself over to escape the pain, moving as easily as if he were a puppet in her hands. He fell to the ground next to Kirk. The first young man didn't move, but lay facedown and limp.

Before Christopher could recover, she bent and wrenched the rebar free from his hands.

"Someone, grab her," the Disciple said. He was trying to push through the people crowding him, but they weren't moving quickly enough.

She waved the rebar in front of her. "Nobody touch me!"

The Disciple was at the point of freeing himself, and Christopher rolled over and struggled to his feet. Eliza dropped the rebar, grabbed Madeline, and ran. To her surprise, Benita came with them, while the others watched in a stupor.

Eliza was disoriented by the still-dim light of early morning, by the violence of the last few moments, by the way Kirk lay face-down, by the force with which the rebar had struck him on the side of the head. That blow had caved in the man's head. It had been meant for her. If Kirk hadn't stepped in front, Christopher would have bludgeoned her to death.

In her confusion, she ran the wrong direction. Instead of flee-ing toward the road, she found herself farther back in the dump, ducking between piles of tires. By the time she realized her mistake, she was turned about, with mounds of tires all around her. She wished she hadn't dropped the rebar.

"Where are you going?" Madeline asked.

"I was trying to go toward the road."

"It's that way," Benita said.

"I know that now." She'd spotted the horizon and reoriented herself. "You should have said something."

"I thought you knew what you were doing," Madeline said.

The three women squatted behind a pile of tires, panting, trying to catch their breath. From the direction of the trailers came shouts, a man screaming. More shouting, a woman screaming this time. A crack, like a two-by-four snapping in two. Eliza's stomach clenched. The Disciple was violently reasserting his control of the cult; more people were suffering because she'd convinced them to resist.

"Eliza?" Madeline asked. "What are we doing?"

"Hold on, I'm trying to think. I don't know that we'd be any better off on the road, not unless Caleb left the key in the truck, and I don't think he'd be that dumb."

"Caleb?"

"The Disciple. If we ran down the road, they could hunt us down in the truck. And it's so flat, that even if we got off the road, they could see us, at least until we got to the dry wash. They'll have water, and they'll catch up with us before long. We might be better off here."

"It wouldn't matter," Benita said in a flat voice. "There's no escape either direction."

"We're not finished yet."

"Yes, we're finished. We've made our choice, and now we'll be burned with the wicked."

Eliza took Benita's face in her hands. She had no time to be gentle. "Listen to me. Either wake up from your coma and do something to keep yourself alive, or go back there and take your chances with the sheep. What's it going to be?" Benita said nothing, and Eliza continued, "Good. Now, we're not going to let them win, right? If anyone dies, it's not going to be us. I don't care if we're three girls. Caleb Kimball—I'm not going to call him the Disciple again, because he's not a disciple of anything, he's a nutcase, that's all—he isn't going to lift a finger. He's going to stand back and order his minions to do the dirty work. But they're weak in the mind, they showed that just now. They can't do anything."

She had to dismiss the others, she had to make Madeline and Benita strong enough to stand up for themselves. Whether it was true or not, she needed these two to believe it.

"What about Christopher?" Madeline asked.

"He's one man. He's *half* a man. You saw his broken arm. I gave it one pull and he was on his knees, crying like a baby."

"You caught him by surprise," Madeline said. "You can't count on that again."

"So what? He still only has one good arm. We're three people. If he tries to stop us, we'll come at him from three sides. Now let's look around for something to defend ourselves with. We're going to arm ourselves, and then we're going to walk out of here with our heads held high."

Again, Eliza wished she could trust her own words, could trust these two to be strong in a fight. Madeline was starved from her time in the pit; Benita was stronger physically, but weaker mentally. When it came down to it, if Christopher attacked again, they might be no more than a distraction.

They groped around the edge of the pile of tires. Eliza's hands found nothing useful: torn bags of garbage, rusting cans, a doll missing its arms, what may have once been a sack of dirty diapers but had dried into hard plastic lumps in the sun. She was about to suggest they continue further into the dump to look for a more fertile pile of garbage, when she stopped.

The shouting had stopped from the direction of the trailer. She strained to hear any voice or movement, but all she heard was the sigh of a light breeze. There was something in the air, an acrid smell.

The other two women had stopped as well, and then Benita whispered, "It's Wormwood. It is about to fall from the sky."

"What are you talking about?"

"When the third angel sounds his trumpet, a great star will fall from the heavens and—"

"I know the Book of Revelation," Eliza interrupted. "That's not what I mean."

She caught a stronger whiff. Like diesel fuel and burning rubber. Whatever it was, there was no star falling, even though she caught herself checking the sky, half expecting to see a meteor streaking across the heavens. It was something from the dump itself, someone burning something nasty. She could taste it in her mouth when she breathed.

"Eliza Christianson," a voice cried out. Caleb Kimball. He sounded maybe twenty yards away, among the piles of tires to her left.

She pulled the others down, made a quieting motion. Benita's eyes widened in terror, and her fingernails traced the scars on her left forearm. Madeline grabbed her wrist and squeezed, shaking her head. Benita closed her eyes and nodded.

"I know you're in there," Caleb yelled. "I'm not going to pretend to forgive you, say that if you give up, everything will be okay. You are beyond forgiveness—now there's only justice and the burning of the wicked. But God says the other two can go free. Send them to me, and I will bless them and send them to wait with the other Chosen Ones."

"He's lying," Eliza said. "Christopher is with him and he'll kill us all."

"You said Christopher would be alone," Madeline whispered. "You didn't say we'd have to face the Disciple."

"Caleb Kimball is only a voice. Remember what I said about Christopher. Grab his arm and yank like you're trying to pull it off."

"We need weapons."

"Come on. This way."

She urged the other two to their feet, and they made to run at a crouch toward the next pile of tires to their rear. Eliza planned to get around back and search again for a weapon of some kind. But just as they moved, the Disciple stepped around the pile and they froze.

To Eliza's surprise, Caleb Kimball stood alone, without any other Chosen Ones, or even Christopher. Soot smudged his forehead, and the back of one of his hands had a red burn. The sky was brightening quickly now; the morning light caught and amplified the wild gleam in his eyes. He held the rebar in his hands, and Eliza could see bits of hair and blood clinging to the edges, where it had crushed Kirk's skull and perhaps someone else's as well.

He saw her looking at the rebar and grinned. "And now, Eliza, it is your turn to die."

CHAPTER TWENTY-FIVE

As the sun rose over the Spring Mountains, David saw a black column of smoke curling into the sky northwest of Las Vegas. Jacob took the car at a bone-rattling pace over the road, seeming to catch every rut, pothole, and patch of drifting sand. A pair of tumbleweeds had snagged against the bumper when they found the ranch road fifteen minutes ago, and these clung to the bumper, pieces occasionally breaking off and flying over the windshield. He kept having to spray and wipe to clear away the film of dirt.

David and Miriam studied the map pages as best they could from their jarring place in the backseat. David had to stop and close his eyes every few minutes to fight against the nausea. Hard to tell if it was the withdrawal or motion sickness, or some combination of the two.

The road started to curve away from the smoke, and Jacob asked in a worried tone, "Are you sure this is the right road?"

"It has to be," David said. He squinted through the window in the direction of the rising sun to try to find the edge of the ghost subdivision where he lived. He thought he could pick out the pink stucco of an abandoned McMansion at the edge of his cul-de-sac.

A few minutes later, they cut across the dry wash and he was sure. Miriam told Jacob to stop the car, jumped out, and inspected the sand in the wash before they continued. "Footprints," she said. "They go back toward the city, then end here. This has to be it." Sure enough, the road cut left again, and soon they were clattering directly toward the growing pillar of smoke.

The smoke had become something biblical. It was a column that twisted and curved into the sky, like the burning of Gomorrah. Curls of fire climbed the column like the fiery hands of the damned trying to claw their way out of hell. The acrid smell of burning rubber came in through the air-conditioning. David lifted his shirt to cover his mouth and nose.

The fire would be visible from the city; no doubt someone had already noticed and called it in. But how long would it take fire trucks to come out here from the city, or even a helicopter to lift off and fly over to investigate? By then it would be too late.

"I think we've found our firebug," Miriam said in a low voice.

"Either that, or the end of the world," David said.

"It might be the end of somebody's world," Jacob said.

His hands gripped the steering wheel, and his face was grim. David was worried enough about Eliza—he could only imagine what Jacob was thinking. No doubt blaming himself, for a start. How had he been fooled into thinking Eliza could handle these nutcases on her own? Their sister had matured into a young woman with confidence, strength, and intelligence. A beautiful young woman, too. In fact, she might have a brighter future than Jacob if she could find her way in the wider world outside of Blister Creek and Zarahemla. She didn't seem to be wracked with the same self-doubts that troubled Jacob.

But still. David had a cast and bruised ribs to remind him of the attack outside his house. He could see their grim expressions, remembered the chilling silence as they'd kicked him half to death. If Jacob had seen the attack, would he have let Eliza go?

They came upon the compound, a double-wide and two silver teardrop trailers. It was a filthy place, surrounded by the refuse of an illegal dump in the desert: wrecked and rusting cars, appliances, old mattresses, hundreds of empty water bottles, old clothing. And piles of tires everywhere. They covered the roofs of the trailers and lay stacked in and around the compound.

The fire came from two of the largest tire mounds, side by side and each at least ten feet tall and twenty, maybe thirty feet across. The flames met in the middle and became a single roaring column, the pillar of fire and smoke that had guided them to the compound. A dozen young men and women stood in front of the trailers, watching the tires burn. They were close enough they had to feel the heat roiling off the fire, had to be choking on the fumes. Even in the car, enough came through the air-conditioning system to coat David's mouth with the oily, bitter taste of burning rubber. The car pulled to a stop, but few turned to look their way. The rest seemed mesmerized by the fire.

"And you sent her here?" David muttered. But the words sounded hollow in his ears.

You did it, too. You knew what they were capable of, and you let Eliza follow them into the desert.

Right, because anyone could stop Eliza, once she'd set her mind to something. As he stared at that twisting column of smoke and fire, it was the only thing that gave him hope. They wouldn't take her without a hell of a fight.

* * *

Eliza stared at the Disciple with cold fury. "You're only one person. There are three of us." She gave a sharp look to the others. "If he comes at us, we charge him. Together. Go for his eyes. Bite, kick. Whoever gets that metal bar, hit him until he doesn't move again."

He smiled. "You're wrong, Eliza. You're only *one* person. These two aren't with you. I'll show you. Benita!"

"Leave her alone!"

"The time has come," he said. "Go join the others."

Benita stiffened. Eliza grabbed her wrist. "Don't listen to him."

"I speak for God! Do not deny it or you will burn in hell this very day. Look! The fire is here. Wormwood is falling from the heavens. Find the others. Join them now. Do not stay with the wicked while the Lord cleanses the earth."

Benita made to leave, and Eliza wrestled with her arm. The woman's face was a mask, slack and dead. Eliza read despair and self-loathing in her eyes. It was the same thing she'd heard in Madeline's voice in the pit.

"Don't listen to him, please, wait. Madeline, help me." The other woman stood frozen while Eliza struggled to hold Benita.

"And you!" the Disciple roared. "Madeline Caliari, you have been weak, but there is still time. Time to obey God, to stand with the Chosen Ones. If not, you shall surely be destroyed. The fires of hell shall burn you for time and all eternity. Go, quickly!"

And now it was Madeline who was abandoning Eliza. She stiffened, just like Benita had. Eliza let go of Benita and grabbed Madeline instead. "Don't do this."

Benita walked away past the Disciple, who watched her go with a look of grim satisfaction. He didn't look happy, not really. Did a man like that ever enjoy happiness, even of the fleeting variety? It was a look of confirmation, of a man so immersed in his own righteousness that he permitted himself a small moment to see his belief confirmed.

Madeline hesitated. She stared after her friend, who had disappeared toward the fire raging a few dozen yards away. The air shimmered with heat. It had to be a hundred degrees here already, and with every step, she had to feel the power of the flames, an insatiable hunger to devour anything in its way.

"He's not a prophet, he's a madman. Madeline, you're strong, remember. You got out of the pit, you beat Christopher."

"You can't stop her," the Disciple said. "You're nothing, you're nobody. So you've got a few twisted words and a way of sowing doubt, but you're still just a girl. Madeline!" His voice was blunt and hard, like a hammer. "Go, hurry."

A shudder worked its way through Madeline's body. She looked again toward the fire, which consumed the east side of the dump and had spread to another pile of tires. It roared like a desert sandstorm. Flaming pieces of paper climbed the column of smoke, and ash and cinders dusted down on their heads. It looked as though a crack had split in the skin of the world and the very fires of hell forced themselves to the surface as the infernal realm worked to devour the earth. Eliza couldn't shake these thoughts from her mind, even as she knew that Caleb Kimball was responsible for the fire. What was he doing?

She tightened her grip on Madeline's arm, but the other woman shook free. Grim satisfaction spread again across the Disciple's face. "You see. You're done, you're alone."

"No," Madeline said. It was only a whisper, but a moment later, it came out stronger. "No, she's not."

"Madeline," the Disciple said, his tone sharp.

Madeline suddenly screamed. "Shut up! Get out of my head. You're nothing, you're not a prophet, or a man of God. You're a monster, a twisted, horrible thing, and I should have never listened to you, and when you took me into the back room and made the others watch, I should have taken a knife and shoved it through your throat. There's nothing wrong with me, I'm not a wicked sinner, I don't need to be purified or sanctified—the only mistake I made was listening to you. Do you hear me, you're nothing, *nothing!*"

"If that's the way it will be," the Disciple said, "then so be it. May Satan consume your souls."

He came at them suddenly, the rebar pulled back over his shoulder to swing.

*　*　*

David, Jacob, and Miriam tumbled out of the car and headed toward the trailers. David wished he had Jacob's calm, purposeful stride, or the way that Miriam carried herself as if she were still an FBI agent, the prairie dress belying the catlike way she moved, the gun that appeared in her hand. Inside, he wondered, did their hearts pound and their knees shake in fear? Or was he the only coward in the group?

The people watching the fire started to file toward the larger trailer. A few of them turned as the newcomers approached, and David recognized faces from the attack outside his house. The faces that had encircled him in silence, while boots laid into his face, ribs, and head.

One of them was the man he'd come across spilling out of the back of the co-op truck. He'd given some silent signal to the others, and they'd attacked at once. He stood between David, Jacob, and Miriam and the rest of the group. One arm dangled by his side, and burns stained his forehead and one cheek, as if he'd splashed himself with cooking oil. Two young men lay at his feet, facedown in the dirt, and a young woman sprawled a few feet away, neck twisted at a strange angle. Her face was such a gruesome mess that David had to look away before he got sick.

The man with the injured arm held something in his good hand, but it was hard to pick out through the swirling black smoke that poured off the tire fires to their left. Heat cooked the desert air around them.

David looked through the crowd and stopped. *Benita.* She met his gaze, and his heart raced at the unexpected contact.

What he saw in her eyes terrified him. It was the look she'd had on the roof of the residential tower that night they'd slipped away from the party. They'd overlooked the glitter of the Strip, and she'd climbed to the edge and leaned over, her eyes a dazed, nihilistic stare like the one she wore now. *Drop me,* that look said. *Let go of my waist and watch me fly.*

"Benita, please. It's me, David. Whatever you're doing, stop. Come with me, we'll talk it out."

"Don't come any closer," she said.

"Benita, no."

But as he tried to get closer, the man with the injured arm stepped between them, and it was too late anyway—she was climbing the cinder block steps and entering the trailer to join the others. The door closed.

As soon as it was shut, the remaining man gave a glance further into the dump and a frown crossed his face, as if he'd expected one more person. He lifted his good hand, and David saw that he held a butane lighter with a long tip. He bent to touch it to the base of one of the tire piles stacked outside the door of the trailer. David, Jacob, and Miriam started toward the trailer, but before they could cross the fifteen or twenty feet, the tires burst into flame, so quickly they must have been doused in lighter fluid or gasoline.

The man squared his body to block their path. Already, the fire was spreading along the tires that surrounded the trailer, although the building itself hadn't yet caught. "You'll have to get past me, first," the man said. "There are three of you and I'm injured, but I'll put up a fight. It will be too late."

"I'm sorry," Miriam said. "We don't have time for that." She lifted her gun. "Move or die."

"And you're going to shoot an unarmed man? I don't think so." He smiled. "The problem with threats is you have to be prepared to carry them out, and not just bluff. I can see on your face that you're bluffing."

"Boy, are you a bad judge of character," Miriam said. Her gun barked twice in succession, and the man fell backward, good hand flying to his chest. A look of surprise crossed his face, even as the blood burbled out of his mouth.

David gaped. Beside him, Jacob started toward the man, rolling up his sleeves, as if forced by his medical training to intervene. Miriam grabbed his arm, and he looked up at her, blinked, and then he was in control again. He nodded and looked away with a grim expression. Already, David could see the light fading in the dying man's eyes as his spirit slipped from his body, speeding toward its eternal reward. Or punishment.

"Don't just stand there like a pair of idiots," Miriam told them. "Eliza might be in there. You have to get them out." She turned to cover the dump with her gun, while Jacob and David ran toward the burning trailer.

CHAPTER TWENTY-SIX

The Disciple swung the iron bar. The women stood side by side, Eliza still holding Madeline's wrist. Eliza ducked backward and pulled Madeline, who didn't move as quickly. The bar struck her a glancing blow across the side of her head, and she fell with a cry.

The momentum of the swing and the partial miss turned the Disciple at an awkward angle, and Eliza rushed forward and shoved him. He stumbled backward, but didn't lose his balance. He brought the rebar around again, like a backhand in tennis. Eliza tried to jump back a second time, and he didn't have as much force to the swing, but it hit her on the shoulder. She fell.

He came at her again. Madeline lay on the ground, moaning and clutching the side of her head. Eliza scrambled away on all fours, and when he was over her, ready to swing down, she gave him a mule kick with her right leg and he fell back. She turned and grabbed him around the legs while he was still unbalanced. The two of them tumbled to the ground. He wore a surprised expression, like he hadn't expected her to fight back. The rebar flew out of his hands and landed to one side.

Eliza only had the advantage for an instant. He recovered quickly and flipped her onto her back. He was too strong. He held her with one arm and got the other one free, then slammed his fist into her temple. Pain exploded in her head.

"Madeline!" she cried.

The other woman had rolled over. A trickle of blood ran down the side of her face, but she hadn't caught the same kind of blow that had killed Kirk in front of the trailer. She looked up, blinking, and crawled toward Eliza and the Disciple.

Eliza fought for her life. He beat her about the face, and some of the blows landed. She got her knee up into his groin, then a forearm across his throat, and for a moment, she pulled free, tried to crawl away. He dragged her back down.

Madeline reached Eliza and handed her something heavy. It felt solid in Eliza's fist. She brought it around with a cry. It crushed him in the nose, and he fell back with blood spurting from his face.

Eliza tried to get to her feet, but she felt shaky and sick. Her head ached, and she was bleeding from her ear. She looked down at the object in her hand. It was a piece of concrete the size of her fist, a jagged, aged chunk, like something torn up from an old patio before being dumped in the desert.

The air was so thick with smoke that she had a hard time catching her breath. Her eyes watered. A wave of black smoke rolled down over the Disciple, and he coughed as he rose to his feet. He groped around on the ground and found the rebar.

"Caleb Kimball!" she shouted. "In the name of the Lord, I command thee to stop."

He drew back. A moment of confusion crossed his face. "No, you can't. You don't—"

"I do." She regained her feet, kept the block of concrete in her hand. "The Lord sent me to bring you back to Blister Creek."

One hand gripped the rebar and the other went to his nose, now streaming blood. He looked down at his hand, and then anger flashed over his face and he met her gaze. "You liar."

"Did you know I killed your brother?"

"What?"

"Gideon Kimball. The Lord told me to kill him."

"What? That was you?"

"He dragged me into Witch's Warts, was going to make me his wife. The Lord spoke to me then, Caleb. You know that, don't you? And do you know what He said?"

"What did He say?"

Eliza said, "'I have marked Gideon Kimball for destruction. Kill him now.' And so I did. I took a piece of sandstone and I crushed his skull. And you know why He told me to come to Las Vegas and find you? Because you have been marked for destruction, too."

And with this, she charged him. He brought the rebar up, but too late. Her words had stunned him, made him doubt just long enough to get under his defenses. She hit him on the side of the head with the concrete. The blow landed hard enough to break off a corner. He went down.

The Disciple looked up in fear and confusion as she came down for another blow. He was done, she could see it in his eyes. It was almost certain that if she spoke with that commanding voice again, he would cower and tell her to go, he wouldn't bother her again. But Eliza was injured, Madeline, too, and somewhere out there were Christopher and the others. She couldn't take the chance that he would regain his senses and order the other Chosen Ones to hunt her down.

Eliza hit him again. And then again. She kept swinging until it was over.

* * *

Eliza pushed through the smoke and the air so hot it felt like it could burn her flesh. She held Madeline's hand, and the two of them ran with shirts over their mouths and coughing. They came to the trailers, now burning, surrounded by tires, also shooting up flames.

"Stop!" a voice shouted.

It was Sister Miriam, gun in hand. As she recognized the figures, she lowered the gun. "It's you, thank heavens. Jacob! It's Eliza!"

Jacob and David were at the trailer door, trying to pry it open, and they turned with a look of naked relief. She realized they'd thought she was inside, ready to burn to death.

"Where are the others?" she shouted.

"Inside," David said. "We can't get them out!"

The people in the trailer didn't have long, maybe seconds, before it would be too late. The entire east side of the double-wide burned, and one of the smaller trailers had just caught fire, as well. The heat from the surrounding blaze was intense, and even here in the clearing, the smoke was so thick that all five of them coughed and struggled for breath.

Dead bodies lay on the ground. Kirk, his head bashed in, another man and a woman, and finally, Christopher. Blood still trickled from his mouth and flowed from his chest to the ground.

David and Jacob tried to kick in the door, but without success. Jacob leaned his shoulder in and rammed at the doorframe. It held.

"Benita!" David cried. "You don't have to do this. Open the door."

A face appeared at the window, parting the blinds. It was Benita, staring out at them, while the fire licked around the window frame. Her face was blank, like someone already dead.

Madeline let out a cry and ran from Eliza's side to the door. She grabbed it and twisted in vain at the knob, as if she could somehow pry it open where David and Jacob had failed. She banged on the door with the flat of her hand, crying for her friend to open up. And still the face stayed at the window.

Eliza came up to Miriam. "Can you shoot out the lock?"

"I tried that already; it's no good. They've got it latched up top and slid something in front."

Eliza remembered the bars installed on the trailer door. She'd wondered why they'd tried to fortify the trailer and now realized why. It was designed as much to keep people in, keep them from panicking when they saw the fires and trying to escape, as to keep people out.

"There's no one else behind me," Eliza said. "Nobody alive. Put the gun away, let's help."

By the time they reached the door, the fire consumed the front of the trailer. Benita stood at the window watching through the bars, coughing, arm lifted to her mouth. Fire reflected off her face.

Madeline's face was a mask of terror as she and David pounded on the door, begging Benita to open it.

Life itself is too painful to bear, Madeline had said. *Sometimes, suffering feels like an escape.*

Benita was ready to leave that pain behind. They'd entered the trailer willingly, knowing they would be burned alive, convinced the fire would cleanse their sins and carry them to a tranquil place where there would be no more suffering.

The fire forced them back one by one, first Miriam and Eliza, then Jacob, with a fist slammed against the door and a final cry of desperation. He grabbed David and pulled him back. His brother struggled. Finally, they grabbed Madeline and pulled her away.

Burning tires spilled from the roof. One of the mountains of tires behind them started to break apart. A helicopter thumped overhead, but the smoke was too thick to see it. The smoke was choking now and the heat so intense it felt like Eliza's shirt would catch fire. The need to escape the heat and smoke overwhelmed everything else.

"We've got to go," Jacob cried. "Now, before it's too late."

Part of the roof of the trailer collapsed, and then Eliza heard a horrible new sound over the roaring fire. Screams. The sound was like an animal, screaming in pain and terror, a rising, wailing shriek. For those inside the trailer, Wormwood had fallen.

* * *

Jacob led them through the smoke. Eliza's eyes were a mass of stinging tears and her lungs burned. A foul, chemical taste filled her mouth. She let her feet carry her numbly away from the spreading fire. The screams continued at her back. At last, they were safely away from the fire and could no longer hear the cries of the dying over the roar of the fire. They spent a few moments bent over, coughing, spitting the bitter taste from their mouths.

"Eliza," Jacob said. "Where are you hurt?"

She looked down and saw what a mess she was. "Most of it is someone else's blood. He's dead now."

"We have to get out of here," Jacob said. A defeated tone clouded his voice. "We did what we could—now we have to keep from getting tangled up in all this."

The helicopter circled around the fire to the east. How long before police and fire trucks found their way down the old road to the illegal dump? It was early morning and news would just be reaching the authorities, but they clearly didn't have much time.

"They'll figure out what happened," Miriam said. "Some of those bodies were in the clearing; they won't be totally consumed. You can't burn away the evidence so easily."

Madeline said, "There are other Chosen Ones, some who were in the city and survived. They know the Disciple was planning for the end of the world. Nobody will come looking for you."

"Only if we get out of here," Jacob said. "We can't do anything more. We got who we came for, that's what matters."

Eliza could tell by his anguished tone that he didn't mean it. He wanted to win—Jacob needed a complete victory, and both as a doctor and a human being, he would probably torment himself about the people who had died, who might have been saved if things had gone differently. And maybe if Jacob had come instead of Eliza, that would have happened. But she didn't think so. She guessed they'd all be dead, anyway. And Madeline, too.

The fire continued to spread through the dump. There had to be fifty thousand tires here, if not a hundred, and Eliza had seen a tire fire in Alberta, knew how hard they were to extinguish.

Jacob led them toward the car. They squeezed into the vehicle, and Jacob tore down the dirt road, hammering at every pothole. Eliza sat in front with Jacob, turning occasionally to study his grim expression or glance over her shoulder at the fires of hell raging at their backs. Gradually, the air cleared.

But Eliza couldn't get the stench out of her mouth. It would stay there through the long drive back to Blister Creek, and later, when she stood under the shower, scrubbing her body with soap until it ached, she could still smell it in her hair and skin, still taste it even after she'd brushed her teeth three times. She heard the screams and the awful cracking of the chunk of concrete against the bones in Caleb Kimball's face.

Only after she threw up twice in the shower, then came out, cleaner but drained and shaken, did she start to feel better. Jacob found her later the next evening, sitting on a bench on the porch, listening to crickets in the night air. She cried in his arms as she shared the horror of her ordeals, while he told her how proud he was of what she'd done.

When she finished crying, she was strong again.

CHAPTER TWENTY-SEVEN

Jacob had underestimated law enforcement. He'd seen so many cases where people had pulled off crimes while the authorities remained oblivious, that it had been a shock the first time he'd realized that law enforcement was not a single, monolithic entity, but a collection of thousands of individuals with varying intelligence, organization, and resources. He got a reminder of that lesson when they found him in Blister Creek less than twenty-four hours after the escape from the burning cult compound.

Sitting on his father's porch, debriefing Eliza about the horrors she'd survived, he'd felt a cold lump settle into his stomach when the black Lincoln Town Car pulled up to the curb. Eliza glanced at Jacob, then went into the house to warn the others.

Jacob rose. The driver was a woman, the passenger a huge, muscular man. Both wore dark suits. They carried themselves with confidence, but moved with a certain wariness as they studied their surroundings from behind sunglasses. Jacob felt a surge of relief. FBI agents Krantz and Fayer.

It wouldn't be accurate to say they were friends. They'd worked together to uproot the conspiracy at the heart of Zarahemla, but the agents had disappeared once the investigation concluded. Just as well; Jacob had plenty of work, and he didn't need the distraction. But during the investigation, they'd come to rely on and even trust each other. He wondered if that would hold up now.

Agent Fayer came up the porch first and held out her hand. "Jacob, you look well."

He took her hand. "Thank you. You too."

"I've never been here. The red cliffs are stunning. No wonder nobody wants to leave."

"Thank you. You're in…well, a good mood."

"Not so hostile, you mean?" Krantz said in his distinctive rumble, shaking Jacob's hand as well.

Fayer smiled. "I've undergone sensitivity training. Glad to hear it's had some effect. I'm going for the kinder, gentler approach these days."

Krantz snorted. "Kinder and gentler? Two weeks ago some slimeball tried to cop a feel and Fayer gave him a knee to the groin. I think one of his testicles actually popped out his left nostril."

Jacob laughed, as much in relief as at the joke. Their demeanor was friendly, and some of his worry evaporated.

Eliza returned to the porch, and Agent Krantz stood a little straighter. "Hello, Eliza. How are you?"

She beamed. "I'm fine, how about you?"

"Doing great."

"How are those coffin nails?"

"Uhm, still working on that." He looked sheepish. "But only eight cigarettes so far this month. My goal for next month is five. After that...well, we'll see."

"Give me a call when you've smoked your last and we'll celebrate." She touched a hand to his arm. "Good to see you, Steve."

Jacob raised an eyebrow. *Steve?* He was not surprised to see that Krantz still had his eye on Eliza, but Jacob hadn't expected that goofy expression on his sister's face. Good thing Father wasn't out here, or Abraham Christianson might find himself under charges for assaulting an officer of the law.

Agent Krantz turned to Jacob after they'd finished pleasantries and taken seats on the veranda with a pitcher of lemonade and the overhead fans turned on. "As big of a mess as Zarahemla turned out to be, someone decided we weren't screw-ups after all. We've been assigned to a special cult investigation team."

"Is that a promotion?"

"I guess, if by promotion you mean we have new, more powerful people to suck up to, longer hours, and the same old pay."

"In that case, congratulations!"

Krantz smiled, and then his face turned businesslike. "So you know what this is about. I trust you'll help in any way you can."

Jacob considered. Maybe it was a trick from the FBI's bag, but he felt relaxed by their friendly approach. They trusted him after their work at Zarahemla, but he could easily take the approach his people usually took toward law enforcement: stonewalling, lying, and denying. He was not proud of the small ways in which he'd engaged in this tactic in the past. Or, he could trust that they'd done nothing wrong, that cooperating could help dozens of people gain closure about the deaths of their family and friends.

He gave a nod to Eliza to indicate his intentions. "We'll help in any way we can. My only hope is that you can minimize our role to the public. We just can't take another media swarm. It's corrosive."

"We'll do what we can," Krantz said. "But you know how things get. They reach a tipping point, and then it goes nuts. Maybe nobody will make the connection."

"Here's the first big piece of information, if you don't have it already. The guy who ordered the suicide pact was a Lost Boy, one of Elder Kimball's sons."

Krantz whistled. "That's one fu—I mean *messed up*—family."

"The family is full of bad seeds," Jacob said, "and Eliza seems to be on a mission to crush their skulls in, one at a time."

Fayer whipped out a digital recorder. "Whoa, you'd better back up."

"Sorry, Liz," Jacob said. His sister had winced at this last part. "Are you good? Do you want to wait?"

Her mouth formed a thin line. "I'm good. Let's do it now, get it over with."

The other three stayed silent while Eliza related her story. She left nothing out, and Jacob got an even more complete picture than he had earlier. The details were beyond ugly, and his throat constricted when she described how they'd tried to "sanctify" her in the back room. And the horror of the pit in the desert was almost worse. He had mild claustrophobia, nothing serious, but enough that the thought of lying in his own filth, naked in the darkness, terrified him. And yet his sister had immediately set about trying to escape. Had actually done so.

Eliza continued to the horrific conclusion, when she'd crushed the Disciple's head with a chunk of concrete. For the most part, she relayed the details in a calm, almost detached manner, but during this last part her voice tightened and she had to stop. Jacob refilled her lemonade glass. She took a long drink and then filled in the part about the people willingly entering the trailer to wait for Wormwood to fall.

Jacob closed his eyes. Those screams, those people he couldn't save. One voice haunted him, a young man's voice, calm above the chaos. *The Lord is my shepherd, I shall not want. He maketh me to lie down in green pastures, he leadeth me beside the still waters.* And then a woman screaming, screaming, and he couldn't hear the young man for a long moment. When she stopped, he heard, *Thou preparest a table for me in the presence of mine enemies, thou annointest my head with oil.* And then the fire, the screams, the collapsing building, and the voice was silenced.

Where's your priesthood power now? Jacob thought. *If you're so good, if you can heal a man with a blessing, why couldn't you stand like Alma and Amulek, command the prison walls to fall around you?*

Or were the miracles of the Book of Mormon and the Bible from a closed book? Were the only miracles left the quiet ones, the unprovable?

He was still reliving the horror at the trailer and thinking about that blessing of David on the porch when his sister finished.

There was a long moment of silence, and then Fayer cleared her throat. "That's one heck of a story."

"It's not a story," Eliza said.

"That's not what I mean. It fits what we've been able to piece together from the crime scene. And I'm sure the other details that come out will corroborate. But that you survived all that, got Miss Caliari out…I'm impressed. If you ever want to leave all this—" she gestured at the polygamist compound and the desert around them, "—you've got a future in the FBI."

Jacob said, "That's what Sister Miriam already told her."

"We could use someone else on our team," Krantz said. "Someone with an inside knowledge of religious cults."

"I'm flattered," Eliza said. "I don't think now is the time, but I'll file that away. You never know."

"We need more details, of course," Fayer said, "but that's a start, and we appreciate your cooperation. Is Agent Kite around?"

"Sister Miriam?" Jacob shook his head. "She went into St. George to meet Madeline Caliari's mom at the airport."

"I want to hear her side, as soon as she gets back. There are more layers to this story, and we won't stop until we peel them all back."

* * *

The real Allison Caliari was nothing like the woman who had approached them at Zarahemla. She got out of the car after Miriam parked in front of the Christianson ranch and looked around with a wary expression. Allison was short, with a dark bob, not unattractive, but more of a soccer mom than the glamorous woman who had appeared at the Zarahemla compound. Not the same woman at all. Madeline had called her mother the moment they'd arrived in Blister Creek after fleeing Las Vegas.

Eliza watched the woman staring at two of her father's wives in prairie dresses, pushing double strollers toward the park, before she caught sight of her daughter coming down the steps from the porch. Both mother and daughter let out a cry and ran toward each other. There were tears, embraces, chatter from both of them.

"What do you think?" Eliza asked Jacob.

"I don't know what to think," Jacob said.

Agents Krantz and Fayer had gone inside to interview Father. Near as Eliza could tell, Abraham Christianson didn't know anything, but that wouldn't stop him. He'd be blustering, denying, arguing for the sake of arguing. It would take two hours to extract two minutes of information.

"I spent more time digging around the Internet, and most of it is true," Jacob continued. "Allison Caliari really is the head of an online group searching for children lost to cults. Madeline really had been sucked into their group, and Allison really had been desperate to find her. Except the real Allison Caliari thought her daughter was still in the Northwest, or maybe California. She hadn't figured out the Las Vegas connection, or realized that the Disciple was a Lost Boy or connected in any way to Father's church.

"That's weird enough," Jacob continued, "but think about this. Here is the head of an online group dedicated to tracking and following Chosen Ones. They have the advantage of pooled knowledge, they've listed their attempts to follow cult members around, discovering how they would eat garbage, sleep in Dumpsters or under freeway overpasses. They hired people to track and kidnap their children in order to reverse brainwash them out of the cult. And they still never found the Las Vegas compound."

"Which means," Eliza said, "that whoever the imposter is, she knew more about the Chosen Ones than a group dedicated to studying and exposing the cult. How is that possible?"

"An ex-member of the group?"

Eliza considered, then shook her head. "That woman is too old. Not one of the Chosen Ones was older than twenty-five, near as I could tell. She really did look like someone's mother."

"I don't like it. It's too slick. Someone maneuvered us into this position, tricked us into sending you off to Las Vegas. Whoever it was knew so much she probably knew about the cleansing, the sanctifying, the purifying. And didn't care if she sacrificed you to the cult. For what?" His face turned grim. "Whoever it is, she's no friend of ours."

"It was worth it," Eliza said. "I saved Madeline Caliari. I'd do it again."

"You really mean that?"

"I do. If I didn't, the things I saw would make me go insane." She forced a smile. "The last thing we need around here is another religious nutcase."

"Hmm, what's the female version of the Disciple in King James English?"

"I don't think the Bible gives us a word for that. Women are either daughters, wives, or whores."

"Come on, is that all? Surely the language allows the gentler sex to be possessed by demons."

"That's true, I'd forgotten. We can be witches, after all."

His voice turned more serious. "There's something else that's bothering me, Liz. Did you realize you've killed two sons from the Kimball clan now, and in much the same way?"

"Bashed in their psychotic brains with rocks, you mean. Yes, I'm aware."

A raised eyebrow. "You're taking this awfully well. No post-traumatic whatever-you-want-to-call-it?"

"Not yet. I'm trying to keep it light, or we're back to crazy and possessed by demons. But no, I won't take it well, not when I get a chance to chew it over. But what's this about Gideon and Caleb? Can it wait? Do we need to talk about it now?"

"I don't think it can. The problem is, there's a third brother out there, if you haven't forgotten. Where is he? What's he doing?"

Eliza felt her mouth go dry. *Taylor Junior.* Her would-be husband, the survivor of the Lost Boy conspiracy, who'd disappeared after Gideon's death and Elder Kimball's arrest.

Jacob nodded. "Fernie will be here in a couple of hours. We need to talk to her. And Miriam, probably David, too. And have a serious discussion about Taylor Junior."

* * *

"And you're clean?" Miriam asked as she and David walked with Diego around the side of the ranch house. Jacob and Eliza stood on the porch, having an animated chat about something. David drew up short.

"Where would I get stuff around here? You haven't been giving me anything."

"A junkie has a way of sniffing out drugs, David. If you don't want to be clean, you'll find something, somewhere. You'll steal from the medicine cabinet, you'll dig around in the household cleaners until you find a way to mix up something nasty. You'll do something." She looked him in the eye. "Can you promise you're clean?"

"I'm clean. It's hard as hell, but I've done it so far. Haven't smoked, snorted, swallowed, or injected a thing since Jacob's blessing."

"Good. I have faith in Jacob's priesthood power, but you still have to do everything you can. That's the way the Lord works."

Was it the Lord? He could see Miriam's whole plan laid out. She'd conspired with his father to bring him to Blister Creek, feed him drugs, and then bring Jacob down to cast out his demons with a blessing. Could that possibly be the Lord's work? And yet here he was, making a valiant fight against the demon that entrenched itself in his soul.

Diego held each of their hands in an unrelenting grip. He still wasn't talking, but there was nothing wrong with his appetite. He looked up at David with wide, unquestioning eyes. David felt something stir as he met the boy's gaze.

This was what a father felt, he thought. A fierce desire to protect his child from harm, to destroy anyone who would hurt that child. A part of him was glad those people had died. Especially Caleb Kimball and the other one—what was it?—Christopher. What kind of monster would starve a child, try to burn him alive?

He looked up to see Miriam watching him. "They'll take him away," she said in a soft voice. "Look for his family. Diego has relatives somewhere. Everybody does."

"Maybe. But if not..."

"If not, do you think they'll let him stay with polygamists?"

"I'm not a polygamist. You aren't, either. Maybe together..."

"David."

He said nothing, just waited for the inevitable. This was where she said something she couldn't take back, where she pulled away. The moment was gone, she was just another follower of his brother, and if his instincts were right, she'd imagined herself the wife of a great leader. Why a woman with her strength and intelligence

would want to be the second wife of any man—even Jacob—he
couldn't quite understand, but whatever else Miriam was, she was
a believer.

She cleared her throat, began again. "David, there's something
going on here, something around your brother. He's gathering
people. They find him, whether they are looking or not. Fernie,
Eliza, me, and now you. Maybe even Diego. If the Lord wants it,
he'll stay with us."

"You believe that?"

"I do. But I also know that many are called, but few are chosen.
You've been called, but will you accept the calling? Or will you
fall back into sin? If you regress, if you choose Satan, I won't have
anything to do with you."

"And if I accept the calling?"

"Then I'll go to Jacob and ask if I can be your wife."

David stared at her, and then a smile spread across his face.
"Isn't that backwards? The drill goes: first the prophet decides, then
he tells the husband, and then the woman gets the word. I don't
know about Jacob, but nobody has asked me yet."

Miriam blushed, her confident expression dropping for the first
time he could remember. "That is, I mean, if you want, well, I
didn't mean to…"

He came around and put his free hand on her cheek. Diego
stood between them, looking up at each of them in turn. "I do
want it, Sister Miriam," David said. "I want it more than anything,
and that's why I think I've got a chance to beat this addiction."

He wanted to kiss her then but knew she'd pull away. *Not yet,*
she'd say. *You need to prove it first.*

David vowed not to disappoint her.

CHAPTER TWENTY-EIGHT

They followed the footsteps through Witch's Warts. After the first hundred feet or so, beyond where boys came to hunt lizards or carve their names in the sandstone with butter knives, there were few footsteps, and it wasn't difficult to find where the Disciple had come through with Diego. A pair of large prints, and a second pair, lightly pressing the sand. In the other direction, a single set of tracks.

Jacob and Fernie went first, speaking in low tones. Miriam and David followed. They held Diego's hand, one on either side. The boy still wasn't talking, but he had warmed to Miriam and David, never leaving their side now that Madeline had returned to Oregon with her mother. Everyone knew it was only a matter of time before Child Protective Services came for him. Hopefully, they'd located one of the boy's relatives, so he wouldn't simply pass into foster care.

Eliza lingered behind, caught up in memories. She'd done her share of exploring the fringes of the sandstone maze as a child, remembered one time when she was thirteen when a second cousin had led her to a sandstone arch, tried to kiss her. She'd pushed him away, laughing. His hurt look had been sweet, really. She wondered what had become of him. A Lost Boy, she thought.

But the violence of her abduction at the hands of Gideon Kimball subsumed all other memories. Witch's Warts felt sinister to her now. The whisper of the wind sounded like gossiping voices, and the hoodoos were like silent sentinels, frowning down on the party. Water from last month's rain still collected in sinkholes eaten into the rock, the dark sheen on their surfaces hiding unknown depths. Most would be a few inches deep, but she saw one at the convergence of so many rivulets that looked like it concealed a pit deep enough to drown in. A sinkhole like the one where Gideon had murdered Jacob's grandfather, where he'd then met his own death at Eliza's hand. She looked away.

"Are we looking for anything in particular?" Miriam asked. "Because we're probably trashing a lot of evidence."

Jacob stopped. They stepped into the shade of a massive thrust of sandstone. Eliza shivered. The others would be enjoying the cooler air out of the sun. She'd just as soon stay in the open.

"Nothing specific," he said, "but I have some questions about Witch's Warts. As far as I can tell, Caleb Kimball wasn't a party to the original Lost Boy plot to take over the church, but he knew his way across. I don't know if he entered Blister Creek at night, but he certainly left at night. How did he find his way through this maze in the dark? We didn't see any flashlights."

Eliza said, "He said an angel led him."

"Not likely."

"A demon, then. Someone."

"I'm not ready to ascribe supernatural elements to Caleb's delusions," Jacob said. "Anyway, there's something about this place that's allowing enemies in and out of Blister Creek."

"We should just fence off the whole thing," Eliza said. "Then it can never be used for that again."

"It's eighteen square miles," he said. "That's a lot of fence. And this isn't our land, anyway. Abraham Christianson is the prophet in Blister Creek."

"I don't know about the rest of you," Fernie said, "but I'm ready to go back to Zarahemla." She rested a hand on her pregnant belly. "That's our home now, and I don't want to have my baby in Blister Creek or bring my kids down, either. There's too much scheming going on here, whether it's Elder Christianson or the Lost Boys."

Jacob put a hand on her arm. "It's not that easy. We're intertwined with Blister Creek, and not just spiritually. I'll bet ninety percent of the people at Zarahemla have cousins here, brothers, sisters, parents, children. We're trying to provide a sanctuary for these people, and for those who've been driven out of their community. Remember what you said about being atomized?"

"I remember," Fernie said softly.

"That's our purpose." He turned back to the others. "We're gathering a community. The righteous, the wicked, the wanderers. Those who are lost and those who are found. I don't know how many people we need to bring into our common cause, or even why, but I accept that now."

Eliza looked at Jacob with the others gathered around him. Somehow, they came to his side: Eliza, Fernie, Sister Miriam, and now David and even Diego, if it was the will of the Lord. Each one refined by fire, purified—she would reclaim that word from the Chosen Ones—and fiercely dedicated to Jacob's cause.

"An army of the righteous," David said. A half smile played at his lips. "And I suppose Eliza is your chief henchman. Bashing in the heads of the Kimball brothers, one by one, like so many zombies."

"Come on, be serious," Eliza said.

"I *am* serious. Well, not the zombie part. I don't know what's going on, I'm just glad to be on the right side of the conflict for once."

"Who is this Taylor Junior I've heard you talk about?" Sister Miriam interrupted. "Is he the other Kimball brother mixed up in the fraud thing a few years ago?"

Jacob nodded. "He disappeared after Gideon Kimball died and the FBI arrested the father, Elder Kimball. I got caught up in things for a few years, finishing school, my residency, then the events at Zarahemla, and almost forgot about him for a while."

"I never forgot about Taylor Junior," Eliza said. "Father wanted me to marry him. The man tried to force himself on me—you can bet I didn't forget. And nobody ever caught the jerk. I bet he still plans to marry me and take his place as head of the church. To reclaim what he thinks is his."

"One more name and picture for the Book of the Lost," Jacob said. "Taylor Kimball Jr. And we'll move him to the front of our search. I want to know where he is and what he's doing."

"It might take a while," Miriam said. "He could be anywhere."

David shook his head. "I don't think so. He's a Lost Boy. Either he's busy destroying himself with drugs and alcohol, or he's still scheming. He'll have others. Lost Boys, maybe wives. And they'll be in the desert. Always the desert."

"We're desert dwellers, too," Jacob said. "We're more than a match for whatever they've got."

As they retraced their steps, Fernie took Eliza's arm and held her back. "You see what's happening, don't you?"

"Jacob is starting to believe."

"Not all of it. There's just a crack in his armor, caused by what happened when he gave David a blessing."

"But he's starting to believe there's a higher purpose," Eliza said. "That we're doing something here."

"And he's gathering his followers. You, me, Miriam, and now David. Smart, capable people. We can repair a car engine, grow our own food, shoot firearms. We live in a walled compound."

"You believe it, don't you?" Eliza said. "You think he's the One Mighty and Strong, and you think the world is coming to an end."

Fernie fell silent, then slowed Eliza down again, until they walked a good fifty feet behind the others. "You know I'm a dreamer, right? That sometimes my dreams tell me what I should do, or seem to hint at bad things before they happen."

"What did you dream this time?"

"I was walking through Salt Lake City, and the streets were empty. Huge snowflakes fell from the sky, and then I realized they were flakes of cold ash. They coated the streets. The windows had blown out on the office towers, and I could smell sulfur. I heard Jacob calling my name. He came walking beneath the Eagle Gate, his boots leaving footprints in the ash. I started to run toward him. And then I saw someone or something following him. It was a shadow that slipped from building to building. I felt a lump of ice in my stomach, and I couldn't open my mouth to scream a warning." She hesitated. "I woke up just when the shadow had reached his side."

Eliza licked her lips. The skin on the back of her neck prickled and she shivered, even though it had to be eighty-five degrees. "Sometimes a dream is just a dream."

"Or just a nightmare, in this case. I know," Fernie added. "But this dream faded slowly. I can still smell that sulfur, if I think about it."

"Does it mean something?"

"Maybe," Fernie said. "I think it might be *the* something."

"What do you mean? Do you think the end is coming?"

"I don't know. Do you?"

"People have been predicting the end of the world for a long time," Eliza said. "Probably started about five minutes after they figured out how the world began. They've all been wrong so far."

"Everyone is wrong about the world ending until it does end." Fernie hesitated. "Are you staying with us this time?"

Eliza thought it over. She planned to return with them to Zarahemla, then go back to Salt Lake, register for classes, and look for a job. And yet she felt the pull of her own family and people. In spite of everything, even knowing her father would try dirty tricks to get her into a polygamist marriage with one of the members of his quorum, she couldn't deny she felt some of the same things that bound Fernie to the lifestyle.

"I don't know."

"I think you do know. I think you're planning to go back to Salt Lake, am I right?"

"Yes," she said, with some hesitation. "It's the right place for me now."

"We'll support you, of course. But be careful."

Eliza remembered the men who'd approached her at Red Butte Gardens. She hadn't thought about them since getting swept up in Caleb Kimball's cult. Those men knew where she worked, and while they weren't guilty of anything beyond weird behavior, it was enough to give her pause. And she remembered the woman who had come to Zarahemla, pretending to be Allison Caliari, who had manipulated Eliza into infiltrating Caleb Kimball's desert cult. Why?

"I'll be careful," Eliza said. "I promise."

They were emerging from Witch's Warts, just to the side of the temple. A glint caught the angel Moroni on the main tower and hit her eye. Her thoughts were a jumble of images: burning tires, Benita staring out from the window, the glassy look in Caleb's eyes when she'd crushed in his skull. She'd seen that look on Gideon Kimball's face, too. Two brothers dead, the more dangerous one still alive.

Taylor Junior, where are you?

EPILOGUE

With the FBI back in Blister Creek, Abraham Christianson decided that the Ghost Cliffs were too dangerous a meeting spot. He scowled whenever he saw their Lincoln driving around town. They sat in the diner, munching burgers and coming out to sit on the hood of their car and eat creemies, just watching people pass. Brother Peterson refused to serve them at first, and Brother Wentworth at the gas station wouldn't pump their gas, until Abraham intervened and told the town to cooperate. But his blood simmered when he saw Agent Krantz smoking a cigarette on the sidewalk near the chapel.

Worse was when they came to the house. He'd been forced to sit with them in his den while they subjected him to an array of tedious interviews. Agent Fayer had grilled him again last night, reminded him of his promises to the federal prosecutors during the last investigation. She was LDS—Salt Lake Mormon—and with her Mormon background knew all the right questions to ask. *Did you know Caleb Kimball? When was the last time you saw him? Has he had any contact with his father in prison? How about Taylor Junior? Know anything about him? Tell me how Blister Creek deals with apostates. Do you believe that the Lord might someday tell you to kill a man?*

Abraham told the truth as often as he could, lied when that was impossible. Some of their questions drew uncomfortably close to facts that he would just as soon keep concealed. Other questions were clearly designed to trap him in a lie. He saw these traps and sidestepped them.

Agent Fayer kept after him relentlessly, coming back to questions, digging deeper and persisting when he tried to deflect her onto less fruitful avenues. She occasionally tried to force his temper. He only just managed to hold his emotions in check.

One time, she rose to her feet just as Agent Krantz entered, carrying a beverage in a thermos, which he insisted was hot chocolate. No doubt it was coffee. He'd have thrown the man out for that if he thought he could get away with it. Fayer gave Krantz an exaggerated shrug as the two agents passed at the entrance to his den. She leaned forward and whispered in Krantz's ear, and then the two of them glanced back at Abraham Christianson.

Krantz leaned back in the chair recently vacated by his partner. It groaned a protest at his extra weight. "I want to apologize for my partner. She can be overzealous at times. I know that you want to cooperate, and I promise we won't carry on with this any longer than necessary. Now, where were we? Oh, yes. Caleb Kimball's troubled childhood. I think you were saying something about the time he poured gasoline on a dog and set it on fire."

"I'm tired, Agent Krantz. I know that exchange with Agent Fayer was theater for my benefit. And I know the tag-teaming is designed to wear me down, and that you might take turns playing good cop, bad cop. I've got a ranch to run, and another one in Canada to worry about, as well as a church to shepherd. Perhaps if you told me what you're looking for, we could save each other a lot of time."

"I'm looking for Taylor Kimball Jr."

"You are? Whatever for?"

He was surprised in more ways than one. And alarmed. For a moment, he thought that Krantz had been speaking to the woman, that he'd figured out what Abraham was doing in pointing Eliza toward the desert compound outside Vegas.

"You mean apart from bringing him to justice on charges of fraud, conspiracy, attempted murder, and accessory to murder? Isn't that enough?"

"But why now? It has been several years. I can see why he'd be on a most wanted list somewhere, but is this really an active investigation?"

"There are a few loose ends that are…troubling, to say the least. We know how the conspiracies work among the Lost Boys. So now we have a Lost Boy—another Kimball son, no less—at the heart of a doomsday cult. They made a suicide pact, and there are few survivors. We're trying to piece together if this is more like Heaven's Gate or Jonestown."

"I'm not sure I see the difference," Abraham said.

"The Heaven's Gate cult killed themselves with little warning. In March of 1997, thirty-nine people destroyed themselves, believing it was the only way to exit their human bodies and join the spaceship trailing the Hale-Bopp comet."

"How could anyone believe such a thing?"

"Indeed," Krantz said, dryly. "People believe the craziest things." He cleared his throat. "Jonestown is more horrific, of course, with over nine hundred people dead at their compound in the South American jungle, including children murdered by their own parents."

"Yes, I know all about drinking the Kool-Aid."

"Flavor Aid, actually, but that's close enough. They'd murdered a congressman and felt the walls closing in. The cult leaders decided that now was the time for everyone to die, but it might not have happened if not for outside pressures. Is that what happened here? Your daughter came and upset the balance, and so they all burned themselves alive, afraid the authorities would soon be moving in?"

"Please, don't say that to Eliza. She's going to blame herself enough as it is."

"I won't. And I don't believe it, anyway. These people wanted the end to come. And even if Eliza sped up the timeline, they are responsible for their own actions. She did nothing but try to help people leave the cult. But that doesn't answer the question of what was going through the feverish minds of this so-called Disciple and his followers."

"There's a third model, of course," Abraham said. "Your assault on Zarahemla."

"You're a smart man, Mr. Christianson. You saw right where I was going. Yes, the third model is Waco, Short Creek, Ruby Ridge, Zarahemla. The cult leader that defies authorities to come in and attack. The faithful have God on their side. The authorities have firearms and military tactics. And of course, you know which side always wins. Including at Zarahemla."

"Let's be clear," Abraham said. "You won—or *thought* you won—in Zarahemla only because the Lord didn't intervene in the way His saints expected. But make no mistake that the events furthered His purpose. We don't always understand that purpose."

"Fine, I understand why you feel that way. From my perspective, I look across the desert southwest and I see a much larger conspiracy brewing. Most of the people haven't vocalized their feelings, and they don't always connect it to Brigham Young's original defiance of the federal government."

"You've been reading your Mormon history."

"I have, and I know that when the Mormons first moved into the Salt Lake Valley it was part of Mexico. After the war with the Mexicans, the federal government moved in to take control and Brigham Young threatened to burn Salt Lake to the ground and fight a civil war against the government. He backed down, of course. Brigham Young surrendered political authority, and his successors eventually disavowed polygamy. But I look around and I see tens of thousands of fundamentalist Mormons who never bowed their heads. They are growing in numbers and strength. And I wonder if there won't come a time when your birthrate pushes that number into the hundreds of thousands, maybe millions."

"Sounds like paranoia to me."

"How many children do you have, Abraham Christianson? I count thirty-six, but I'm sure I'm missing two or three."

More than two or three, actually. Between here and Canada, grown and still living at home, Abraham boasted forty-five children, maybe forty-six, depending on whether Katherine had given birth yet or not. Probably not. Katie's pregnancies invariably went past term.

Krantz nodded. "You see my point. I give the Christiansons, the Cowleys, the Griggs, the Johnsons, the Phipps, the Kimballs, and the Birds about five generations, and you'll have enough people out here to cause some serious trouble."

"You and I will be long gone by then," Abraham said. "And I'm guessing the Second Coming will arrive before then, anyway."

Agent Krantz stood up. "Maybe, maybe not. Just make sure you don't do anything to speed it along. Thank you, sir, for your cooperation."

* * *

After that exchange, and the worry that other agents might be staking out Blister Creek, Abraham decided to meet the woman in Beaver, at the cattle auction. He took two of his sons with twenty steers in trucks. While the boys were in the auction, he stepped out of the tent and its suffocating smell of cattle and manure and walked through town. Heat shimmered off the pavement, and he stayed in the shade of the cottonwood trees that lined the street. He stopped at the old county courthouse, a handsome brick building with a clock tower, built in more optimistic times. Beaver had been declining for more than a century now. Not coincidentally, he thought, since the time Salt Lake had abandoned plural marriage.

It filled him with sadness to think about what might have been. If not for a few faithful, the Principle would have been lost. Maybe the day would come when the righteous would fill these old towns again—Beaver, Manti, Price, Richfield, Delta, Ticaboo—and fulfill the original vision of Brigham Young.

He was sitting on the steps when she found him. She didn't stand out, thankfully. She'd traded her BMW for a Taurus, and wore a skirt and a long-sleeved shirt. A little higher collar, more conservative hair and she could have passed for a member of the church. Maybe it was the clothes, but he thought he saw a hint of the same nostalgia he was feeling in her expression.

"Do you ever feel regret for the path you've taken?" he asked as she took a seat next to him.

"Of course. Doesn't everyone?"

"I don't know, maybe. Usually, no. What other path would I take?"

"It wouldn't hurt you to be a little more self-reflective, Abraham Christianson."

"Self-reflection leads to crises of faith, to letting go of the Iron Rod. I can't afford that kind of lapse. My *people* can't afford it."

"It's a good thing your son doesn't feel that way," she said. "He'd be beyond dangerous. A man with that intelligence, who inspires that much love from people, with a singular purpose to control the world around him. A very good thing Jacob is not like you in that way."

"What you just described is exactly what I hope he'll become."

"What, a monster?"

He bit back his reply. "We'd better stop this line of conversation. It isn't fruitful."

"Well, what should we talk about? You don't want to discuss how the Utah Jazz bombed out of the playoffs again? Or who is going to win between BYU and the U this year? Gas prices are going through the roof again. What about the alligator that guy was keeping in his bathtub in St. George? Crazy, huh?"

He wasn't going to let her goad him again. "Whenever you're ready."

"So, no chitchat. Yes, it worked. We dangled your daughter like bait and drew our prey."

"Tell me."

"Only two people left the trailer encampment after Eliza arrived. One was a young man who returned with three others. I believe that all of them burned to death in the tire fire."

"And the other person?" Abraham asked.

"A young woman. She left with the young man, they met the other three, and then she split off. I thought her the most likely suspect. Here is her picture."

She reached into her purse and removed a color printout of a young woman entering a grocery store in what he supposed was Las Vegas. Yes, there were slot machines visible through the window. He recognized her face.

"This girl is my first cousin, once removed," Abraham said. "I can't remember the last time I saw her. I thought her family had joined the TLC. One of the girls went over to the Kingston Clan."

"Looks like you were wrong."

"I suppose so," he agreed with some reluctance. "And then what happened?"

"I stayed with the girl."

"And you were sure at this point?" he asked.

"Reasonably sure. We knew he had a woman on the inside already, and we knew they were stalking your daughter. But I took precautions, just in case I was wrong. I'd hired people in Las Vegas.

One man kept an eye on the compound—he was the one who called in the fire once it was clear what was happening. Another associate followed the others. They never left each other's presence before returning to the trailers. I kept after the girl." She returned to her purse and pulled out a second picture. "The girl met this man. I believe they are married."

Abraham Christianson looked at the picture and his blood turned cold. It was as if an evil spirit had come out of the purse with the picture and lingered in the air between them. He didn't need a spiritual sign, but the sun took just that moment to duck behind a cloud and a shadow fell over the courthouse.

The man's hair was longer, the beard trimmed away until he was as clean-skinned as Jacob or David. But the eyes were the same.

"He made some calls," she continued. "Another few hours and he'd have been ready for his own assault on the compound to rescue your daughter. If you can call it rescue, what he likely planned to do with her."

"And you know where he lives?" he asked.

"Not yet," she said, "but now I know how to find him."

Abraham folded the two sheets of paper and tucked them into his back pocket. He had to get back. On the off chance that the FBI had followed him to Beaver to see if he were really planning to go to the cattle auction, he didn't want them searching for him. They might learn how he'd lied to them, and that was one more problem than he needed at the moment.

"So what now?" she asked.

"We don't have any other choice. Either we find him and destroy him, or we wait for him to come to us. And then we're in trouble." He rose to his feet. "We'll talk soon. If anything comes up, you know how to find me." He walked away without looking back to see if she'd returned to her car or waited on the courthouse steps, watching him.

But a block away, he couldn't resist pulling the second picture out one more time to look into the face of evil. The man was getting into his car, turning slightly, as if sensing the presence of a camera and looking up to fix the person behind the camera in his memory. Those eyes, that look that every man in his family had. Only he no longer stood in the shadow of others, he had become the one who controlled all of Abraham's enemies.

Taylor Kimball Jr. And now Abraham wondered. Was he looking into the eyes of the Antichrist?

-end-

ABOUT THE AUTHOR

Michael Wallace was born in California and raised in a small religious community in Utah, eventually heading east to live in New England. An experienced world traveler, he has trekked through the Andes, ventured into the Sahara on a camel, and traveled through Thailand by elephant. In addition to working as a literary agent and innkeeper, he previously worked as a software engineer for a Department of Defense contractor, programming simulators for nuclear submarines.